TWELFTH NIGHT SORCERY

The Cambion Club, Book 2

Anne Rollins

ARE YOU SIGNED UP FOR DRAGONBLADE'S BLOG?

You'll get the latest news and information on exclusive giveaways, exclusive excerpts, coming releases, sales, free books, cover reveals and more.

Check out our complete list of authors, too!

No spam, no junk. That's a promise!

Sign Up Here

www.dragonbladepublishing.com

Dearest Reader;

Thank you for your support of a small press. At Dragonblade Publishing, we strive to bring you the highest quality Historical Romance from some of the best authors in the business. Without your support, there is no 'us', so we sincerely hope you adore these stories and find some new favorite authors along the way.

Happy Reading!

CEO, Dragonblade Publishing

Additional Dragonblade books by Author Anne Rollins

The Cambion Club
Garden Folly Magic (Book 1)
Twelfth Night Sorcery (Book 2)

Beau Monde Secrets Series
Secrets at Selwyn Castle (Book 1)
Discovery at Dogwood Cottage (Book 2)
The Incident at Ingleton (Book 3)
The Case at Castle Rock Cove (Book 4)

CHAPTER ONE

January 5, 1817

"YOU LOOK SPLENDID," Lady Grantly told Honora. "That shade of blue really brings out the color of your eyes."

Honora studied her reflection in the mirror. Her underdress was a simple satin round gown in a dusky shade of blue-gray, but layers of turquoise tulle had been draped strategically about her body, emphasizing her hips and bust. The latter of the two certainly benefited from emphasis, but she privately thought she could have done without calling attention to her hips. They were prominent enough on their own.

"You are right about the color," she told her mother, "But I doubt anyone will know I am supposed to be Aphrodite."

Roses and pearls were associated with the Greek goddess of love, so her pearl earrings and the white rosebuds in her hair might clue in a savvy observer. But Honora did not think the guests were likely to be at their most observant tonight. The Duke of Belmont was known to be liberal with the spirits at his parties.

"It does not matter," her mother replied. "All that matters is that you look like the jewel you are." She smiled somewhat mistily into the mirror. "Isn't it marvelous? My oldest child on the verge of receiving a proposal of marriage!"

Honora shuddered and looked down at her hands. Her evening gloves had been dyed to match the sea-foam of her costume, as had her slippers and half-mask. She picked up the mask and put it on. Now her costume looked complete.

But her mother shook her head. "Darling, don't you think you look better without the mask? We want people to see your lovely face."

"It is a masquerade ball, Mother," Honora said, trying to be patient. "Masks are *de rigueur*." And a mask was essential to her plan. She could not carry out her scheme if everyone at the ball knew who she was. "Besides, the costume looks better with the mask."

Her mother sighed. "As you wish, dear. The duke will know who you are, anyway." There was a distinct smugness to the curve of her lips.

"Precisely." Honora injected her tone with as much fake cheer as she could manage. "He is the only one who matters." When she realized she had unknowingly clenched her hands into fists, she forced herself to relax. She had never been as good at acting as her sister Dora, but tonight she needed to give the performance of her life.

Lady Grantly smiled and kissed Honora on the top of her head. "My baby," she said sentimentally. "Shall we go up to the ballroom?"

Honora answered with a nod. She followed her mother up the broad flight of stairs that connected the first story with the second. The double doors of the ballroom stood wide open, and the sounds of Twelfth Night festivities could be heard all the way from the floor below.

Because it was a masquerade, the butler did not announce the guests. But everyone turned and stared when Honora and Lady Grantly entered the ballroom. Honora's mother wore a black domino over a black silk dress. According to her, that costume signified "Night." Honora suspected Mama had chosen it merely because she already had the garments left over from a previous masquerade.

"I don't see the duke," her mother said fretfully. "It will be hard to find him in this press."

"He will find me." Honora shuddered. Belmont seemed to

have some kind of sixth sense where she was concerned. He always knew which dinner party she meant to attend, or which day she chose to go to the local assemblies. In the past, he had avoided such rural amusements; he did not usually socialize with the local gentry. But ever since their first meeting at a hunt ball, he seemed to inevitably show up to dance with Honora or to take the seat next to her in the drawing room. It was one of the things Honora particularly disliked about him.

Though, to be fair, she had taken a disliking to Belmont the first time she spoke to him. For a man of his age, he was quite attractive, but she had found him off-putting from their first encounter. There was something she did not like about the shifting, shimmering lights of his aura, though she could not explain what bothered her. She only knew he seemed like someone she ought to avoid.

Unfortunately, the duke did not feel the same way about Honora.

"Let us enjoy the ball in the meantime," she told her mother.

She prayed the duke would ignore her long enough for her to act on her plan. Fortunately, it was not his habit to hover over his quarry for the duration of a party. He preferred to stalk her from the sidelines until he judged the time was right.

Even with a mask on, Honora had no trouble attracting dance partners. But she found it difficult to concentrate on the steps of a cotillion or country dance while searching for the perfect accomplice. The very masks that allowed her a necessary measure of anonymity also scared her. Anyone at all could be behind a mask. What if she chose someone worse than the duke? She was not naïve enough to think he was the worst man in the world, after all; merely one of the worst of her acquaintance.

But, she reminded herself, there was an enormous difference between a one-time indiscretion and a lifetime of matrimony. Her stomach roiled as she remembered her panic yesterday. She had been caught with her back to a wall and no one in earshot while the duke pressed unwanted kisses against her face.

The worst of it had been the way he smiled afterward, as if he were *pleased* by her distress. As if her reluctance added some relish to the kisses he stole. If he treated her so disrespectfully now, when they were not yet betrothed, how would he treat her when she was his wife?

Anything would be better than that. All she had to do was find a man who would serve her purpose for tonight. What the stranger did tomorrow would be none of her concern. Surely, she could tolerate anything for the span of an hour? Hopefully, less.

Even so, Honora rejected one prospect after another. Sometimes the problem was that she recognized the men flirting with her. She could not take the risk that they might recognize her, too. Other times, she found something unsavory about the individual in question. Perhaps he had an annoying laugh. Or maybe he seemed to sweat too much. She passed over more than one prospect because the gentleman in question had already tippled overmuch. A drunken man might be more willing to play a part in her scheme, but he might also be more dangerous.

Honora grew increasingly anxious as time passed. Being in crowded rooms always tended to fatigue her, but tonight her uneasiness had an additional cause. She had seen the Duke of Belmont several times, though they had yet to meet face-to-face. He was dressed as Hades, bident in hand, with one of his Italian greyhounds trotting at his side, costumed as Cerberus. He kept his distance from her for now, but more than once she caught him looking in her direction. At any moment, he might decide the time had come to approach her. She had to act *now*.

The duke was not the only man who caught her eye. A man dressed as Bacchus, sporting a toga and a crown of wax fruit, also kept attracting her notice, though he did not pay the slightest attention to her. Perhaps it was *because* he kept so steadily looking past her that her eyes were drawn to him.

She could not otherwise explain why she kept finding him in the crowd and staring at him from a distance. He was taller than average height for a man, standing above most of the guests, but not strikingly so. He was built on square, brawny lines—a little heavyset—but not so broad as to stand out in the crowd for that reason, either.

The only thing at all distinctive about Bacchus was that his aura was spangled with the flickering lights that indicated a possessor of magical talent. The density of those shifting sparks suggested that he was a fairly powerful magician, but what fascinated Honora was that his magic looked like neither sorcery nor wizardry, but something in between the two that she'd never seen before.

She wished she could pull the stranger aside and ask him how his magic worked and what he could do with it. Unfortunately, a crowded ballroom was not really the right place for that conversation. Her mother had spent hours drilling Honora on appropriate ballroom talk, and she had not forgotten those lessons. It was not considered polite to talk about magic in mixed—magical and nonmagical—company. People who possessed only mundane talents might feel left out.

Still, she kept noticing him. When her eyes scanned over the increasingly drunken crowd, they always paused and lingered on Bacchus. Eventually, his eyes met hers. Perhaps he read some of the interest in her face, despite the yards that separated them. In any case, Bacchus began to slowly work his way towards her, pausing to greet people on the way. She forced herself to stand still and smile, waiting for him to come to her. Her heart pounded more heavily, and her hands began to sweat.

As the stranger approached, her confidence melted away. Could she really carry out her plan? She knew so little about such matters! But she had to do it soon. Her mother had hinted that the duke intended to propose before midnight so he could announce his engagement at the unmasking. Bacchus might be her only chance to escape.

Here he was now, towering over her. This close, he seemed much larger than he had looked from a distance. He could have made two of her. His hair was a warm, rich brown color and it curled a little. Really, he made an ideal Bacchus.

"Madam, do I know you?" His voice sounded exactly like what she would have expected: deep, cultured, a little lazy. Typical English aristocrat. What was it, then, that constantly drew her eyes towards him?

"I do not think we have ever met." Honora would have remembered him, if only for his unusual aura. "But perhaps we ought to become better acquainted?" She had planned her script ahead of time, but the words sounded patently phony.

To her surprise, though, her feeble attempt at flirtation worked. A smile lit up his face as he bowed to her. Half his face was hidden by a mask, but even so, she could see that his smile transformed his face, making him far more handsome.

"In that case, would you care to dance?"

She returned his smile, relieved by the success of her plan. "I would like that very much."

They joined in the next country dance. He danced very well, which initially surprised her, until she reasoned that there was no reason why a large man should not move lightly. Wasn't a tiger just as agile as a housecat?

Bacchus asked her for another dance after that, and she accepted, because she increasingly suspected he might be the ideal accomplice. At least, he seemed more attractive than her other options. He spoke and acted like a sober man. He did not reek of liquor or stink of unwashed body. He touched her politely and respectfully and, though he looked at her appreciatively as she danced, his eyes met hers rather than wandering about her body as some men's eyes did.

After the second dance, Honora thought there was a real danger she would pass out from sheer nervousness. She'd not had so much as a single drink tonight, but all the lights and sounds of the crowded room were making her dizzy. Now was the time to act, but she had no idea how to accomplish her goal. She had never done anything like this before. She opened up her fan in an attempt to cool her flushed face.

"Can I get you a drink, perhaps?" her unknown swain offered. He certainly had good manners.

Yes, he would do. Best not to put it off.

"What I would really like," she said hesitantly, "is to go somewhere quieter and cooler to catch my breath." She fanned herself furiously. That, at least, was not pretense. She was burning up.

He stared at her, as well he might. Genteel young ladies did not ask unknown gentlemen to leave the ballroom with them. "Do you wish me to escort you to the gardens?" he offered doubtfully. "It is rather cold tonight."

Much too cold, she silently agreed. A January night was no time for lingering outdoors, no matter how attractive the grounds might be. More importantly, the garden would be too private for her purpose. No one else was likely to roam the grounds at this season.

"Perhaps an uncrowded corridor, if we could find one?" Frankly, Honora was amazed she could utter those scandalous words.

All of this was so very unlike her. All her life, she'd done her best to follow the strict rules governing young ladies of the gentry, though they often confused her. Her inquisitiveness sometimes led her to ask questions her mother considered inappropriate, but she had never deliberately transgressed the bounds of propriety the way she intended to do tonight.

"As you wish." The stranger offered her his arm, and they slipped out a side door into a hallway bustling with servants. The servants glanced past them, apparently not at all concerned about guests leaving the ballroom.

Bacchus seemed to know where he was going. He led her up a narrow back staircase, then into a long corridor. Belmont Court was so large that although she had toured the public rooms yesterday, Honora had not seen this hallway at all. Judging from the rows of doors along the wall, these were probably bedrooms.

Once they were out of earshot of everyone, Bacchus turned

to her. "Does this suit? No one is likely to disturb you here."

"Yes." In fact, she worried it might be *too* private for her purposes. Her assignation would only be useful if other people learned of it. "Thank you."

She peered up at him doubtfully. She had chosen her accomplice and gotten him alone, but she had no idea what to do next. None of her lessons on etiquette had ever covered seduction.

"Is there something I can do to help you? Or—" His voice sounded hesitant, uncertain. "Were you looking for a little Twelfth Night *diversion*?" He gave the last word a suggestive emphasis.

Honora hoped her mask concealed the shame burning in her face. "Yes." She felt immensely relieved that he had suggested it himself. She would not have known how to ask. "If you don't mind." The moment the words left her mouth, she wished she could take them back. She was beginning to feel sick to her stomach. Her heart pounded so loudly, she half-worried Bacchus would hear it.

The unknown gentleman smiled again, but it did not seem like a mocking smile—not that she could easily tell, with a mask covering the top half of his face.

"How could I mind an invitation from so beautiful a woman?" he said gallantly. "I do not typically engage in liaisons with strangers, but I will make an exception for the goddess of love herself. I imagine one of these rooms is empty—" He turned to the nearest door and reached for the handle.

"Not in there!" Honora protested, her voice sounding strangled. He stared back at her, his mouth hanging open in surprise. "Isn't it more adventurous to, er, stay out here in the corridor?" She tried to keep her voice low, sultry, and seductive. But she merely sounded as if she had a head cold.

He recoiled, his eyes widening. "You want me to take up you against a wall?" Even the mask on his face could not conceal his shock.

"Yes." Honora felt reckless, terrified, and horrifically embarrassed. But she had to go through with this. It would be better than the alternative. At least, it could not possibly be worse.

He shook his head. "I don't usually do this sort of thing," he said slowly. "Madam, have you considered that if we are caught, your good name will be ruined?"

"Yes, I am aware of that." That was, in fact, the whole point. She needed to blacken her name so thoroughly that the Duke of Belmont would want nothing to do with her. "I am not afraid of the consequences."

He stared at her in silence for what seemed like an eternity. She watched his Adam's apple bob as he swallowed nervously, and she steeled herself for rejection.

Instead, he bowed to her again. "Very well. I do not usually court scandal, but it is Twelfth Night, after all. For tonight, I am your faithful votary, Aphrodite." He stepped closer and reached for her mask.

Honora opened her mouth to protest. This was humiliating enough with a mask on; she did not want the stranger to see her face. But she remembered in the nick of time that it would be better if she were unmasked when they were caught. She needed to be recognized. The duke knew she was dressed as Aphrodite, so he might figure out her identity once he heard rumors about the assignation, but she did not like to rely on that hope. Better to be certain.

So, she made no protest as Bacchus removed her mask and tossed it aside. Instead, she smiled tremulously at him.

Instead of returning her smile, he frowned. "How old are you?" All the gallantry had fled his voice.

Honora cringed at his unexpectedly sharp tone. "Twenty-one."

His frown deepened. Honora bit her lip. Ought she have lied and given an older age? But people generally thought she looked younger than her actual age. If she claimed to be, say, five-and-twenty, he might not believe her.

"And your husband? Is he here tonight, too?"

Her jaw dropped. He thought she was committing adultery? Well, of course he would think that. An aristocratic wife violating her marriage vows was more plausible than a virginal debutante trying to seduce a stranger.

"Yes, my husband is here tonight." It was not much of a lie. She was on the verge of becoming betrothed, which was the next thing to being married. And her almost-fiancé was the one hosting the masquerade. "But he will not care what I am doing. We do not interfere with each other's lives."

The man stared at her for another long moment. She wished she knew what he was thinking. His dark eyes, shadowed by the mask, gave little away.

"You ought to have chosen a better husband," he informed her. "A man who leaves you to wander a party alone and dally with strangers does not deserve to be married to you."

"No doubt you are right about that." Honora could tell she was about to start babbling, but she could not stop the words pouring out of her mouth. "You don't mind, do you? That I'm married?" At the back of her mind, a little voice began to whisper that this was all going to be very awkward if Bacchus ever found out who she really was.

But would he find out? Surely there must be a way for her to get caught without—no, he would have to find out. If someone saw and identified Honora, he would discover who she was. Then he would know she'd lied about being married. But he might figure that out anyway when it became obvious that she had no idea what to do with a man in bed.

Was this plan going to work? But it *had* to! She clasped her hands together anxiously.

He did not miss that gesture. He sighed and shook his head again. "You seem nervous. What do you say we go back to the ballroom and forget this ever happened?"

She opened her mouth to protest, but he forestalled her.

"I am not in the habit of dallying with married women, any-way. I really think it would be for the best if—"

Just then, one of the guestroom doors opened a crack, and a peel of tipsy laughter rang out. Bacchus swore. He grabbed Honora's hand and, before she understood what was going on, he bundled her into the nearest guest room. The door slammed shut, plunging them into darkness.

CHAPTER TWO

OLIVER VALANCE HUDDLED behind the bedroom door, his heart pounding. Aphrodite's gloved hand still rested in his. Even as he panicked at their near discovery, he also noticed how small her hand was compared to his. From a distance, she had not seemed particularly diminutive, but up close, he dwarfed her. She'd been blessed with generous curves, but she was shorter than most grown women.

She looked young enough to be a debutante, too. Was she really one-and-twenty, or had she lied about her age? He wasn't sure he could trust any of what she'd said. Something about this situation seemed fishy, even apart from the way Valance seemed to have taken leave of his senses. He had been a fool for a pretty face before but tonight set a new standard for his folly.

But then, he had never before seen a face like hers.

Raucous laughter pealed in the corridor. "Who was that?" a woman asked.

"God knows," a man replied. "Didn't recognize 'em. Hope they didn't recognize us." Both strangers laughed again. Their footsteps gradually faded as they walked away.

Valance waited until the hallway fell silent, willing his heartrate and breathing to slow down. "We are safe," he finally announced. "They didn't recognize us."

It had been utter folly on his part to unmask the lady in the hallway. He realized that now. He had been so intent on seeing her face that he hadn't considered the consequences. All he could think about was that Aphrodite must be radiantly beautiful under her blue-green mask.

And he had been right. It was rare to see a grown woman with that pale, nearly-white shade of hair. It was equally rare to see eyes that so vibrantly blended blue and green. The combination of hair and eyes would have made Aphrodite stand out in any crowd, even apart from the graceful shape of her cheek bones or her charming retrousse nose. She was right that they had never met before. He would have remembered her.

"Ah, so we were not discovered," Aphrodite said softly.

Something about her voice worried him. He peered down at her, but in the darkness of the room he could not read her face.

"I suppose we are fortunate not to have been caught and identified," she continued.

Why, he wondered, did she sound disappointed? She ought to be glad they'd gotten away without being caught! In any case, Valance had had enough of a scare for one night. His desire for Aphrodite had built since the moment their eyes met across the crowded ballroom, but the shock of nearly being caught felt like a bucket of cold water. He no longer felt at all lustful.

Time to end this dangerous game. Now, before someone got hurt.

Valance cleared his throat. "We should go back to the ballroom. Next time we might not be so lucky." Aphrodite made no response. As the silence stretched out, Valance began to worry again. "Madam? Are you unwell?"

"I do not know what to do," she whispered.

Valance closed his eyes, silently wishing he were snugly tucked into his own bed, back in Russell Square. Aphrodite was not his problem to solve. "Go back to your husband," he suggested. "And next time . . ." Who was he to give marital advice to a stranger? *He* had never been married. "Next time, think twice before you sneak off for a tryst."

She sighed so softly he almost missed the sound. Then she

cleared her throat. "No doubt you are right. But I need a moment to collect myself. You may go on without me, sir."

"You want me to leave you here?" He drew his brows down unhappily.

"Yes, please."

Was it his imagination, or did her voice tremble? Although Valance's eyes had adjusted to the dimness of the room, he still could not interpret her expression. But her tone made him uneasy. Something felt off.

"I really think I should escort you back to the ballroom. Who knows who you might encounter in one of these back hallways? Some of the guests have already had too much to drink." He did not like to imagine what might happen to her if she met the wrong man.

"I am not going back to the ballroom." Her voice had grown more confident.

"Then where are you going?" His words hung in the air, unanswered. "I know it isn't any of my business, but—"

"That is right," she said crisply. "It is none of your business where I go or what I do. But if you are not going to ruin me, I must come up with a different means of escape, so please—"

"Ruin you?" he repeated, startled. "You *want* to be ruined?" She did not answer. Her silence gave him time to recall something even more disturbing she'd said. "What do you mean, *escape*? Are you trying to get away from someone?"

She hesitated for so long, he thought she was not going to answer him. Finally, she said, "That is my concern, not yours. If you are not going to help me, please leave me alone to figure this out."

How was he supposed to help her when she would not say why she needed help? He tore off his ridiculous crown of wax fruit and tossed it on the floor so that he could run a hand through his hair. The strangeness of the situation frustrated him. It would be easiest to do as she asked and leave her behind, but that did not seem right.

"Damn it all," he grumbled. "You're making this my business!" She'd made it his business the moment she asked him to accompany her out of the ballroom. Having escorted her away from light and safety, he felt he had an obligation to see that she came to no harm.

Time to shed a little light on the situation. Fortunately, Valance had had pockets sewn on the inside of his toga, though they disturbed the hang of the fabric. Now, he dug around in a pocket for a pencil and a scrap of paper. The darkness made it difficult to write words, but he could work this spell with a single rune. He drew a swift, sloppy starburst symbol on the paper, pouring his magic into every stroke of the pencil. As he finished the last stroke, a silver witchlight burst into being above him, illuminating the guest room.

"How did you do that?" Aphrodite did not sound scared or surprised, merely curious. "I did not hear you utter any incantations. But that was sorcery, not magecraft, wasn't it?"

"More or less," he said, feeling self-conscious. He had not expected to have to explain his unusual gift. "I work magic by writing words or drawing symbols rather than by speaking, chanting, or gesturing. It's a rare form of sorcery."

Some of his instructors at Oxford had, in fact, considered it to be more akin to wizardry than to sorcery. Wizards and witches used materials when they worked magic; sorcerers used only words. Valance did not need eye of newt and wing of bat—or the more normal herbs and crystals used by wizards—to work his spells. But he could not work magic unless he had a writing implement and a surface to write on. In a pinch, he could use a stick to scratch symbols into the dirt. But he had never been able to cast spells by speaking, the way most sorcerers could.

"How strange." She tipped her head back to study the witchlight. "Your light is very well made, though. Bright and efficient. You didn't waste any power."

"Er, thank you?" Valance had not expected to have his spellcasting critiqued, either. Most people could neither see nor work magic.

Aphrodite peered up at him, a wrinkle forming between her brows. "By any chance, are you able to cast concealment spells?"

Valance stared. "What do you mean? Conceal what?"

"Could you conceal a person?" Aphrodite clarified. "Make it so other people wouldn't notice someone? Or at least, so they wouldn't recognize that person? Like a magical disguise?"

"I have never tried to do that." It ought to be within the scope of his talents, but he had never had a need to conceal someone. "Why do you ask?"

"I need to get away from here tonight." She spoke matter-of-factly, as if she discussed nothing more concerning than the order of the dances at the ball. "It would be easier to leave if people did not recognize me. If servants see me and identify me, the—I mean, someone might be able to track me down."

Valance narrowed his eyes. "What exactly are you running away from?"

Rather than answer him, she stared down at the floor and twisted her hands together. The soft glow of his witchlight illuminated the anxious lines in her face. She looked on the verge of tears.

All sorts of unsavory possibilities jostled for space inside Valance's head. "Is someone trying to hurt you?"

He could not help thinking of the sad story of Lady Cheverly, whose abusive husband nearly killed their oldest child a few years after she ran off with Lord Markham. Lord Cheverly had eventually been declared incompetent, and his children were placed in the care of a safer guardian but arranging that had been both difficult and expensive.

Men like that deserved to be shot, in Valance's opinion. If he had been Markham, he would have called Cheverly out and put a bullet in his brain. Except that Markham was a truly terrible shot, and would probably have gotten killed by Cheverly, who had decent aim. So perhaps it was best that no duel had occurred.

"Maybe," Aphrodite said at last. "But probably not the way you mean *hurt*." She drew a deep breath. "The fact of the matter is that my mother is trying to force me into a marriage I don't want. I would do anything to escape it." She licked her lips. "I cannot offer to pay you money, but if there is any service I could offer in exchange for your help, I would gladly—"

"Your parents are arranging a marriage for you?" Valance interrupted. "Aren't you already married?"

She froze in midsentence, her mouth hanging open. That was answer enough.

"You lied to me." Valance, appalled by how close he'd come to a gross violation of both manners and morals, could say nothing more.

It was one thing to have a brush with a widow or a negligent husband's philandering wife (though, before tonight, he had always avoided *affaires* with married women). But only the worst of rakes would casually tumble into bed with a gently-reared maiden. Such a liaison would destroy a debutante's chances of a respectable marriage.

Valance clenched his hand into angry fists. What the hell was this girl doing in a bedroom with a strange man? Where was her chaperone? Was she trying to entrap him? He'd heard rumors of girls so bent on capturing a husband that they were willing to trap a man in a compromising position to force a proposal. He had always thought those stories were apocryphal, but that was the only explanation he could think of for Aphrodite's intended seduction. He broke into a sweat as he considered all the possible consequences of this tryst.

"What game are you playing?" His voice, thickened by panic, sounded more like a growl.

Aphrodite flinched. "As I told you, I am trying to escape an undesirable marriage." She swallowed heavily. "I thought the best way of doing that would be to ruin myself, so B—so no one would want to marry me."

"That's the worst way of escaping an unwanted marriage! My God!" He mussed his already-disarrayed hair again, half-wishing he could pull it out in dismay. This plan was worse than anything he'd imagined. "Don't you realize that you will be an outcast from society forever? Your family may disown you. And you will never marry. And . . and . . ."

He could not even begin to list all of the disadvantages of her scheme. It would ruin not only her name, but her family's reputation. She would end up living in poverty with some maiden aunt in a god-forsaken village, never to be seen in society again. And that was if she was *lucky*!

"Yes!" She clenched her fists, as if she were starting to lose her temper, too. "I realize all those things. But it would be better to spend a lifetime as a disgraced spinster than to marry Belmont."

Once again, Valance staggered. Quite literally, this time. He took a step backward and nearly stumbled. "Your parents want you to marry *Belmont*, when he's already buried three wives?"

The duke must be nearly thirty years Aphrodite's senior, and there was no getting around the fact that he was a very nasty customer. Belmont was hard on his horses, short-tempered with his servants, and (if rumor was true) rough with his mistresses. The only positive thing anyone could say about him was that he knew how to host a good party. That was the only reason Valance had come to tonight's masquerade. Belmont was certainly not one of Valance's particular friends.

"Yes." She looked grim, and no wonder. "You see why I have to run away, don't you? He told my mother that he intends to propose tonight."

"I suppose I do see your point." Valance rubbed his temples, feeling a headache beginning to build. He forced his jaw to unclench, hoping to stave off the pain. "But where do you intend to go?"

Aphrodite's face brightened. "London, at first. Then to Bath, perhaps. I attended Miss Merton's Academy near Bath, and I thought my old headmistress might hire me—"

"No one will hire you if you are ruined," he interrupted. "No one wants a fallen woman teaching their children!"

She was going to end up on the streets if she ran off to London with no better plan than this. She probably did not have the skills for any position but that of governess or companion, both of which required an absolutely stainless reputation and sterling letters of recommendation.

Unless—"Are you a witch or sorceress? Have you some practical magical talent?" Magic could ease anyone's way in the world. It might give her a chance for a new life.

But she shook her head. "I wish I did. I can see magic, but I cannot work it."

"Unfortunate." But he ought to have predicted as much. If she were capable of working powerful magic, she would have had more options, and would probably have come up with a better plan.

"Please, sir," the nameless girl said. "Can you help me?"

Valance stared at her in dismay, wishing he had never set eyes on her. Or at least refused to leave the ballroom with her. No amount of physical attractiveness was worth this much trouble.

She must have read refusal in his face, because she sighed, and her shoulders slumped. "At least, will you promise not to tell anyone about this conversation? You must realize that my safety rests in your hands now. If you tell anyone you saw me, or reveal my plans, I may not be able to escape." She swallowed uneasily. "As I said, I cannot pay you in money, but . . ."

"Of course, I will help you," Valance said wearily. No woman deserved to be forced into marriage with the Duke of Belmont. But he could already tell this was going to ruin his plans for the week. If not for longer. "We had better go now."

She blinked at him. "Go where?"

"London, of course. I live in a rather unconventional household," he explained, "and my housemate's sister lives with him. With us."

Aphrodite, probably concerned about the proprieties, frowned. She opened her mouth to say something, but he hurriedly interjected: "It's not what you think." He could not explain the full situation, though; it was not his secret to reveal. "I mean, Miss Carrington has a companion with her to maintain her reputation. It is all entirely above board."

It was, in fact, entirely scandalous. People only tolerated Abigail's behavior because she was an heiress, her godmother having left her a substantial fortune. And she did not care to move in *tonnish* circles.

"In any case," Valance concluded, "you will not be the only lady in the household, so you need not worry about damaging your reputation."

"But the whole point of this tryst was to ruin my reputation!" Aphrodite crossed her arms in front of her chest, boldly meeting his gaze. Whatever she lacked in common sense, she made up for in courage.

Valance shook his head. "You need a better plan." She would not have hatched such a scandalous plot if she truly understood the long-term consequences of her actions. "But we can talk about that later. First, we should get out of here."

Her plan for escape might have flaws, but her idea to use a concealment spell was a good one. He tore a scrap off the paper with his light spell, thought for a moment, then scribbled a few words in Latin. He had to combine elements from a few different spells, as he had never learned any disguise spells. He hoped this cobbled-together script would work. They did not have time to experiment or fine-tune the spell.

He handed the ensorcelled paper to Aphrodite. "Put that in your pocket."

"What will it do?" She stared at the scrap of paper in her hand, then held it up to the still glowing witchlight. She squinted as if trying to read the words. But, not surprisingly, she seemed to make nothing of them. No one could read Valance's handwriting.

"What I *hope* it will do is convince anyone who looks at you that they are seeing a young gentleman of nondescript appearance, rather than a young lady dressed as Aphrodite. But I have no idea whether it will work, because I have never cast such a spell before. It might not do anything at all." It was only right to warn her. To his eyes, Aphrodite still looked like a young woman. He had no idea what other people would see.

"The spell worked," she said confidently. "That is, your magic certainly did something. I just could not tell what."

"Let's hope it does what I want it to do."

Whatever else the spell did, it had taken a good deal of power. His headache was worsening, and his stomach rumbled ominously. Working magic always made Valance hungry, and they had missed supper. But he knew there would be no time for a snack. Sooner or later, someone was going to notice that Aphrodite was missing from the ballroom and come looking for her.

"We should go now," he told her. "I have no idea how long that spell will last. Come with me."

She followed him obediently to his guestroom. His valet, Preston, slept on a cot in the corner of the bedchamber, there being no dressing room. Valance shook him awake.

"My lord?" Preston smothered a yawn. He glanced at Aphrodite and nodded politely before turning back to Valance. "Do you require my assistance?" It was not like Valance to wake Preston so late. Normally he would have undressed himself after a night of carousing.

"I am afraid it is a bit of an emergency," Valance said apologetically. "We need to leave." His original plan had involved staying the night so he could return home by daylight. That was clearly out of the question now.

"Oh. Before breakfast, you mean?" Preston sat up in bed.

Valance was relieved to see that his valet had at least kept his trousers on, though he had gone to bed in his shirtsleeves.

"Now, I am afraid. This very moment. As I said, it is an emergency. I will pack my own bags, if you will be so good as to rouse Gates and have him ready the carriage." They were fortunate to have a bright, gibbous moon tonight—the roads ought to be safe enough for travel.

"As you wish, my lord." If Preston had questions about the

reason for this late-night departure, he kept them to himself.

Valance took off his mask and tossed it carelessly onto the dressing table. He longed to change out of the rest of his costume, but he could not do that with Aphrodite standing right there. He had to make do with covering his costume up with his greatcoat.

"Er, my lord?" Preston asked.

"Yes?" Valance glanced up from his packing.

"Does the situation demand secrecy?" Preston pitched his voice low, as if he feared someone might be eavesdropping outside the bedroom door.

"Yes," Aphrodite said, before Valance could answer. "The fewer people who know of our departure, the better."

Preston's eyes widened. "Yes, sir," he said, addressing Aphrodite. He seemed to genuinely think she was a man. Apparently, the disguise spell was a success.

Valance began to feel more hopeful. Perhaps they could make a clean escape. Once he got to London, he would learn more about Aphrodite's family. There must be a grandparent, aunt, or uncle willing to take her in even if her parents wanted nothing to do with her. But most likely, she exaggerated her parents' determination to marry her off. It was against the law to force a girl to marry against her will, wasn't it? At least, it ought to be. Probably all she needed to do was explain the matter clearly, and her parents would accept her decision. They would have to be monsters to force her to marry a man like *Belmont*!

Valance grew increasingly confident about their chances of escape as it became clear that his coachman was also fooled by the disguise spell. Gates, like Preston, had no clue that Valance's traveling companion was a young lady rather than a young man. No one stopped them or called after them when they left the hall and climbed into Valance's carriage.

Preston sat up on the box with Gates, leaving the inside seats to Valance and his companion. Only now did Valance realize how awkward it was to be alone with Aphrodite under these circumstances. Merely an hour ago, she had tried to seduce him. He supposed the gentlemanly thing to do would be to pretend none of that ever happened. All things considered, it was just as well they had been interrupted before he could so much as kiss her.

"You might as well get some rest," he suggested. "It will take us a few hours to get to London." That was why he had planned to stay the night at Belmont Court. People came from all over the country for these parties, even though Belmont lived in an out-of-the-way corner of Kent. Whatever his other faults, Belmont was a generous host.

"I know." Aphrodite hastily covered a yawn. "If you don't mind, I think I will try to sleep." She leaned against the wall of the carriage and tucked the lap robe about her. Then she closed her eyes, and to all appearances, fell asleep quickly.

Valance stayed awake, too jolted by the rough road to slumber. Instead of sleeping, he thought about how to reunite Aphrodite with her family. For the first time, it occurred to him that by running off with her—traveling alone, inside a closed carriage, for hours—he might have already compromised her. Of course, their time alone in a bedroom together would have been enough to compromise her, but he hoped no one ever learned of that. Taking her home with him might be scandal enough. There would be chaperones in Russell Square, but the two of them were unchaperoned now.

What would he do if her family demanded some sort of satisfaction from him? What if her father or brother called him out? What if they insisted Valance marry her? Between Miss Manfield's rejection last summer and Valance's most recent quarrel with his mistress, he'd had enough of the fairer sex for now. He was not sure he had it in him to pursue a new courtship.

Valance stayed awake the entire ride, searching for a solution that would allow Aphrodite to escape with her good name intact, while leaving him with his freedom. But the pounding of his head made it hard to think at all.

It must have been past three in the morning when they finally rolled up to the Carrington family's townhouse. Aphrodite still slept with the lap robe tucked about her. She must be freezing, as she had not brought a coat with her. Valance felt a pang of guilt. He ought to have either offered her his greatcoat or worked a warming spell for her. He had not even thought of that.

"We are here," he said quietly. "Madam?" She did not stir, so he put a cautious hand on her shoulder and shook her awake.

"What?" She recoiled from him and stared back, wide-eyed. "Who are you? Where are we?"

"I am Lord Valance." He used the same soothing voice he would have used for one of Roderick Carrington's young daughters. "We are in London, in Russell Square. Not far from the British Museum. I live here. We will tuck you into our spare bedroom and figure things out tomorrow." Or rather, today, it being morning already. But they could not solve her problem without a good night's sleep.

"Oh, I see," she said politely. "Thank you very much." She sat up and tried to smooth her hair, which had long since tumbled out of her coiffure.

"My pleasure." He was not at all pleased with the situation, but he could hardly admit as much.

Valance helped the stranger out of the carriage, leaving Preston to carry his valise. The townhouse's front door was locked, but that did not matter. He carried a copy of the house key.

To his surprise, every candle in the front hall still burned. One of the Carringtons—Peregrine, not Abigail—lay on the marble floor, a piece of blue chalk in his hand.

Valance stared at his housemate. "God, Peregrine, what are you doing up?"

"Working magic."

Valance rolled his eyes. He could see that much. Peregrine had drawn half a pentacle on the floor. On his right side was a pile of candles waiting to be lit, while several pouches of herbs lay on the left. It looked like a major magical working. What Valance could not see was why the magic had to be done at three in the morning. Peregrine often kept odd hours when he was deep into a project, but this seemed excessive even for him.

Before he could clarify his question, Peregrine continued.: "What are you doing here? I thought you were staying in Kent till tomorrow."

"It's already tomorrow," Valance reminded him. "And I had to leave early. Due to an, er, emergency."

"Yes, I needed to leave Belmont Court in a hurry." Aphrodite gazed down at the pentacle, too. "His Lordship was kind enough to transport me. Look, I don't mean to tell you how to go about your business, but I think that line is a little crooked." She pointed to indicate one of the yellow chalk lines.

"Oh. So it is! Perhaps I messed it up because I haven't slept tonight. Thank you for telling me." Peregrine stared up at Aphrodite and cocked his head to one side. "Who are you, then? And why are you glamoured to look like a man?"

CHAPTER THREE

"YOU CAN TELL I'm not really a man?" This fascinated Honora. As far as she could tell, no one else had been able to see through Lord What's-His-Name's disguise.

"You certainly look like a woman to me," the new stranger replied. He had hair a lighter shade of brown than her rescuer, and he was built on more slender lines. She guessed him to be roughly her own age, or perhaps a little older. "That is, you are dressed like one. But what is all that blue-green fluff on your dress? Are you supposed to be a plant?" A line formed between his brows as he studied her costume.

"I'm supposed to be Aphrodite, emerging from the sea. It was my mother's idea." Honora wrinkled her nose. She had wanted to be a ghost or a mummy. Something that involved a lot of wrappings. Something that wouldn't attract attention. But she had, as usual, been overruled. Her mother wanted everyone to notice Honora.

"But why would you add a glamour over your costume?" the stranger continued. "No one can see the costume because of Valance's spell. Why wear a costume if no one can see it?"

"*You* can see it," Honora pointed out. "How can you see it if other people can't?"

"Oh, that's because I'm a better magician than Valance," he explained. "His magic is not strong enough to hide something from *me*."

Lord Valance (she tried to commit his name to memory this time) made a rude sputtering sound. "There's no need to insult me! I have never worked this spell before, and I didn't have time to perfect it. If I had known—"

"I'm not trying to insult you," the stranger interjected. "I am merely answering this young lady's question. Your spell was very well-made and I am sure it fooled most people, but it was not strong enough to fool *me*."

Lord Valance, unconvinced, shook his head. "Anyway, do you know if there's an empty bedroom I can put Miss, ah, the unknown lady, in?" His eyes shifted in Honora's direction.

The stranger furrowed his brow. "Both guest rooms are being used for storage right now. But Susan and Abby are out, so you could probably use one of their rooms."

His lordship's mouth fell open in dismay. "What? Since when? Where did they go?"

"They went to Surrey yesterday. Susan's cough was getting bad and Abby thought the country air would help. But I think she was also cross because I made a mess in the dining room."

Lord Valance's face fell into anxious lines. "What exactly did you do in the dining room?"

"I was trying to figure out how to catch fireballs with magic," his friend explained. "My first spell did not work right, and some of the furnishings got burnt. But I figured out how to fix the spell, so you need not worry. It won't happen again."

"Why would you want to catch fireballs?" Honora asked. What a fascinating idea! But what did he even mean by "fireballs"? A ball made of fire? Or a ball *on* fire? Or something else?

"I'm trying to make a trap to catch a falling star. That's what this is." He gestured to the chalked pentacle on the floor. "Since there is no meteor shower tonight, I had to make my own meteorites for practice."

"Oh." Honora frowned. She had many questions, and she did not know which to ask first. She was particularly curious about how one could produce home-made meteorites. But the placement of the pentacle also confused her. "Wouldn't you have to put the trap outside to catch a falling star?" She had never heard of a meteor shower inside a townhouse.

"No, part of the spell involves transferring the meteorite directly into this room," he explained. "That way, I won't have to stand on the roof to collect it."

"Peregrine, you do not want a meteorite to land inside the house." Lord Valance stared at the pentacle and tapped his foot, scowling.

The strange gentleman had been studying the chalked lines on the floor, but now he glanced up at his housemate. "Oh, good point. I suppose it might make a mess. Or damage the floor."

"Precisely," Lord Valance agreed. "Your sister would be un-happy. So would Susan. So would I, for that matter. I am sure this is an excellent spell, but there must be a better place to work it."

Peregrine-What's-His-Name sighed. "Very well. I suppose I will have to do this on the roof after all. But that is not very convenient. You know perfectly well that I've had bad luck working magic on rooftops." He began to scuff out the chalked lines. Then he peered up at Honora. "Who are you, again? Have I met you?"

"No, we have not met." There was nothing distinctive about the stranger's physical appearance. The bronze lights that twinkled and shifted in his aura indicated that he was a powerful wizard, but apart from that, his aura looked perfectly ordinary. Still, Honora thought she would have remembered him.

"I am Honora Grantly, the daughter of the late Sir Isaac Grantly." Introducing herself violated half a dozen rules of etiquette, but there was no one here who could make a proper introduction between them.

The wizard got to his feet, dusted off the knees of his trou-sers, and bowed quite properly. "Very pleased to make your acquaintance, Miss Grantly. I believe I met your father at the Cambion Club a couple of years ago. All the Carrington men are members, even my older brother."

She acknowledged his bow with an inclination of her head. "That is quite likely. My father usually did visit his clubs when he came to town." He had belonged to Boodle's, too, but he had visited the Cambion Club more often.

Mr. Carrington said, "The Grantlys tend to be either mages or sorcerers if they have magic. Which are you?"

Asking someone about their magical talents (or lack thereof) was considered bad manners, but Honora saw no reason not to answer. "I am technically a mage, but a very limited one. I can see both magic and auras, but I cannot work magic of any kind."

Her father, being a sorcerer rather than a mage, had only been able to give Honora a little instruction on reading auras. He had been more successful at teaching her how to analyze spells. Her magical sight had been keener than his, so she had sometimes assisted him with his work.

"That's a shame. We could have used another sorcerer here. I could have used help with this spell, in fact." Mr. Carrington gestured down to the half-erased pentacle. "This is quite the magical household, you know. My sister is a witch, and I am a wizard, and of course Valance is whatever he is. There's no word for his type of magic. Susan does not work magic, but she is very good about tolerating magical experiments," he added as an afterthought.

"And who is Susan, then?" Honora found it difficult to keep all these names straight.

"Oh, she is my sister's lover." Mr. Carrington's face did not lose an iota of composure as he made this revelation.

Honora blinked and rapidly readjusted some of her assumptions. Having been to boarding school, she knew perfectly well that some girls fancied other girls. But she had thought that was a stage people outgrew. Apparently not?

"*Peregrine*, you cannot introduce Miss Taylor that way! You should refer to her as your sister's companion." Lord Valance rubbed his bloodshot eyes. "Abigail and Susan would not want strangers to know about their relationship."

"I know that!" Mr. Carrington said indignantly. "I would never refer to Susan that way when talking to a stranger, but since this young lady is your friend, I assumed she would keep the information in confidence." He smiled hopefully at Honora.

"Oh, no, we are not friends," Honora explained. She knew nothing about Lord Valance other than that he had an unusual means of working magic.

"My apologies. Are you Valance's new mistress, then? Did he finally dismiss Cherie?"

Lord Valance threw his hands up in the air. "She is not my mistress! She is a respectable young lady!" His scowl deepened.

Honora opened her mouth to ask who Cherie was, but at the last minute, she thought better of the question. It was not her business how many lovers Lord Valance kept. (But was it her imagination, or did Mr. Carrington look disappointed at this news? Curious.)

Mr. Carrington's misunderstanding gave her a good idea, though. She would be thoroughly, absolutely ruined if people thought she was Lord Valance's new mistress. Perhaps he would be willing to set her up in rooms and visit her often enough to ruin her reputation? That would be an enormous expense to him, though, particularly if he already kept a mistress.

Honora sighed, wishing she had access to her fortune. Everything would have been easier if she'd had money. But the money left to her under her father's will was held in trust for her by Uncle Robert, who shared Lady Grantly's enthusiasm for the marriage to Belmont.

Lord Valance turned to Honora. "The hour is very late, and I think we all ought to go to bed. This conversation will make more sense after a good night's sleep."

"Possibly." Honora suspected that so complicated a situation would be difficult to explain under any circumstances. But sleep could not hurt, and it might very well help.

"Peregrine," Lord Valance continued. "You and I had better spend the night at an inn, so as not to compromise Miss Grantly."

But Mr. Carrington shook his head. "Absolutely not. You know I hate sleeping anywhere but in my own bed. My apologies, Miss Grantly," he added, turning back to Honora. "I am sure it is awkward for you to stay here without a chaperone."

"I do not mind the impropriety," she assured him. It would, in fact, be perfect. If she spent the night here without a chaperone, she would be thoroughly compromised. "I am trying to ruin my reputation, you see."

"Really?" Mr. Carrington raised his eyebrows. "Is that difficult to do? I was rather under the impression that it was difficult to *avoid* being ruined, if one is a woman. There are so many things a lady is not allowed to do!"

"I am finding it more challenging than I expected," Honora admitted. She cast a sour glance at Lord Valance, who could have been more helpful about the matter. Why on earth would he worry about preserving her reputation when she had made it clear she wanted to blacken it?

"I suppose it is too late to do anything about the matter tonight. We will just have to hope tno one learns you were here unchaperoned." Lord Valance rubbed his temples, as if he had a headache. "In that case, allow me to show you to your room."

Honora followed her host upstairs to a large, well-appointed bedroom, part of the master suite. Most unfortunately, the bed had already been stripped.

"Well, damn," he said. "You can't sleep here."

"Where is the bedding kept?" Honora asked practically. "I can make the bed myself." She had never made a bed in her life, but it could not be too hard, could it?

Lord Valance lifted the lid on the wooden chest at the foot of the bed. "The bedding ought to be here."

Honora peered inside too. The chest was empty, with not a blanket or sheet in sight. They walked through the dressing room into the second bedroom, but that bed was in the same state. Though she poked about in the room for a few minutes, no bedding could be found. No one could sleep in either of these rooms tonight.

"I suppose the maids must be laundering the sheets," Lord Valance said. "I am sure there are extra sheets and blankets somewhere, but I don't know where the linen closet is. I don't own this house, you understand. It belongs to the Carringtons. I only live here." He shrugged apologetically.

"Why *do* you live here?" Honora knew nothing about this particular neighborhood, but she knew that Bloomsbury was not one of the fashionable parts of the West End. Most noblemen would have preferred Mayfair or Marylebone.

"The Valance family has never owned a townhouse," Lord Valance explained. "And I have known Peregrine and his sister all my life, because their estate borders on mine. And"—he hesitated for a moment, and finished—"I dislike living alone."

"I see. Well, is there a sofa in the drawing room I could sleep on?" Exhaustion weighed Honora down, making it hard to think clearly. She desperately needed rest. And after that? She would figure out the next steps tomorrow.

Lord Valance sighed. He had been doing that rather a lot since their arrival. "I will sleep on the sofa. You can sleep in my room."

Reluctance dripped from his voice; he clearly did not want to give up his bedchamber. Who could blame him? Honora had yet to meet the sofa or *chaise longue* that actually provided a good night's sleep.

"That is not necessary," Honora assured him. "I will be fine on a sofa." She smothered another yawn.

"Nonsense. You are a guest here. I cannot ask you to sleep in the drawing room."

He strode out of the room as if the matter were decided. She tagged after him, feeling too tired to argue further. His room lay up another flight of stairs. It was smaller than the other bedrooms, and had been papered in rather somber shades of brown and gold. Privately, Honora thought it was one of the ugliest wallpapers she'd ever seen.

"In case you are wondering," Lord Valance said, "I am not the one who decorated the room. I believe this room used to belong to Carrington's younger brother."

"I see." Honora *had* wondered. Perhaps the Carrington family eccentricities included unusual taste when it came to home decor.

"Good night, then. We can speak more in the morning." He left in a hurry, as if he were glad to get away from her.

Honora could scarcely blame him for that. She had attached herself to him like a barnacle, when in fact there was no reason why he should help her. It was very generous of him to let her stay here at all, given that they had met only a few hours ago.

Everything seemed to be working out quite well, she thought as she stripped down to her shift. She had gotten away from the duke, and after tonight she would be so thoroughly compromised that Belmont would not offer for her. She was safe for now, and in the morning, she could figure out her next steps.

Honora climbed into bed and tucked herself in, shivering. No fire burned on the hearth, but the counterpane was soft and thick. It ought to keep her warm enough. The faint odor of some scented soap or cologne hung about the bedding, but it was not an unpleasant smell. Far from it.

She fell asleep as soon as her head hit the pillow. It had, after all, been a very long day.

CHAPTER FOUR

January 6, 1817

VALANCE WOKE UP far too early. Judging from the position of the sun in the winter sky, it was not yet noon. But at least he had slept away the last of last night's headache. Since he left the masquerade before he had too much to drink, he was not the least bit hungover. On the contrary, everything looked much clearer by the light of day.

Yesterday, helping a woman who wanted to escape an unwanted marriage had seemed like the chivalrous thing to do. Today, Valance wondered what could have possessed him to take Miss Grantly home with him. His intentions might have been for the best, but in bringing her to Carrington House without a chaperone, he had thoroughly compromised her, and ruined his own good name—a possession of which he had always been proud.

Maybe he ought to have taken Miss Grantly to a respectable hotel. Last night, he had decided against that, because he was afraid his disguise spell wouldn't last long enough to protect her. If people realized she was a young lady rather than a gentleman, they would think it scandalous for her to arrive at a hotel at four in the morning, without any luggage nor a maid to accompany her. Still, that might have been better than letting her spend the night in a house with two young bachelors and no chaperone.

Failing that, he could have deposited her at the home of one of his few married friends. That might have been the least damaging option. Unfortunately, he did not think any of them were in London at the moment. Sir Roderick Carrington rarely left his country estate, and Lord Markham's first child was only a few months old. If the Markhams came to London at all this spring, it would be later in the Season. In any case, Valance hadn't thought of that option last night.

Instead, Valance had made the worst choice possible, with no better excuse than that he had been too exhausted to approach the problem logically. He could only see one way to mend the damage, and it was a step he would rather not take. But it was early yet. Maybe he would think of a better solution once he woke up more thoroughly.

He rang for Preston, who brought him a hot cup of coffee and rolls that had long since gone cold. "The dining room is unusable at the moment, my lord, so I thought you had best eat in here."

Preston's face looked pained, as it often did since Valance moved into Carrington House. Preston approved neither of Russell Square nor of the eccentricities of Valance's housemates. Valance, on the other hand, much preferred living with his friends to living alone in a bachelor flat. He liked having people on hand for a spontaneous game of chess or cards, or to use as a sounding board for talking through the latest problem with his magical research. Peregrine understood magical theory better than anyone Valance knew, including most of his Oxford professors.

"My lord," Preston continued, "May I ask why you did not sleep in your bedchamber last night?"

Valance spoke around a mouthful of stale bread. "You should not ask." It was not for a servant to question his employer. "But since you *have* asked, I might as well explain that my bedchamber is currently occupied by a young lady."

"A young lady?" Preston's carefully cultivated wooden expression slipped, revealing how startled he was. More than startled: dismayed.

"A *respectable* young lady," Valance qualified, wanting there to be no misunderstanding about Miss Grantly's status. The servants would not treat her well if they thought she was a member of the *demi-monde*. "Miss Honora Grantly, daughter of the late Sir Isaac Grantly. I am afraid the reason for her visit must remain secret." Mostly because he could not think of any plausible explanation.

"I . . . see," Preston said slowly. "How long will she be staying?"

"I do not know," Valance admitted. That depended on whether Miss Grantly would see reason. And on whether he could think of a way to preserve her reputation. "Do you happen to know where Mr. Carrington is?"

"I believe he is still asleep," Preston said. "I have yet to see him this morning."

Valance found Peregrine in his own chamber on the first story. There were as many books in his bedroom as in Valance's, but Peregrine, being a wizard, also kept a mortar and pestle, boxes of chalk, and other *materia magica* on his shelves. This made his room seem more cluttered than Valance's, despite being larger. It was also more tastefully decorated, because unlike Cosmo, Peregrine had let his older sister choose the wallpaper and drapery for him. Abigail had excellent taste.

Peregrine had fallen asleep still fully dressed in yesterday's clothes, but at least this time he'd made it to the bed. He had been known to doze off at his desk while working out a formula.

"Peregrine!" After years of friendship, Valance knew better than to shake his friend awake—Peregrine did not like unexpected physical contact. Valance waited for him to stir and open his eyes before speaking further. "I'm sorry to bother you, but I need your advice."

"Hmm?" Peregrine mumbled sleepily. "You don't usually want my advice." He sat up, yawned, and stretched.

"I know." Valance was more likely to approach Abigail with his problems. He had grown up thinking of her as being wiser than himself, though she was only two years his senior. "But I'm in a bind and I need to talk to someone."

"Yes?" Peregrine swung his legs over the edge of the bed and rolled his head from side to side to stretch his neck. "What's the problem?"

Valance took a deep breath. "What on earth am I going to do about Miss Grantly?"

"Oh, is she still here?" He sounded surprised.

"So far as I know." Valance had not thought to check, but it seemed unlikely that she had gone anywhere. Did she even have somewhere to go? "She spent the night in a house with two bachelors and no chaperone. She will be ruined."

"I suppose that's true," Peregrine agreed. "You are going to have to marry her."

Valance groaned. That was precisely the outcome he wanted to avoid. If Miss Grantly was willing to ruin herself to avoid one unwanted engagement, she probably would not want to jump into a different unwanted marriage. And Valance had certainly not planned to marry anyone at all yet. He was only four-and-twenty, and he intended to enjoy his liberty a little longer. Being a bachelor meant endless possibilities for bedmates. In fact, he'd already started making a list of courtesans he might approach after he dismissed Cherie.

"Can't you think of any other solution?" he begged.

"No, I can't." Peregrine yawned until his jaw cracked. "I may think of something after breakfast. I will let you know."

Valance did not feel particularly optimistic, but he distracted himself by bringing his valise to an empty bedroom and ringing for Preston to shave him and dress him. After having worn that ridiculous mythological costume for so long, it was a relief to change into his normal, comfortable morning clothes. Since Miss Grantly was asleep in his room, he had to make do with the clothes in his bag. He had packed his things hastily last night, so his clothes were considerably rumpled, but he still felt much better once his cravat had been neatly tied.

He went looking for Peregrine again, finding him the process of tying his own cravat. Peregrine did not employ a valet, as he did not particularly care about the tie of his neckcloth or the shine of his boots. He still contrived to look perfectly respectable when he wanted to do so.

"Did you think of any better solution?" Valance asked, though he did not have much hope.

"I did think of one alternative, but I don't think you'll like it." Peregrine darted an uncertain glance at him out of the corners of his eyes.

"Oh?" Valance suspected Peregrine was right, but he could not help being curious about this alternative solution.

"If you don't want to marry Miss Grantly, you could set her up as your mistress." Peregrine peered at his reflection in the mirror rather than looking Valance in the face as he made this suggestion.

"*Peregrine!*" Valance was horrified. "How would that help? I am trying to *avoid* ruining her!" Besides, he already had a mistress, though things had been rather rocky between them for the last few months.

"I know you are trying to avoid ruining Miss Grantly," Peregrine said patiently, "but I think it is probably too late for that. If you don't want to marry her, setting her up as a mistress would at least give her a chance to gain valuable skills she could use in her future career."

"In what future career? As a *courtesan?*" Peregrine always did tend to think outside the lines, but this idea was worse than anything Valance could have imagined.

Peregrine shrugged. "I've heard such work pays well for women who are attractive and agreeable. And Miss Grantly seems to be both, don't you think?"

"Attractive, yes," Valance agreed. There had, after all, been a reason why he followed Aphrodite out of the ballroom. He had wanted her even when half her face was hidden by a mask. Valance would not admit to Miss Grantly being agreeable, though. A truly agreeable woman would not upend his life this way.

But all of that was beside the point. "Peregrine, you cannot propose that a respectable young lady become someone's mistress merely because she wants to avoid an uncomfortable marriage."

"I suppose not," Peregrine agreed. "In that case, you will have to marry her. I don't really see any way around it." He met Valance's eyes and twisted his mouth into a rueful smile.

"Neither do I." Valance scowled and scuffed the floor with the tip of his boot. He hated feeling trapped. Probably Miss Grantly hated it even more.

"Besides, you—"

"Don't say it!" Valance could guess what his friend was about to say, and it was something he had heard often enough from his mother. He did not need to hear it from Peregrine, too.

But Peregrine ignored his warning. "You need an heir. You will have to get married eventually. You might as well marry Miss Grantly, since you have compromised her. It would be the most honorable thing to do."

"I wish your sister were here," Valance grumbled. Abigail was every bit as intelligent as her brother and more socially savvy. She understood the rules of the *ton* quite well, though she sometimes ignored them herself. If there was a way out of the situation, Abigail would find it.

But Abigail and Susan were probably ensconced by the fire in the comfortable morning room at Carrington Abbey, spending time with the rest of the family. For a brief moment, Valance wished he were in Surrey, too, lounging in his own billiard room or library, without a care in the world. Except that if he were at Dreadnaught Hall, he would have to deal with his mother, which usually meant a whole series of headaches.

Valance sighed and walked away. What he needed was something to clear his mind. Since Miss Grantly seemed not to be awake yet, he could not speak to her. He might as well spend the time working.

Peregrine used the library as his workroom, and Abigail had

claimed the study for her witchcraft, so Valance had taken over the breakfast room as his work space. He had filled it with bookcases and used the round breakfast table as his work area. There he went to soothe himself by working on what he called, for lack of a better word, his runes.

As Valance had explained to Miss Grantly, he cast spells by writing words rather than speaking them. But drawing a single symbol was faster than writing a phrase, and it used less paper. Therefore, he was trying to develop an alphabet of easily-drawn symbols with which he could cast his most frequently-used spells.

He had mastered the rune for a witchlight long ago, but fire was proving more challenging. If he drew a flame on a piece of paper and put magic into it, the paper itself caught fire. That could be useful in some situations, but he wanted a more controllable flame.

Today, he experimented by drawing different variations of the flame symbol. Some of them didn't work. Some of them worked in the way his usual fire rune worked: by causing the paper to burst into flames, singing his fingers and leaving scorch marks on the table.

"What are you doing?"

Startled by the unexpected voice, Valance flinched. Miss Grantly stood on the opposite side of his worktable, intently studying his most recent spell paper. He hadn't even heard her enter the room.

"Why is it so smoky in here?" She wrinkled her nose.

"I am trying to develop a symbol for fire, because sketching a rune is faster than writing out a whole spell. But the spell works a little too well, if you catch my drift. The paper catches fire." He gestured at the charred paper and ash littering the table.

Valance would have happily continued explaining his rune system, but he knew they had more important things to talk about. "Never mind that. We need to talk about your future."

"Oh, I don't think I need to worry about my future any-more." He had not invited Miss Grantly to sit down, but she took a seat anyway. "The Duke of Belmont will not want to marry me after I have spent a night here without a chaperone. I am thoroughly ruined." She sounded pleased.

Valance rested his head in his hands for a moment. "So," he said cautiously, "what exactly is your plan now? Will you go back to your family?"

She shook her head. "I shouldn't think they would want me back. Not after this. My mother will be extremely angry with me." He could not argue with that, so he remained silent. "I told you, I am planning on going to Bath to visit my old school. Miss Merton will be able to help me."

"And *I* told you that no headmistress in the world is going to hire a woman who has been ruined," Valance reminded her. "The scandal would reflect poorly on the school."

She shrugged, not seeming the least bit fazed by this objection. "Perhaps I will find other work, then. I am good at sewing. I used to make my own dresses. Only for wearing in the country, of course," she clarified. "I have never been to London before. In any case, I am sure I can find work as a seamstress if all else fails."

Valance sighed. "Do you have any idea how little seamstresses make? Or what long hours they have to work? Or what they do when their eyesight begins to fail?" He had heard Abigail discuss the plight of working women many times, so he was well aware of what a pittance most seamstresses earned. Hat making and lace making were no better.

She frowned. "Eyesight? Oh, I hadn't thought of that. I do need reading glasses for fine work. I had to leave mine at Belmont Court. I will have to replace them somehow." She sighed. "I suppose there were a few gaps in my plan."

"Your plan was nothing *but* gaps!" Of all the things she had to worry about, she was fretting over her missing spectacles? "You didn't think any further than getting away from Belmont, did you?"

"No, I didn't." She picked up a scrap of paper and began shredding it, steadily looking away from Valance. "The other day, as soon as he got me alone for a moment, he backed me into a corner and kissed me." She shuddered. "And he kept doing it after I told him to stop. No, I didn't think further than getting away from him before he tried that again."

"What a blackguard," Valance said, though the word hardly seemed adequate for the duke's villainy. "Someone ought to call him out." Such an assault did explain the haste with which Miss Grantly fled the masquerade. No wonder she'd been so desperate to leave!

She shook her head. "My brother is only ten, so I'm afraid I would have to wait a long time for him to avenge my honor. In the meantime, I will find some way to sustain myself."

"If you don't come up with a better plan, you are going to end up in the river," Valance grumbled. The river was where fallen women were said to drown themselves.

"What a nasty thing to say!" She stared at him, her eyes wide. "What have I done to deserve that?"

Frustrated almost past the point of speech, Valance threw his hands in the air. "What have you done? First, you tried to seduce me! Then you ran off with me. And now you're ruined. Do you really think this is going to end well for you?"

He had looked all the consequences of last night's folly squarely in the face, and he did not like what he saw. The aftermath of the masquerade would be only marginally better for Valance. Men's reputations were not as fragile as women's, but there were some things a gentleman ought never do, and absconding with the daughter of a baronet was one of them. He would be labelled a rake.

Miss Grantly crossed her arms in front of her chest and frowned. Even her frown was graceful. For some reason, this irritated Valance to no end. How could she look so perfect and yet behave so obstinately?

"I think it will end better than marriage to Belmont would have ended," she replied. "Everyone says he killed his first wife and made it look like an accident. And the second one died in childbirth. And the third one . . ."

Valance interrupted. He'd heard all the rumors, too. "They say he refused to call a physician because he thought she was faking her illness. By the time he realized the truth, she was too ill to be cured."

The third Duchess of Belmont's death had been the talk of all the clubs a year and a half ago. But, as no one could prove Belmont had behaved with deliberate cruelty, he had suffered few social consequences. Thanks to his rank, he was still widely received in society.

"Yes, I see perfectly well why you wouldn't want to marry Belmont," Valance admitted. "But why didn't you just turn him down when he proposed? He can't marry you against your will."

She tightened her lips and shifted her eyes. "My mother insists I accept him, and she has leverage over me."

"Leverage?" he repeated, mystified. Did Miss Grantly have some unexpected secrets in her past? A previous *affaire*, perhaps, that had been hushed up? That might explain why she was bold enough to tryst with a total stranger.

"I can't say more than that." Now she sounded miserable rather than determined. "Except that if I don't do what my mother wants, there is someone else who will suffer. Someone I care about. My mother was trying to use that leverage to force me to marry the duke. Refusing him would not work. I needed to make myself unmarriageable." She tilted her chin up boldly and locked eyes with Valance. "Which I have done, thanks to you. I am very grateful for your assistance, my lord."

Valance furrowed his brow as he considered the implications. "What makes you think this person you care about will be safe now that you are unmarriageable?"

"My mother is manipulative, but I don't think she is evil."

Valance snorted. Any woman who would force her daughter to marry the Duke of Belmont, knowing he might have caused the death of two of his previous wives, seemed evil to him.

"I don't think my mother is *malicious*," Miss Grantly clarified.

"Merely ambitious. She would like to move in the finest social circles. Her father was a baron, you see, and I think she always felt that she lowered herself in marrying a baronet rather than a nobleman." She shook her head. "Naturally, Mama's social credit would increase if her daughter became a duchess."

"I see."

Valance remained quiet, considering the options before him. He did not particularly like any of them. He studied Miss Grantly's face as he ruminated. For a woman in a terrible situation, she seemed remarkably calm. That was, he supposed, to her credit.

Moreover, she seemed to know enough about magic not to be uncomfortable living with a magician. Miss Mansfield, who came from a non-magical family, had been scared of Valance's sorcery. When he proposed, she had told him she would marry him only if he gave up magic. It had taken Valance only an instant to choose sorcery over matrimony. The experience had rather soured him on the process of courtship.

But Miss Grantly was the daughter of a sorcerer, so she must be used to having magic about the house. She had been curious about Valance's sorcery, not frightened. And anyone who could talk intelligibly with Peregrine about his meteorite scheme would likely understand Valance's own less complicated magical work.

Really, Valance might do worse. Beautiful young women who came from respectable magical families were scarce, even among the *ton*. And if he married Miss Grantly, his mother would quit trying to set him up with the daughters of her friends. That was worth something.

The silence stretched out uncomfortably until Valance made his decision. He tried to keep his voice light, calm, and conversational, though his heart had already begun to pound. "Of course, your mother's social credit would also increase if you married a viscount, wouldn't it?" he pointed out.

Miss Grantley wrinkled her brow. "What are you talking about? Which viscount would I marry?"

Valance bowed, trying to hide his uneasiness beneath formality. "Me. Since you ran away with me and spent the night here, I am afraid you are going to have to marry me."

CHAPTER FIVE

HONORA LAUGHED, THINKING that to be a good jest. Her laugher faded as she saw that Lord Valance neither smiled nor chuckled. He wasn't joking? Her stomach plummeted. She knew it was rude to stare, but for a long, speechless moment, all she could do was stare blankly at him.

She finally collected herself sufficiently to say, "But you don't want to marry me."

He did not act like a man who had fallen so madly in love with her that he wanted to propose less than twenty-four hours after meeting her. On the contrary, he looked like a man who faced an unpleasant but necessary task, like having a tooth drawn.

"Not particularly, no," he agreed. "Meaning no offense, of course. You might be delightful company for all I know. Er, and I am sure your courage and fortitude are to be commended."

Honora frowned, not at all certain he meant those words sincerely. She did not know Lord Valance well enough to clearly interpret his speech or his expressions. Sometimes she missed sarcasm in a person's voice, particularly with strangers.

"But you know," he continued, "A gentleman can't simply run off with a gently reared female of tender years, then leave her to fend for herself. It isn't at all the thing."

"I am not of tender years." Honora had been out of the schoolroom since she was seventeen. She had neither been presented at court nor debuted in London, but she'd had seasons at Bath and Tunbridge Wells. "I am of age. And you didn't run off with me. You merely gave me a seat in your carriage."

He nodded. "Yes, but everyone else will assume we ran away together. If I don't marry you, they will call me a rake and a scoundrel. My reputation will be tarnished, possibly permanently. You may have wanted to ruin *your* good name, but I prefer not to soil mine."

"Oh." Honora sat in silence, dismayed. She had not considered that aspect of the situation. Of course, her original plan had not been to run away with anyone. She had meant to be caught in *flagrante delicto*, doing something no innocent debutante would ever do at a masquerade. Though that would have damaged Lord Valance's reputation too, wouldn't it? Why had she not realized that?

It had, she realized, been rather selfish of her not to think of the way her plan would affect her partner in crime. She must have assumed—if she had thought about it at all—that any man who would hold a liaison with a stranger at a ball must already be a confirmed rake. Apparently, that was not the case. But how was she to know?

"I have ruined your life," she whispered. "I am so very sorry."

"I forgive you, of course, but I hope you see that you will make my life easier in many ways if you agree to marry me." He lowered his eyes, as if examining the scraps of burnt paper that covered the table. "I can safely promise not to murder or assault you, so I might be some improvement over the Duke of Belmont."

"Anyone would be." Honora shivered at the unsavory memory of Belmont's mouth against hers. Perhaps not literally *anyone*. But certainly, ninety-nine out of a hundred men would be better than Belmont. Wouldn't they? Or was evil more entrenched in society than she knew?

"Well?" His cool, collected tone of voice was belied by the way he fidgeted with the quill in his hand.

"Of course, I will marry you if you really wish it, but you

don't really wish it, do you?" She owed it to him to make this right if she could. But she did not see how marrying Lord Valance would fix anything. It might very well make his situation worse. If he married her, he would forever give up his chance of marrying someone he actually liked. "You could spend your whole life stuck with a wife you don't want."

Valance grimaced. "The same would be true of you, shackled to a husband you didn't want. But it need not be so terrible. I am perfectly willing to let you go your own way, if you like, after . . ." He looked askance at her as his voice trailed off.

"After?" she prompted.

"I do need an heir," he said apologetically. "I have no brothers who could inherit my title. But after we had a son, I would not care what you did. You could have your own household, if you preferred. You could take whatever lovers you wanted, so long as you were discreet."

Honora swallowed uneasily. It was not a particularly appealing vision of matrimony, but it would probably be better than life at Belmont Court. And, she supposed, it would not be worse than most society marriages. People married for economic and political reasons all the time. Perhaps this was no different.

"Very well," she said doubtfully. "I will marry you, if you are certain you really want that."

He gusted a sigh. "Right, then. Well, I had better be off. I want to get to Doctor's Commons while the office is still open."

"You are going to get the license *today*?" she squeaked. She had expected it to take time to plan a wedding—a week, perhaps. A few days at the very least.

"The sooner we get married, the better it will look to the gossipmongers," he said grimly. "If I can get a special license today, we could be married immediately and send the announcement to the papers tomorrow. That would minimize the scandal of eloping."

He scanned her up and down, wrinkling his forehead. "It's a pity you don't have a better dress to be married in."

Honora took stock of her garments. This morning, she had removed the absurd blue-green sea foam from her costume, leaving only the simple silk gown beneath. But you could see marks where she had removed the stitches.

"This is ridiculous," she announced. She could not marry a man the day after meeting him.

"Yes, it is. But I have found that life often is. Particularly," Lord Valance added, "in this household."

Honora, thinking of Mr. Carrington's plan to trap a meteorite in the hall, could not disagree. Why had Mr. Carrington even wanted to capture a meteorite in the first place? She had not thought to ask that last night. Perhaps, if she was to live here, she would get a chance to ask him more about the spell. She had any number of questions.

"I will see you later, Miss Grantly." Lord Valance rose to his feet and inclined his head. "If you need anything, don't hesitate to ask. The butler's name is Babbage, and the housekeeper is Mrs. Dewes. They are both sensible people and they are well used to dealing with the Quality." With that, he walked out of the room, leaving Honora to sit in stunned solitude.

Her mother had been right: Honora had indeed been on the verge of receiving her first proposal—just not from the man her mother wanted her to marry. If this turn of events astonished even Honora, she wondered how her mother would react when she learned of the marriage.

If the Duke of Belmont had not been in the picture, marriage to a viscount would have been quite a social coup for the Grantly family. Honora's father had never really tried to circulate in London society, apart from magical organizations. Most of her parents' acquaintances were members of the gentry, and Honora had expected to marry no higher than that. Only Belmont's persistent notice of Honora over the last few months had led her mother to build such lofty castles in the air.

If Belmont could be forgotten—and Honora certainly hoped she could forget him—Lord Valance would look like a perfectly acceptable suitor. He might not live at a fashionable address, but if he had been invited to one of Belmont's masquerades, he must have good social connections. Honora had no idea what his income was, but he dressed well, so unless he was running up enormous debts at the haberdasher's, he could probably afford a wife.

She frowned as she thought about living expenses. She ought to have asked him about his financial situation before accepting his proposal, oughtn't she? Marrying her would not help Lord Valance financially; her marriage portion was only three thousand pounds. Under normal circumstances, that money would be settled on her, designated to go to her children.

Without a legal settlement in place, would her new husband have control of her small fortune? Or would it still be under Uncle Robert's control? Honora could not remember all the terms of her father's will. But there would be plenty of time to figure that out later. What ought she to do *now*?

She would need to write to Mother to explain what happened, though her explanation would have to be largely fictitious. Mother had never understood why Honora disliked Belmont so much, so she would certainly not understand her running away with a stranger she met at the masquerade.

But it might be better to write that letter after the wedding ceremony so it would be absolutely clear there was no chance of Honora returning to Belmont Court. Better to ask forgiveness than permission, as the saying went.

Honora also needed to purchase new toiletries and new clothes. Mother would probably ship her things to London after the wedding, but it would take time for them to arrive. Probably weeks. So, Honora would need a few morning gowns and evening gowns. But she could not do anything about that, either, as she had no money.

Was there, in fact, anything useful she could do? Must she sit twiddling her thumbs until Lord Valance returned? Ugh! She disliked being passive. Just as she was about to go in quest of a book to read (despite not having her reading glasses), someone scratched at the door of the workroom.

"You may enter," Honora called.

Lord Valance's valet entered the room and greeted her with a bow. "If you please, Miss Grantly, Lord Valance requested that I give you this." He handed her a heavy purse. "He thought you might have some purchases to make," he said tactfully.

"Thank you, ah—?" She arched her eyebrows. She had met him last night, but she could not remember his name.

"Preston, madam."

"Thank you, Preston," she said, relieved that she knew at least one of the servants in the household. "Is there by any chance a footman who can run errands for me?" She did not particularly want to go out in public in this dress. It had not been designed for winter weather.

"I am afraid there is no footman, but either the errand boy, Buttons, or one of the housemaids would be happy to help you." He gestured to the bell-pull in one corner of the room. "You have only to ring and someone will attend you. Or I can carry a message."

"Excellent." Privately, though, she wondered if the errand boy's name was really *Buttons*. And if not, why did they call him that? "If you could send a maid in to speak to me, that would do very well."

She could at least order a toothbrush and toothpowder, not to mention soap and other toiletries. She had not brought so much as a hairbrush with her when she fled. And, she remembered, she ought to send a note to the modiste her mother used on the rare occasions when Lady Grantly came to town.

After Preston left, she peered inside the purse—and promptly gasped. She counted twenty sovereigns, which ought to be more than sufficient for all her needs. While she waited for the maid, she tore a scrap of paper from one of the notebooks on the work table and jotted down her request for Madame Aubert.

Honora fortunately remembered most of her dress measurements. She requested a walking dress, a morning dress, and an evening gown to begin with. And, of course, she would need underthings. She sighed, hoping her mother would ship her possessions to her quickly. She did not want to go through the trouble or the expense of replacing her entire wardrobe.

She had expected to be left in boredom once she sent off the note, but to her surprise, Mr. Carrington called her into the dining room with a question about wall coverings.

"My sister suggested we strip all the paneling and paper the walls instead," Mr. Carrington explained. "But she didn't say what color wallpaper. Or what pattern."

"Er, couldn't you wait and ask her when she gets back?"

Honora turned around in a circle, studying the room. It would have been a comfortable room if not for the fire damage. The room reeked of smoke, and some of the wooden paneling had been blackened. On top of that, a burn mark ran the entire length of the table. She longed to know what exactly had gone wrong with the spell, but was afraid to ask. She hoped Mr. Carrington did not often have such accidents.

Mr. Carrington pursed his lips. "I don't think Abby will come back until the room is set to rights. That's what she said."

"Oh." Honora could understand that. But she thought it rather courageous of Miss Carrington to leave her brother in charge of redecorating the room. She would not have trusted her brother with such a task. Then again, Jack was only ten. "What sort of things does Miss Carrington like?"

Her new housemate shrugged. "She likes pretty things from nature. You know, flowers, leaves, seashells, birds, lizards, and what-not."

Lizards? That was not particularly helpful. Or was it? "What about a green wallpaper," Honora suggested, "in a fern pattern?" Botanical patterns were quite popular, so it should be easy to find something like that. And green was a soothing, restful color.

"Oh, that could work. Thank you." Mr. Carrington smiled broadly. He was not as handsome as Lord Valance, but she liked the way his eyes crinkled when he smiled. "We shall have to replace the table too, I suppose."

"I expect so," Honora agreed. It seemed rather a shame, as the table had been a stately, well-made one, made of mahogany. "And anything you keep will need to be cleaned, to get rid of the smell of smoke." If that was possible.

His face brightened. "Oh, I might have a spell that could help. It's an air purification charm that I invented to keep Susan's room free of smoke and dust. She has rather delicate lungs."

"That sounds helpful." At least, it would be helpful if it worked and did not cause a fire or a mess. But Honora's admittedly limited experience had, so far, led her to mistrust Mr. Carrington's spells.

"Do you want to watch me cast it?" he offered.

"No, thank you," she said quickly. His face promptly fell, so she smiled apologetically. "I'm afraid I have many things to do today." More to the point, she did not want to linger while he worked his potentially dangerous wizardry.

It turned out to be just as well she was free, because to her very great surprise, Madame Aubert and her assistant showed up unexpectedly, carrying books of fabric samples and, even better, two finished evening gowns that Madame thought could be altered to fit Honora. One of them fit so well that Madame's assistant altered the hem then and there, while Honora chose fabric for her other new gowns. They left her with one new gown to wear and a promise that more would be available within the week.

Shortly afterwards, the maid returned with the toiletries Honora had requested. She could finally wash, change her dress, and arrange her hair as best she could without the help of a lady's maid. She frowned at her face in the mirror, wishing her hair curled naturally. Her sister Dora had raven-wing hair that hung in gorgeous curls without the use of an iron or curl paper. Why couldn't Honora have been born with hair like that?

She was still pondering that question when someone tapped

at the door. She expected a servant bearing another message. But when she opened the door, she saw Lord Valance. His eyes widened as he scrutinized her from head to toe. She hoped she didn't look like a quiz in her new gown.

"I am sorry to disturb you," he said politely, "but most of my clothes are in here, and I ought to dress for dinner—"

"Oh, I am done dressing. I will leave the room to you."

But he held up his hand to stop her from leaving. "I brought a friend of mine to dinner. A Mr. Stephens. He is an ordained clergyman, and he is willing to perform the wedding ceremony after dinner. Since we have a special license, there is no need to marry in a church."

"I see." Honora's heart pounded more heavily at this news. So, this was really happening? When they had discussed the wedding a few hours ago, she had not really believed everything could come together this quickly. Maybe she simply hadn't wanted to believe it.

"Will that be acceptable?" His Lordship clasped his hands behind his back and shifted from one foot to another, looking nervous. Probably he was not in the habit of marrying strangers, either.

Now was the time to change her mind, if she meant to do so. Or for him to change his mind. "Are you quite sure you wish to go through with the ceremony?" When she saw his frown, Honora hurried to explain herself. "I am very grateful to you, my lord, but you deserve better than to be married to a stranger. If you wish to back out of the engagement now, I will not think worse of you." He was under no obligation to protect her; after all, she had been the one who tried to seduce *him*.

He shrugged his shoulders, still keeping his hands clasped behind his back. "You also deserve better than to be married to a stranger. Miss Grantly, if marriage to me is unappealing, you have only to say so, and we will find some other solution. Somehow."

His scowl changed his entire face. Normally he had a pleasant, friendly face. Now he looked a little like a grumpy bulldog, minus the jowls. And the underbite. And wrinkles. And fur. And—actually, Honora decided, perhaps it wasn't a good comparison at all.

"But I still believe this is the best course of action for both of us. If, that is, you have no insurmountable objection to me as a husband." He met her gaze steadily as he spoke.

It was impossible to object to someone if you knew nothing about him, Honora thought. But she said only, "I have no such objection, my lord."

"You honor me," he said solemnly.

She bit her lip to keep from smiling at the obvious falsehood. She would have honored him better by not involving him in her ruination. "On the contrary, my lord, I am grateful for your generosity." She very much feared he would come to regret it.

CHAPTER SIX

VALANCE ALREADY DEEPLY regretted attending Belmont's masquerade. Why had he gone to the house of such a monster of a man? He should have stayed home and read a book by the fire, sipping a glass of hot mulled wine. Or he could have played chess with Peregrine. He might even have prevented the fire in the dining room. Everyone would have been happy. Everyone except for Miss Grantly, that is, but as he would never have met her, this would not have disturbed him.

If he had stayed home on Twelfth Night, Valance could have spent a very pleasant afternoon at the Cambion Club today, with nothing more to worry about than what was for dinner. Instead, he'd had one of the worst afternoons he could remember, beginning with a long visit to Doctor's Commons. As a nobleman, Valance was entitled to request a special license, but the Archbishop's staff needed some convincing (and a donation to one of the Archbishop's favorite charities) to get it ready *today*.

After he got the marriage license, he paid a visit to Cherie to inform her that their arrangement had come to an end. He knew better than to arrive empty-handed. He bought his mistress the diamond pendant she had been hinting about, intending it as a farewell gift. He also offered her what he considered to be a generous financial settlement to tide her over until she found her next protector.

Nevertheless, Cherie took the news very badly indeed. To be

precise, she threw a Sevres vase at the wall. She was not malicious enough to actually aim it at Valance, so he did not need to dodge, but the vase was ruined. And, since it had contained both water and flowers, so was the wallpaper.

Cherie also swore at him in French. Her lapdog woke up from his nap long enough to curse Valance out in canine, too.

"Oh, do stop that," he told Cherie. "I know perfectly well you are English. And you know that I know. There is no need to pretend." He ignored the dog entirely, hoping that would prevent his barking from escalating into biting.

She had been baptized as Charity Barber, but she changed her name to Cherie Barbauld when she went on the stage. She did have a French grandmother, from whom she had picked up some choice phrases, but she did not know enough of the language to fool anybody.

"Bastard," she hissed. "How dare you treat me so cruelly? Leaving me destitute and alone?"

"I just gave you a thousand pounds, and I paid the lease for this house for an entire year. You will not be destitute." And he had given her jewelry worth nearly as much over the course of their *affaire*, in addition to her allowance.

"But I will be alone. You have broken my heart!" She threw herself into an armchair and began to cry. She was only a moderately successful actress, but she had long since mastered the art of dramatic tears. If he had not known her so well, he would have thought she wept in earnest.

"Perhaps you can play house with that handsome actor who keeps calling," Valance suggested. Thomas Sowerby was everything Valance was not: svelte, blond-haired, blue-eyed, and charismatic. He even had dimples, for Christ's sake! Valance suspected Sowerby did more than drink tea when he dropped in to visit Cherie, but he had no solid proof of infidelity.

Cherie made a moue of distaste. "Perhaps I am better off alone. All men are selfish, inconstant, and worthless. I pity your wife. A pox on both your houses!"

"God, I hope not," Valance said fervently.

Admittedly, he had frequented brothels before setting up a mistress, but he had always scrupulously used magically-reinforced condoms precisely to avoid the Great Pox. Though he had never had any symptoms of such a disease, he still shuddered at the idea. It would be dreadful to infect one's wife because one had amused oneself too freely as a bachelor.

"It was a figure of speech," Cherie grumbled. "You could not get the pox from *me*. You know you are the only man to have ever bedded me." She pouted her plump lips at him.

There had been a time when Valance would have melted at the sight of that adorable pout, but now it merely irritated him. He wanted to ask some pointed questions about her relations with Sowerby, but he restrained himself. Such inquiries would only drag out this already-painful confrontation.

He cleared his throat. "In any case, I am certain that a woman with your talents will land on her feet. I am very grateful for the time you have spent with me, and I wish you well. But I am afraid I have much to do today, so I cannot linger. Good bye." He hurried out the door before she could hurl more fractured French—or fragile housewares—in his direction.

On the whole, parting from Cherie felt more like a gain than a loss. Valance would no longer have to put up with Cherie's histrionics, her fits of bad temper, or her wandering eye. Let Sowerby have her if he wanted her; Valance felt himself well rid of her.

In truth, he would have broken things off soon enough even if he were not getting married. Cherie ought to have seen the end approaching. Heaven knew Valance had been neglecting her of late: it must have been weeks since his last visit.

After that, he called on his friend Stephens, the only clergy-man Valance knew well enough to ask for such an unorthodox favor. If Augustus Stephens was startled to learn that Lord Valance wanted to get married in a private ceremony that very evening, he hid it well. He offered Valance a glass of wine to celebrate, and then they both took another glass. In fact, they spent rather too much time celebrating over a plate of cheese and biscuits before Stephens dressed for dinner and they walked to Carrington House.

Now that Valance was home, his bride-to-be seemed to be having cold feet. He could hardly blame her. It wasn't as if he wanted to go through with this farce. But what else could he do? He had made the mistake of sneaking out of a ballroom with a total stranger. He ought to have known such a choice would lead to trouble, headache, and scandal.

He was doing his best to minimize the scandal. He could deal with the headache by stopping at George's Apothecary tomorrow to pick up more of their pain lozenges. But he suspected the trouble was only beginning.

As soon as Miss Grantly left the room, he rang for Preston. Then he cast a skeptical glance around his bedchamber. Where were he and his wife going to live after the wedding? They could not live here—the house was full enough with four people. Or, more accurately, it was filled with the possessions of four people, all of whom accumulated books at a rate beyond good reason. Shelf space was in short demand when one lived in a house full of scholars. Abigail and Peregrine both required *materia magica* for their spells, too, so the nursery had been converted into a storage room for magical supplies.

Though, now that Valance thought about it, wasn't there still a bed in the corner of the nursery? If Valance remembered to ask a housemaid to make that bed, he could sleep there tonight rather than in the drawing room. The former nursery smelled strongly of magical herbs, but it would still be an improvement over that awful sofa. He asked Preston to pass the message on to one of the housemaids. That put him in much better spirits. He had not been looking forward to another night on that damn sofa.

To Valance's surprise, dinner was served in the dining room that night. He had feared they would have to eat in the breakfast room, which was already full of Valance's things. But Peregrine had worked some powerful wizardry to get the smoky odor out of the dining room, and though his spell had not been *entirely* successful, the room smelled tolerable now. A tablecloth hid the scarring on the dining room table, and everyone simply pretended not to notice that some of the panels were scorched and the ceiling of the room had been blackened with soot.

Though dinner tasted delicious, the conversation languished. It did not help that the table was so woefully unbalanced. Usually, Abigail prevented her brother from monopolizing the conversation by talking only about his current magical experiment. And if the Carrington siblings quarreled—which happened rather frequently—Susan and Valance would politely discuss music or light literature, ignoring the spirited row going on around them.

Abigail being gone meant she could not quarrel with her brother, which was a blessing, but it also meant she was not there to redirect conversation. Peregrine spent the entire meal explaining his meteorite spell to Miss Grantly. Her eyes grew rounder as his explanation grew increasingly more technical, but she continued to ask intelligent questions.

Valance could not help being a little impressed. Even university-trained magicians had trouble keeping up with his friend. Peregrine's mind worked very well indeed, but it sometimes seemed to operate differently from other people's minds. Valance had always compared it to the way his own magic worked effectively, despite being different from other sorcerers' spellcasting.

With Peregrine deep in conversation with Miss Grantly, Valance was left to talk with poor Mr. Stephens, who spent much of the meal looking confused by all the magical theory. And who could blame him? Peregrine wanted to capture a meteorite so he could investigate a theory that shooting stars contained magical elements not normally found on earth. But as no one had ever provided convincing evidence of that theory (meteorites being rather rare), Carrington's current obsession seemed quixotic, to say the least.

After the dessert course, Miss Grantly turned away from the conversation about astronomical magic and caught Valance's gaze from across the table. "Ought I retire to the drawing room?" There was no hostess to lead the way for her, nor any other women to keep her company.

"I think we ought to skip the after-dinner drinks tonight," Valance suggested, "and get this wedding business squared away." He and Miss Grantly both turned towards Stephens.

"Oh, is it my turn in the limelight?" Stephens smiled benevolently. "Let me fetch my prayer book. And we will need another witness, you know. I suppose one of the servants would do?"

Valance nodded. "Peregrine, can you ring for Babbage and Mrs. Dewes?" If anyone raised questions about the legitimacy of the marriage, the butler and the housekeeper would be the most respectable witnesses.

So, Valance and Miss Grantly stood in front of a pleasant coal fire and said their vows. The only hitch came when Stephens turned to Valance and prompted him: "You'll need the ring now."

"Damn!" Valance had completely forgotten that he needed a ring.

"I beg your pardon?" Stephens glowered at him, no doubt appalled at hearing such language in the middle of a religious service.

"Wait right here." Feeling like the greatest blockhead in the history of matrimony, Valance bolted to his bedchamber to dig around in one of the drawers in his dresser. Ah, there it was—a wooden box, the size of a cigar box, locked tight. But where the devil was the key?

No time to find the key. Valance pulled a scrap of paper out of his pocket, scribbled a Latin phrase on it, and placed it on top of the box. He tapped the paper and the lock clicked open obediently. Inside were several mementos left to Valance by his paternal grandmother: brooches, a mourning ring, a miniature portrait of her husband. *Where was it?* Ah, there—a golden *fede* ring, with two hands clasping, that Valance's grandfather had given her when they were courting.

Valance took the ring and jogged downstairs. Everyone else still stood in the dining room, chatting awkwardly about the weather.

"Sorry," Valance said, still feeling like a fool. "I have the ring." To his great relief, it fit on Miss Grantly's hand. He did not know what he would have done if it had been too small.

Stephens continued with the ceremony. He read the entire service, though Valance thought it was strange to preach a sermon on matrimony when there was no congregation to be edified. Then it ended, and Valance was married to a woman he had met less than twenty-four hours ago.

Oddly, the first thing that came into his mind was: *I'll never have to go to Almack's to dance with debutantes again.* Trousers were not allowed at Almack's, and Valance had never cared for breeches or tight pantaloons. That was one small blessing.

"I wish you both very well." Stephens shook Valance's hand, bowed to Miss Grantly—no, to Lady Valance—and headed home. The night was young, but Stephens did not keep fashionable hours. He worked as chaplain at St. Simon Magus Hospital, and his day began long before noon.

"I expect I'm *de trop*," Peregrine said cheerfully. He disappeared into the library, leaving Valance alone with his wife.

"I suppose that's that." Valance knew the words were inane, but he was not sure what words actually were appropriate for this situation. After all, he had never been married before. "I had better write out the notice for the newspapers before I forget." Publishing an announcement of their wedding could not possibly stop all the gossip their elopement would create, but it might add a touch of respectability to the marriage.

His new wife frowned. "Hadn't we better talk?"

"Talk about what?"

She lifted her brow. "About our life together?"

He rubbed his forehead, feeling a headache beginning to build. Couldn't they talk about this tomorrow? Or next week?

They would have their entire lives to talk, after all. Unless they ended up separating, which seemed rather likely, all things considered.

"Is there something specific you wish to know?" he asked.

Once again, a worried line formed between her perfectly arched eyebrows. "I don't know what you expect of me."

"I don't expect anything of you," he said. "Other than treating me with civility and behaving rationally. I will endeavor to do the same."

She continued to frown. What exactly did she want to hear? It was not as if he could make any kind of declaration of love. He did not know her at all. Or was she worried about how he would treat her? That would make sense, given her reasons for fleeing Belmont. He could understand her wanting reassurance on that point.

"I assure you, my lady, I have no intention of being a tyranni-cal or controlling husband. You are free to spend your days as you like. But if you have any preference as to where you wish to reside, you should let me know." Valance supposed that was something they had better discuss sooner rather than later. He meant to begin searching for new lodgings right away.

"I assumed I would reside with you, since I am your wife." The furrows on her brow deepened.

"Naturally, but I do not own a townhouse. We will have to rent a residence of our own. It may take time to find one, though." Townhouses in Mayfair did not open up every day.

"I thought we were going to live here." She gestured vaguely at the room.

Valance turned his head as he scanned the dining room, which still bore the marks of that fireball spell. She really thought he would expect her to live *here*? With the Carringtons? Leaving aside the fact that the house would be too crowded, living here might further harm her already damaged reputation. Half of London assumed Abigail Carrington was Valance's mistress. (Both Abigail and Valance found that idea laughable, but how was the world to know?) It was best not to speculate about what the other half of London thought.

Valance could not say all of that, so he told her only part of the truth. "This is not a suitable house. There would not be enough room for you. You ought to have a sitting room or morning room of your own, as well as a bedchamber." In marrying him, she had become a viscountess. She ought to be treated like one.

"Oh. I assumed I would sleep in your room." She clasped her hands together, looking surprisingly nervous.

"Of course, you will, for now." He struggled to keep his voice light and pleasant despite his growing frustration.

Did she not see how awkward it would be if he had to enter her chamber to dress multiple times a day? He could sleep in the nursery, but he still needed access to his toiletries and clothing. She would have no privacy. And where would she even put *her* things? That bedroom was adequate for one person, but it would hardly do for two.

"I think we will both be happier if we have our own space," he explained. *Much* happier.

She nodded, though she still looked thoughtful. "I suppose you are right. But I do not particularly care where we live, so long as the house is comfortable. It is not as if I care about fashionable addresses."

"That will make finding a house easier." He smiled, relieved to have that so easily settled. "I will get working on that tomorrow. And you had better write to your family, so they know you have not been murdered." He meant it as a joke, but too late, he remembered the rumors about Belmont's first wife. He ought not joke about murder to Miss Grantly. Or rather, Lady Valance.

Her face relaxed. "Oh, yes, I had better do that now. My mother will be very worried! I suppose there is writing paper in the breakfast room?"

Valance repressed a shudder. The breakfast room was *his* room! He did not like other people using his workspace, but what could he do? His wife had no sitting room of her own. All the more reason why they needed to find a house of their own sooner rather than later. When Lady Valance had her own chambers, she would no longer need to intrude on his space.

"Yes, you will find notepaper there. And I can frank your letters for you, if you remind me in the morning." He turned away, relieved that the conversation was over.

"I will see you later, then," she called after him.

He glanced back over his shoulder. "Yes, later. Good night!"

It did not occur to Valance until he was halfway up the stairs that his wife might have meant she expected to see him later *that* night. Surely, she didn't expect them to consummate the marriage tonight? Given the circumstances, that seemed inadvisable, to say the least.

Perhaps if the new Lady Valance had been an experienced woman—a widow, for example—his decision might have been different. She had, after all, abundant natural charms, and he was as randy as any other newlywed. Or rather, he would have been, if not for that growing headache.

But he had absolutely no desire to bed a frightened virgin whom he had met yesterday. It would take time to build up enough trust between them for that step. She would surely be relieved not to have to fulfill her marital duties yet. Ought he go back downstairs and clear that up? He hesitated at the top of the stairs, considering.

No, his head had begun to pound in earnest now, probably because he had not yet caught up on last night's lost sleep. Though he'd had every intention of writing up the wedding announcement tonight, he changed his mind. He would do best to go straight to bed and sleep off this headache. There would be time enough to discuss bedroom matters later.

CHAPTER SEVEN

IT TOOK HONORA a couple of hours to realize Lord Valance was not going to sleep in her room—or rather, his room, since she was the interloper—that night. While she waited for him, she sat in bed reading *Glenarvon*. Her mother thought this novel was too scandalous for an unmarried girl to read. Honora had been delighted to find it on the shelf nearest the bed.

Reading without her spectacles strained her eyes, but the novel was gripping enough to keep her turning the pages until her candle began to flicker. That surprised her. She had thought it had a couple of hours left in it. She got up to check the clock on the mantel and discovered it was past midnight.

Oh. It seemed her husband would not be joining her tonight after all. She must have misunderstood him. Where on earth *was* he sleeping, then? The sofa in the drawing room? But why? The bed in his room was certainly big enough for two people.

Was he perhaps very shy? If that were the case, though, why would he have left the ballroom with her last night? Lord Valance had seemed perfectly willing to bed her yesterday, when they were not married—when, in fact, he had thought her to be married to someone else. She'd assumed he would be just as eager now that she was his wife. More eager, if anything, since he needed an heir.

To some extent, it was a relief that he had not visited her room tonight. Her mother had always said she would explain the marriage bed to Honora when she became engaged, but of course there had been no chance for such a talk before her hasty wedding. Thus, Honora had only a vague concept of what was involved, based on constricted reading and scraps of gossip picked up here and there. She felt certain, though, that consummating the marriage would at the best be awkward, and at the worst might be awful.

On the other hand, precisely because she knew so little about the subject, she felt deeply curious about it. She had as many questions about conjugal relations as she had on any other subject, and she had assumed some of her questions would be answered tonight. She could not help feeling a little disappointed that the answers to her questions were to be deferred until some unspecified later date.

On top of that, her husband's absence deprived her of a chance to talk to him. She knew very little about him, so she had many questions about his history, goals, and preferences. They were married now, after all. They had vowed to mutually help and comfort one another. Having put Lord Valance in a position in which he felt obligated to marry her, Honora intended to be as good a wife as she could be. But how could she do that without learning more about her husband? Had he meant something different than she had when he said his vows? That was an unsettling thought.

She would very likely have stayed up until dawn wrestling with these concerns, except that she had been up until nearly dawn yesterday and had not yet recovered. Once she gave up on Lord Valance, she blew out the candle and enjoyed her first good night's sleep in days.

HONORA SLEPT UNTIL after noon. She woke up in good spirits, but that changed when a maid informed her that Lord Valance, who'd woken up hours ago, had already left the house on some unspecified errand, leaving no indication of when he meant to return.

She could not help feeling ill-used. Would it have been so very hard for Lord Valance to leave a note for her? Or a message with a servant? She had to remind herself that Lord Valance had only married her because he had compromised her. He had done her an overwhelmingly generous favor in helping her escape Belmont and taking her under his protection. She had no right to complain.

In the meantime, Honora had no idea what to do with herself. She had written a letter to her mother last night. She supposed she ought to write to Uncle Robert as well. But that did not take very long. Just when she wondered what she ought to do next, the butler entered the morning room, leading a tiny dog on a leash.

"If you please, Lady Valance," he said respectfully, "This arrived for his lordship."

"From whom?"

"The messenger did not say. But there is a note." He handed her a piece of perfumed notepaper and retreated, leaving Honora very confused.

There was no name or direction on the outside of the letter, so, after thinking it over for a moment, Honora broke the seal to see what it said. The message was written in a scrawling hand and it included a good deal of seemingly arbitrary underlining.

To the Right Honorable, The Viscount Valance, the note began,

Hoping that your lordship is in good health and not, as I am, suffering from an attack of the nerves after <u>yesterday's Catastrophe</u>. I would send for a physician, but <u>as your lordship knows,</u> I must hoard my limited resources, not knowing whence I will earn more.

(Did the author mean "from whence," Honora wondered, or

"when"? It was not clear from the context.)

I will therefore do my best to suffer bravely. Having been bereft of your favor, I have only my maid to listen to my lamentations. Which, as I am sure you realize, are many.

I am afraid that I must return this gift which you once, in happier times, <u>graciously</u> bestowed on me. I cannot look upon poor Bishop Barkley without bursting into tears at the memory of your perfidy. As he deserves to be cared for <u>properly,</u> I hereby return him to you. Perhaps you can give him <u>to your wife</u> as a wedding present, along with whatever fragments of your cold <u>heart</u> may yet remain beating.

Yours Dolefully,
[Illegible Scribble]

"Bishop Barkley?" Honora glanced down at the dog, who was happily gnawing on the carved wooden leg of the sofa. "Stop that at once!"

Honora used the firm-but-loving voice she would have used with one of her younger siblings. But the tiny dog ignored her entirely. She had to forcibly drag him away from the sofa. He retaliated by wriggling out of her arms and running around the room, barking excitedly.

She knew very little about dogs. Her mother did not allow pets in the house, and her father, being more interested in sorcery than sport, had never kept hunting dogs. She could not tell whether Bishop Barkley was playing a game or trying to threaten her. If it was the latter, his threats seemed ineffective. He could not reach much higher than her ankles.

Yap! Yap! Yap! How could such a small animal produce such a loud noise?

"What is that awful racket?" To Honora's relief, Lord Valance himself opened up the morning room door. "Dear God," he said, in the voice of a man who has seen something too terrible for words, "Why is that vermin in my house?"

"It is not vermin," Honora argued. "It is a dog."

"I know it is a dog. It is, in fact, the worst dog in the world. Why is it *here?*" He directed a fierce scowl at the poor little thing.

"Someone sent it to you, along with this note." Honora handed him the perfumed bit of notepaper.

"You opened my mail?" He glared at Honora. "You cannot read letters from my—I mean, you cannot open mail addressed to me." Once again, he resembled nothing so much as a grumpy bulldog.

"It was not specifically addressed to you," Honora pointed out. "There was no name on the back of the letter."

He turned the paper over in his hands. "I see. She probably meant for you to see it." His mouth settled into an unhappy line as he read the note. Then he crumpled it up and tossed it into the fire.

"You have good aim," Honora observed. If she'd tried that, the note would have fallen short, and possibly a few feet to the left.

"Yes, I used to bowl for my house cricket team at school. And don't tell me that I don't look athletic," he added, "because—"

"I wasn't going to say that," Honora interjected. "Athletes come in all different shapes." The blacksmith who bowled for the village team back home was built on heavier lines than Lord Valance. His stocky frame had never prevented the team from winning, so far as she could tell.

Lord Valance blinked, as if he had not expected that response. "Quite so." Then he cursed. The dog had lifted its leg and was relieving itself on the foot of the sofa.

"Maybe he will grow out of that habit." Honora hoped to console her husband, who looked nearly apoplectic. "Don't all puppies have accidents?"

"He's no puppy! He's a full-grown Yorkshire terrier."

"Are you sure?" Honora knew nothing about Yorkshire terriers, but she had never in her life seen a dog that small. She had simply assumed it was a puppy.

"*Very* sure. I bought him on St. Valentine's Day in 1815, when he was already two months old." He scowled at the dog again. "You would not believe the number of rugs that animal has ruined in his short life."

"Oh." There seemed to be nothing more to say. Even Honora knew a two-year-old dog ought to have been housebroken long ago. "Is there room in the garden for a kennel for him? Maybe he should do better outside." It would not be fair to the Carringtons to let a dog ruin their furnishings.

"He is not going to live with *us,*" Lord Valance asserted. "I will send him to Surrey. My mother can deal with him." He turned on his heel and started to walk out of the room.

"Wait!" She could not let him go now, when she had so many questions. Who knew when she would have a chance to speak with him again?

To her relief, he turned back "Yes? Was there something you needed?" He addressed her politely enough, but he eyed her warily.

"Aren't you going to explain anything?"

He drew his eyebrows together. "What is there to explain?"

Everything! Honora thought. Best to start with something simple, though. "For example, why you were sent that dog?"

He shrugged his shoulders. "You read the letter, didn't you? You know who it was from."

"Your lover?" she guessed.

"My mistress." He averted his eyes, as if ashamed. "My *former* mistress. I broke things off with her yesterday, and it looks like she is still angry." He once again turned to leave the room.

"Why did you break things off with her?" Honora asked. Lord Valance's back stiffened, and he nearly stumbled as he put his foot down. Perhaps he was not so athletic after all.

He faced her again. "I broke things off with her because I got married." He used the sort of slow, patient, gentle voice she associated with parents speaking to children. She clenched her hands into fists at the sound. She was not a child, and he was not her parent.

Honora lifted her chin up before replying. "But I never asked you to jilt your mistress. Under the circumstances, I would quite have understood if you wished to keep one." For all she knew, Lord Valance might have been deeply attached to Illegible Scribble.

"Well, I recall vowing otherwise yesterday! You are, of course, free to do as you like, my lady." This time, the title sounded more like an insult than a sign of respect. "You may, for all I know, be accustomed to meeting strange men in back hallways at every entertainment you attend, but I—"

"How dare you?" Honora snapped. "That was the first time I ever did anything like that, and I only did it to escape Belmont! I thought one night of shame would be better than a lifetime of misery." Her voice trembled. "And you were perfectly willing to accept my invitation. So how dare you stand there and judge me?" She blinked her eyes quickly, trying to hold back angry tears.

He flinched. "You are quite right. I must have taken leave of my senses at that masquerade. I have no other explanation for why I behaved as I did. But what do you think would have happened to you otherwise?" He shook his head. "You would have ended up in the deepest disgrace."

"That would still have been better than being the Duchess of Belmont. And, at the moment, I am not at all certain that being the Viscountess Valance is much better than being disgraced!" She would rather work herself to death as a seamstress than listen to insults from her own husband.

He gasped. "Well, I like that!" The sarcasm in his voice made Honora cringe. "After I spent the entire day making arrangements for your comfort!"

"How was I to know what you were doing, when you left the house without bothering to leave any kind of message for me?" Lord Valance should not get credit for the good intentions behind his errand if he could not even show her common courtesy.

He crossed his arms in front of his broad chest and shifted his weight back, rocking onto his heels. "I was not aware that I needed to account for my every movement, Lady Valance. Since I am, after all, a grown man of four-and-twenty. Nearly five-and-twenty," he added, as if that would impress her.

Honora snorted. He was only three years older than her. That did not give him much of an advantage. What right did he have to act superior?

"In the future, I will submit all my plans in writing to you, so you can approve them or not, as you see fit. Will that suit?" He raised his eyebrows in an exaggerated expression of inquiry.

"Now you are being childish." Unsettled by the anger in his eyes, Honora looked away from him. It was as well that she did so, because she caught Bishop Barkley chewing on the fire irons. "Stop that!" She spoke more sharply than she intended, because some of her anger at Lord Valance carried into her voice.

Bishop Barkley glanced up at her and wagged his tail, but then promptly resumed his gnawing.

"You will break your teeth," she grumbled as she picked the dog up. She had to pull the poker out of his mouth.

"He is more likely to break the fire irons," Lord Valance predicted. "He destroys all he touches."

"Perhaps he was spoiled?" Honora could see how it might be easy to spoil a dog as adorable as this one. That is, as adorable *looking*. She did not find his behavior at all appealing.

"Oh, almost certainly." Lord Valance grimaced as he studied the dog. "Must you cuddle that beast? I have too many memories of him biting me." He shuddered theatrically.

"Does he bite?" That surprised Honora. Aside from his earlier barking fit, he'd seemed friendly enough.

"He only bites men."

"Very wise of him." Honora kissed the dog on the head. Perhaps he had reason to bite Lord Valance. His Lordship had shamefully deserted the dog's owner, after all. Maybe Illegible Scribble spoke the truth when she wrote about his heartlessness.

She lifted her eyes to see Lord Valance staring at her with

something like horror on his face. "Did you just kiss that dog because he bit me in the past?"

This accusation came so disturbingly close to the truth that her face burned with shame. "No, I just thought you were being too hard in what you said about him."

"He doesn't understand what we are saying! He's a dog!" Lord Valance threw his hands in the air to punctuate his point. But Bishop Barkley took offense at that and began barking at His Lordship.

"See, he knows you are his enemy." She smiled down at the dog. "He must be smarter than he looks."

Lord Valance eyed the barking dog with disdain. "Don't get attached to him. I plan to send him to the country posthaste. There will be absolutely no lapdogs in the house on Curzon Street."

"But you told me you were not going to be a tyrannical husband," Honora started to remind him. Then she realized the importance of his words. "What house on Curzon Street?"

"That was my main errand today," he explained. "I met with my solicitor and informed him of our marriage. He is going to write up a new will for me, so you will be provided for in case of my death. When I asked him to look for a house for us, he said he already knew of one. It belongs to Lord Bloxom, who never uses it. The previous tenant had to break his lease when he left the country for health reasons."

"Will we need to furnish it?" That would take time and money. Honora stared down at the floor, uneasy at the thought of all the money Lord Valance might be forced to spend because of her.

"No. It is furnished already, but of course you may make additions if you wish. That is," he added more hesitantly, "if it meets with your approval. Would you like to see it now?"

She pulled a face. "I would, but I don't have suitable clothing. I haven't any walking dresses. Nor any cloaks or pelisses. They will not get here until later this week." She tugged on one of her short sleeves to demonstrate the inadequacy of her gown. She would freeze if she left the house wearing nothing but a thin silk gown.

"Hmm." Lord Valance looked her up and down. "Right. You cannot go out in public like that. Wait here." He walked out of the room with no further explanation. He did not seem to be in the habit of giving very satisfying explanations for his conduct, did he?

But this time Lord Valance returned quickly, carrying a thick wool cloak.

"I borrowed this from Mrs. Dewes," he explained. "She stands about as high as you do, I think."

"Oh, thank you!" Honora had grown tired of being stuck in the house.

She reached for the cloak, but to her surprise, Lord Valance tucked it around her himself, bending his head close to hers as he fastened it. He stood so close, she could smell the citrus and spice of his cologne. It was the same scent that had clung to his bedding.

She peered up at him, startled by his proximity. When their eyes met, the corners of his mouth quirked up. She returned the smile uncertainly, suddenly very aware that although he was more or less a stranger to her, legally, he was also her husband. Now he seemed entirely *too* close. She took an involuntary step back. When he glanced away, she found herself able to breathe freely again.

"Let's go," he said. "My solicitor will be waiting for us."

They headed to the waiting carriage, and, traffic being light, they shortly reached Curzon Street. The house looked much like other London townhouses: narrow, tall, with steps leading from the street down to the lower level and up to the ground floor. It was made of red brick rather than blocks of stone.

Lord Valance did not bother knocking, but walked right in. They found a respectably dressed man with salt-and-pepper hair waiting for them in the dining room. He had been reading over some paperwork, but he greeted them with a smile. Valance introduced him as Mr. Watson.

Mr. Watson walked them all over the house, explaining to Honora the pros and cons of every room. Honora found it difficult to keep all the information straight, but she could see with her own eyes that this was a comfortable house that had been furnished with good taste. It boasted a separate breakfast room and dining room on the ground floor, but the dining room was smaller than the one in Russell Square.

"I don't know how much you intend to entertain?" Mr. Watson asked. "This might not be adequate if you want to host large dinner parties." He shifted his eyes back and forth between the two of them.

Honora caught Lord Valance's eye. He raised one eyebrow in a silent question.

"I have no desire to host large dinner parties," she said. "Maybe small groups of friends?" Not that she had many friends to invite. She knew a few young women from boarding school who spent the Season in London, but those would probably be her only acquaintances in town.

Lord Valance looked relieved by her response. "I think this room will be adequate," he told Mr. Watson. "It seems comfortable."

When they reached the first story, Mr. Watson became distracted by a window that had been carelessly left open. While he went to investigate, Valance led Honora into the master suite.

"I knew we should lease this house when I saw this room," he told her, smiling smugly.

Honora turned around slowly, studying the room. It was papered in a shade somewhere between blue and green. The bed was hung with heavy curtains that would keep out the winter chill, and there was a pretty escritoire in one corner. Comfortable though the bedchamber looked, she could not imagine how it had won him over.

"It is quite charming," she acknowledged.

"Take a closer look at the wallpaper," Lord Valance advised.

She walked up to the wall, her husband trailing a step behind. "Oh, it's a rococo design. Seashells. How pretty!" She still did not understand what was so special about the wallpaper. Was she missing something?

"Yes, seashells. Perfect for my Aphrodite!" He bent down to brush his lips lightly against her cheek. Then he walked through the door that separated the two bedrooms, leaving her frozen with astonishment. She wonderingly reached up to touch her cheek. Perhaps Lord Valance was not as indifferent to her as he had seemed. Interesting.

CHAPTER EIGHT

THREE DAYS AFTER the wedding, the Duke of Belmont paid a call on the newlyweds at Russell Square. Valance felt certain this was the first time so high ranking a nobleman had ever visited Carrington House. He thought it likely to be the last, as well.

Most fortunately, Lady Valance was not at home. She had gone to her modiste to try on her new clothes. Peregrine was meeting a friend at the Cambion Club, and Abigail and Susan were still in Surrey. Valance thus received the duke in the drawing room, alone.

"To what do I owe this pleasure, Your Grace?" he asked.

"I came to express my felicitations." The duke gave him a wintery smile. His silvered hair and the snowy folds of his cravat accentuated the frost in his expression.

Belmont dressed in such style that Valance immediately felt like a country bumpkin, though, in fact, Valance's coats were made by Weston. But, as Valance did not have the narrow-waisted build popularized by dandies (and he refused to wear a corset to achieve it), he probably did not do full justice to Weston's work.

"I am honored, Your Grace." Valance gestured to an armchair. "Won't you take a seat?" The duke sat down, his back ramrod straight. Valance sank into a chair across from his. "Now we can have a comfortable coze." He casually stretched his legs out, and was pleased to see the duke's smile fade in the face of his nonchalance.

No doubt the duke had expected to intimidate Valance. Well, he need not know how Valance's heart pounded. Valance reminded himself of his grandfather's saying, "A Valance should fear nothing but God." It was an unofficial family motto. Well, Belmont might be a demon of a man, but he was no deity.

For a long moment there was no sound but the snap of the fire. Then the duke broke the silence. "Perhaps you are unaware, but I am a friend of the Grantly family."

"You surprise me. Lady Valance seems to view you in quite a different light than that of a friend." Valance propped his head up on his hand and smiled broadly.

The duke's mouth tightened. Every trace of *his* smile had fled. "There seems to have been a misunderstanding between Miss Grantly and myself."

"If you refer to the eldest daughter of Sir Isaac Grantly, forgive me, but I must correct you. She is the Viscountess Valance now." Valance let his own fake smile drop away, too.

Belmont nodded courteously "Yes, of course. My mistake. You are fortunate in your choice of wife, Lord Valance."

"I am." This time, Valance's smile was genuine. It warmed his heart to know that he, a mere viscount, had stolen Belmont's chosen bride on the eve of their betrothal.

Lady Valance must be one of the most beautiful women in England, and Belmont was unquestionably one of the most powerful noblemen in the kingdom. And yet the lady in question was Lady Valance now, not the Duchess of Belmont.

In marrying Miss Grantly, Valance had very likely made the greatest coup of his life. Not that that had been his motive at the time. In fact, he had not even considered his actions in that light. He had been primarily concerned with salvaging Miss Grantly's reputation, along with his own good name. But it pleased him to view the elopement as a victory now, especially as Belmont seemed to grow increasingly uncomfortable the longer Valance beamed at him.

The duke shifted position in his chair before speaking. "Nevertheless, your sudden nuptials surprised many people. I have naturally spoken to the Grantly family about the matter. Since the young lady disappeared while under my roof, I could not help but feel responsible. And do you know what I found? Even the young lady's mother was unaware of any attachment between you and the former Miss Grantly."

Valance considered his answer more carefully this time. He did not want to tell any lies that could be easily disproven. He could not, for example, claim to have met Miss Grantly in town last season, because she had made it clear she had never been to London. He might have encountered Sir Isaac at the Cambion Club before his death—Lady Valance had mentioned that her parents sometimes came to London for brief visits—but if so, he did not remember the man.

On the other hand, Valance could not reveal the truth about how he met his future wife. No one must know that Miss Grantly had propositioned him with the express purpose of ruining her reputation.

"Our acquaintanceship was of the briefest, it is true," Valance admitted. "Such is often the way when *young* people fall in love, is it not? The deepest attachments may form in a surprisingly short amount of time."

Valance knew he was talking nonsense, and Belmont must know it too, but his words nevertheless had an effect. Belmont, who must be nearly fifty, flinched at Valance's emphasis on the word "young."

"No doubt that is true," Belmont snapped. "I only hope the young lady does not regret her impulsive decision. If she does . . ."

"If she does?" Valance narrowed his eyes. Were they finally getting to the real reason for Belmont's visit?

"I do not usually take other men's discards," Belmont said coolly, "but I would make an exception in the case of so rare a prize as Miss Grantly. Excuse me—I mean Lady Valance, of course." He smiled mockingly. "If ever she tires of you, Lord Valance, or you of her, I should be very happy to take her off of your hands."

If Belmont intended to rattle Valance, he succeeded. Valance sprang to his feet, clenching his fists. His immediate impulse was to break Belmont's nose, but he forced himself to use his words—and to choose them carefully. "I think you forget something, Your Grace."

"Do I?" Belmont rose from his chair so gracefully that Valance felt a twinge of envy. Belmont was rumored to be an excellent fencer, and it showed in his supple movements.

But Valance was significantly larger than the duke, both in height and breadth, and he was as much a Corinthian as he was a scholar. Though he did not fence, he regularly boxed at Gentleman Jackson's. He pulled himself to his full height to emphasize his physical advantage.

"Three somethings, in fact," he explained. "First, Lady Valance is a human being with free will, not a prize to be traded between noblemen. Second, the lady has made it abundantly clear that she prefers my company to yours. And thirdly, she is my *wife*. You will touch her over my cold, dead body."

"That can be arranged." Belmont spoke softly, but his cold blue eyes remained locked with Valance's.

"Oh, can it?" Valance took a step closer to Belmont. Before he could say anything further, a black-and-gold blur detached itself from the hearthrug and launched itself at Belmont, barking furiously. Bishop Barkley had taken offense at His Grace's threat.

Unfortunately, Bishop Barkley was too small to reach any higher than His Grace's boots. Even more unfortunately, the duke reacted by kicking at the little dog, as if he had been no more than a dirt clod in his path. Bishop Barkley ducked in time to evade the blow. He scurried back to Valance, his tail between his legs.

Valance trembled with rage as he scooped the frightened dog

into his arms. "You have been very straightforward with me. Allow me to be equally plain, Your Grace. If ever you harm anyone or anything in my household—anything from the rats in the cellar to the bats in the attic—I will shoot you where you stand."

Belmont responded with only a chuckle.

"You may laugh," Valance said more calmly, "but you can ask anyone you like, and they will tell you I am reckoned to be the best marksman in my club." That was not saying much: the Cambion Club catered to magicians and scholars rather than athletes. Still, Valance was a good shot by anyone's standards.

Belmont's confident smirk faded. "In any case, Lord Valance, I beg you to keep my words in mind. And do remember, for your own sake, that people who cross me often come to regret it." His hard, clipped words were a threat, not a warning.

"I will keep that in mind, sir, but I beg you to remember *my* words. I do not speak idly . . . I wish you a good day, sir." Valance spoke cordially. He even smiled, though he longed to kick Belmont out of his house. He followed the duke all the way to the door to make sure he really left.

Once the door shut behind Belmont, Valance looked down at the shivering terrier in his arms. "I hope he didn't hurt you. You all right, boy?"

Bishop Barkley wagged his tail and licked Valance's face. He took that to be a "yes."

"Let's go to the kitchen and see if there's some steak for you. I believe you've earned it, you brave boy!" Bishop Barkley could not have understood his words, but he recognized the friendliness in Valance's tone, and his tail wagged with greater abandon.

Valance whistled as he wandered toward the kitchen in search of a treat for himself as well has his dog. It was not every day that he stood up to a murderous duke. He felt he had acquitted himself well in the encounter, all things considered.

CHAPTER NINE

O N MONDAY, A little over a week after they first met, Lord and Lady Valance moved into the little house on Curzon Street. The house came with a core staff of servants, and Mr. Watson moved heaven and earth to quickly hire other servants for them, including a lady's maid for Honora. She had never had a lady's maid of her own before. At home, her mother's maid or one of her sisters helped if she needed assistance. It was, she admitted, nice to have Clack's help unpacking her few possessions.

Honora's wardrobe had increased, thanks to her recent purchases, but she still anxiously wondered when her things from home would arrive. She particularly missed her spectacles, since she got a headache if she read without them for too long. Given that she normally read for at least a few hours a day, that constituted a significant problem.

She had not yet received a reply from her mother, though Honora had written twice: first to inform her mother of the unexpected marriage, then to share her new address. But that changed the Friday after they moved into their new home. The footman brought her a letter while she was still breakfasting with Lord Valance. She had no need to read the direction; she recognized the handwriting at once.

"It is from my mother." She set it aside to read after they finished eating.

Lord Valance lifted his eyes from his plate. "You need not stand on formality. I do not mind if you wish to read it now."

"I would not be so rude." She smiled cheerfully at him. She normally disliked mornings, but today she felt disposed to be pleasant to all the world, including her husband. Really, he was quite charming. He had let her bring Bishop Barkley to the new house, despite his objections to the dog. Ever since that first day of marriage, he took the time to tell her where he was going and when he would return, or at least left a message for her.

Everything would have been fine, except that his lordship treated Honora with the same detached civility with which he would have treated a stranger. With the sole exception of that brief kiss on the cheek the day they toured the house, he never touched her at all; never uttered any endearments; never showed more interest in her thoughts or actions than was demanded by common courtesy; never, in short, treated her like his wife.

She must have misunderstood his intentions. She had thought he meant this to be real marriage, even if it were to end in separation once he had an heir. Their first week of matrimony made it abundantly clear that he meant to be a husband to her in name only.

But that was no reason to treat him with disrespect. On the contrary, Honora felt all the more guilty about how her poorly-planned scheme for escaping Belmont had embroiled Lord Valance in her affairs. He did not deserve to have his life disrupted, and she thought it very kind of him to avoid any allusions to the damage she must have done to all his goals and plans.

So, she courteously waited until after breakfast to open her mother's letter. But before she could read it, she was waylaid by the housekeeper, who had questions about tonight's menu and concerns about the quality of chicken the poulterer had delivered. Then her maid wanted to discuss the state of Honora's wardrobe. Clack had been disturbed by how few gowns hung in Honora's wardrobe, and she wanted to know when the rest of Honora's clothes would arrive. Honora wondered that, too.

After that conversation, the butler wished to talk to her about hiring a second footman, though Honora had doubts about whether so small a household needed more than one. She was happy enough to pass that question on to Lord Valance to decide.

Consequently, it took a couple of hours before Honora found time to sit down to read Lady Grantly's letter. But reading the contents was like having a bucket of cold water poured over all her hopes and dreams.

My Dear Lady Valance,

I will no longer call you "Honora," for it seems your late father chose poorly when he selected your name. I am glad he did not live to see the day you brought such dishonor into the family. Have you no respect for the reputation of your brother and your sisters? Your shameless behavior reflects poorly on all of us.

Daughter, what were you thinking? Even now I cannot believe you eloped with a man—a stranger to the family—in the middle of the night! When you disappeared from the masquerade, I feared you had been abducted or murdered, but the reality was far worse. I nearly had an apoplexy when I received your letter.

For years, I labored to bring you into society and help you form eligible connections. Just when I had arranged a most advantageous match for you, you chose to spoil all my plans by running away! I do not know how I can ever hold my head up in society again. We are lucky His Grace the Duke of Belmont has not brought legal action against us for misleading him as to your intentions.

Under the circumstances, I do not feel I can in good conscience visit you, nor welcome you under our roof. We cannot give even the appearance of condoning your scandalous behavior. Doing so would materially damage the prospects of your sisters—all your sisters. What damages your good name soils theirs as well.

Similarly, I shall not be able to return your possessions to you. To do so would look too much like a mark of approbation. I have requested that Mrs. Potter donate your clothing to chari-ty. Your books have already been taken to the nearest bookseller. As for your saddle horse, Squire Browning wishes to purchase her for his daughter, and I hope she may have good use of her.

I pray you do not repent of your hasty wedding. From all I have been able to learn, Lord Valance is a known libertine who keeps the most disreputable company. Should you discover that he makes a poor husband, you have only yourself to blame.

I must ask that you not write to any of your siblings again. Their future must be protected at all costs.

Sincerely,
Prudence Grantly

Honora did not know how long she sat there, staring at the letter. The strain of reading her mother's fine handwriting without her glasses might have given her a headache under any circumstances, but she thought the pain she felt now came as much from the pressure of unshed tears as from eyestrain.

Honora had known her mother would be scandalized by her original plan to ruin herself. As she told Lord Valance, her family would want nothing to do with her if she were caught in amorous congress at Belmont's masquerade. She had been willing to accept that as the price of escaping Belmont. But she had thought—she had let herself believe—that her immediate marriage to Lord Valance would prevent her mother from disowning her. She thought she had salvaged some remnant of respectability. And she thought Dora would be safe from any repercussions.

She had been so very wrong about everything.

The paper in her hand shook as Honora's body was wracked with tears. It was the first time she had cried since the night of her elopement. Until now, there had not seemed to be any reason to weep.

"My lady, I am going to the club, but I will back—my lady?"

Lord Valance stood in the doorway, clad in style from his carefully-arranged curls to his brightly-polished Hessian boots. "Is something wrong?'

Honora sat up straight and tried to stop shaking. But she could not. Nor could she answer Lord Valance. He walked into the room and sat down beside her on the sofa, looking concerned. She handed him the letter, thinking it would explain the situation better than she could. He read it twice, then wadded it up and tossed it in the fire, as he had done with the note from Illegible Scribble.

"If that is how your mother treats you, I should think your life would be better without her in it." He pitched his voice low, but spoke with assurance.

Honora wished she had some of Lord Valance's confidence. She could only shake her head. "If it were only her, maybe. But I am cut off from the whole family. My sisters. My brother. Our home." Her horse, Ladybird. Her books. Probably all of the correspondence she had saved from years of writing to her school friends would be tossed out or destroyed, along with her diaries. She could never have any of it again.

She sniffled and blinked her burning eyes. "I don't even get to keep my spectacles."

Lord Valance cursed softly. "Don't be daft. I will buy you a new set of spectacles. If you want to ride in Hyde Park, I will get you a saddlehorse. All of those things can be replaced."

Once again, Honora shook her head. According to her mother, Grantly Manor would be forever closed to her. Nothing could replace her childhood home. She reached up to scrub her tear-damp face, and her husband handed her a clean handkerchief.

"Thank you," she mumbled.

Very much to her surprise, Lord Valance wrapped one arm around her and pulled her closer to him. "What your mother says does not matter. You are my wife now."

She leaned against him, desperate for reassurance. He smelled of soap and citrus, and his embrace felt both soft and solid.

"And we will make a new home for ourselves." His arm around her tightened.

"Will we?" Honora asked doubtfully. Certain things about their marriage would have to change for this house to feel like a home.

"It might take some time," Lord Valance admitted. "We hardly know each other, do we? But yes, I hope we can eventually become comfortable together."

Honora smiled. "I would like that."

It was one thing to enter into a marriage of convenience; that was not so very uncommon. Many couples married without loving each other. Sometimes they managed to form quite comfortable households. But it was quite another thing to live one's life in a fake marriage, without even a semblance of affection or an attempt to know one's spouse. Honora would have minded *that*. She had vowed to be Lord Valance's wife, not merely his housemate.

She still did not understand why a man who had been willing to tumble into bed with her at a Twelfth Night party without even knowing her name should drag his feet about consummating their marriage. But she supposed he had his reasons. Perhaps, after all, he *had* been attached to Illegible Scribble. He might need time to grieve the end of that *affaire*.

But—she wrinkled her brow—if that were the case, why would he have been willing to be unfaithful to his mistress at the masquerade? Strangely, she had never wondered about that before. On Twelfth Night, she had been so intent on her plan of ruination that she had not spared much thought to the motives of her accomplice. Was Lord Valance simply a philanderer by nature? Her frown deepened as she speculated.

"Is something wrong?" Lord Valance asked.

Honora peered up at him, intending to ask him about his past behavior. She found him studying her, his forehead creased with concern. Something about the directness of his gaze made her feel unexpectedly shy.

"Nothing is wrong. I was just wondering why . . ." Her voice trailed off because she did not know how to word her question so it wouldn't sound like a condemnation.

On Twelfth Night, Lord Valance's decision to leave the ballroom for a tryst with a stranger had certainly served Honora's purpose. If the rumors of Belmont's cruelty were true, it might even have saved her life. But once she had married Lord Valance, Honora couldn't help thinking that his lack of fidelity to his mistress might indicate a significant character flaw.

"Why what?" His dark brown eyes looked soft and kind.

Honora took a deep breath. "Why did you leave the ballroom with me on Twelfth Night?" At the last minute, she decided not to add "when you already had a mistress." For all she knew, courtesans might not expect fidelity from their protectors. Perhaps he had committed no wrong against Illegible Scribble.

Lord Valance drew back from her, removing his arm from around her shoulders. "Why do you want to know that?"

"I am trying to better understand your character," she explained. For some reason, her answer seemed to bother him even more than the original question.

"I assure you that my behavior on Twelfth Night was not at all in character! I can only assume I had too much to drink."

"Really? You didn't seem tipsy to me." There had certainly been a great deal of inebriation at that party, but Lord Valance had neither spoken nor moved like a man under the influence of too much wine or punch.

"Really." He truculently lifted his chin. "But since you are asking personal questions about our first encounter, Lady Valance, let me return the favor. I wish you would explain why you chose *me* for your ridiculous scheme."

Honora drew in a sharp breath. She could not explain that. She quite clearly remembered the way "Bacchus" kept drawing her attention, but she had never understood why. She intended to answer "I don't know," that being the most honest answer, but she never got the chance. Their butler opened the door before she could respond.

"Mrs. Valance," Weller announced.

"*Damnation!*" Lord Valance hissed the word so softly, Honora was not entirely sure she heard him correctly.

Honora stared at him, then examined the middle-aged lady who had entered the room in the wake of the announcement. Mrs. Valance was tall—taller than Honora, at least—and dressed in black silk. Her eyes and hair were nearly the same in color as Lord Valance's, although her hair had begun to gray at the temples.

Mrs. Valance's aura looked very different from her son's, though. When Honora focused on the radiance surrounding her mother-in-law, she saw a rainbow of spangles similar to most people. Mrs. Valance's aura showed none of the silver, bronze, or gold lights that would have indicated magical talent. Somehow, her aura looked less inviting than her son's, though Honora could not have said why.

Lord Valance slowly rose to his feet. "Mother! What a pleasant surprise!"

CHAPTER TEN

OTHER'S TIMING WAS absolutely dreadful. Valance had been on the point of abandoning his planned afternoon at the club in order to spend the day with his wife. It would not be right to leave her alone after receiving that heartless letter. Besides, there were things they ought to talk about—conversations he had put off for too long.

Between moving to a new house, making his will, meeting with his man of business to make sure his financial affairs were in order, and writing to all the many people who would expect to be personally informed about his marriage, Valance's first week of wedded life had been busier than expected. He had not neglected his wife, of course. He made certain to always be home in time for dinner, and he kept his evenings free of social engagements.

But somehow, he never seemed to know what to say to Lady Valance. Theirs was such a peculiar situation: strangers forced into close proximity with each other. He did not know her well enough to know how best to treat her. He had done his best to give her space, not wanting her to feel trapped in this marriage. He'd meant it when he said he did not intend to be a tyrannical husband. But he had no idea what kind of husband he ought to be.

In truth, he had no idea how to be married at all. The worst of it was that those few of his friends who were married had generally made love matches—sometimes in the most romantic way—and were thus not in a position to advise him on his marriage to a stranger. Even if they had been in town, which they were not.

Had Sir John Carrington been alive, Valance would have written to him on the subject, he being the happily married man whom Valance had known longest and best. But Sir John had been dead nearly three years. Sir Roderick was the only one of the three Carrington brothers who had yet married. Sir Roderick was also the member of the family whom Valance knew least well, so he felt reluctant to approach him for advice.

And now, before he could even begin to get his marriage sorted out, his mother had arrived for an unannounced visit. That did not bode well. Even so, Valance allowed his mother to embrace him, and he kissed her cheek respectfully, if not precisely affectionately.

"Mother, what brings you to town?"

"The Season, dear boy! What else?" She smiled affectionately at him.

Valance frowned. "It is only January!" The parliamentary session would begin soon, yes. But the social whirl of the Season would not reach its height until after Easter.

"Yes, but I have so much catching-up to do with my friends. You know it has been years since I have spent any time in London. But now you have a proper home of your own, it will be much easier to visit you!" She beamed.

Valance's heart sank. "You mean to stay here, then?" *For the whole Season?* A faint pulse in his forehead promised more pain in the near future.

"If it is no imposition!" The smile on Mother's face suggested she was certain it would be no imposition.

Valance glanced at his wife, hoping for some indication of her opinion. This was her home, too. He ought not force her to deal with an unwanted guest.

"Of course, you are welcome here, Mrs. Valance," his wife said graciously. She had already risen to her feet to greet her new mother-in-law. "We have a guest room that should suit you well."

Valance's shoulders slumped in silent despair. He had hoped his wife would object to the proposed visit. And he had doubts about how satisfied his mother would be with either of their guestrooms, which were smaller than what she was used to.

"Oliver," his mother reproached, "you have not properly introduced me." She scrutinized Lady Valance from head to toe, but her expression gave no hint of what she thought of her new daughter-in-law.

Valance cleared his throat. "Ah, yes. Mother, this is Lady Valance. Miss Honora Grantly that was."

"I am so very happy to meet you, my dear. You must tell me everything about how you and Oliver met, and what he did to win your heart. I have heard so little about the matter, you know." She smiled at Lady Valance, but the sharp look she darted at her son made it clear she meant to rebuke him.

Lady Valance's eyes widened. She turned to catch Valence's gaze. He stared back with equal dismay. Somehow, they had forgotten to work out a convincing story to explain the scandalous elopement and the subsequent wedding. Why on earth had they not at least gotten their stories straight?

Valance took a deep breath, hoping to draw on all his powers of creativity. "There is really nothing to tell, Mother. We met at a party and I was so immediately smitten with Miss Grantly's beauty, intelligence, and daring that I lost no time in proposing. Quite romantic, really." Technically, he spoke the truth, at least if one defined "smitten by her daring" to mean "absolutely appalled by the outrageousness of her plan."

Was it his imagination, or was his wife struggling not to laugh at that description of their meeting? Yes, he saw her mouth twitch. She put up a hand to hide her reaction, but her amusement still shown out of her eyes. The corners of Valance's lips automatically curled up in response.

"Unfortunately," Valance concluded, "the Grantly family's

personal affairs forced us to marry quickly, so we were not able to inform you of the engagement."

"Personal affairs?" His mother cocked her head to one side. She glanced from Valance to his wife.

"Of a very private nature, I am afraid," Valance added hastily. "I am sure you understand."

His mother wrinkled her brow. She had a charming frown, and she knew how to employ it to good effect. "But Oliver, I do *not* understand. I am very happy to see you married, dear boy, but why could you not have given me some warning? I had no idea you intended to set up house for yourself."

"I am afraid that is my doing, ma'am," his wife interjected. "Circumstances beyond my control left me in immediate need of a new home, and Lord Valance graciously provided one. I am afraid I cannot reveal any more about the situation." She sounded genuinely sorry about the need for discretion.

"There, you see, Mother? All perfectly explainable!" Valance smiled his most reassuring smile. He wished he'd inherited more of his mother's acting ability.

It sounded like a threadbare explanation even to him, but it was not as if he could tell his mother about his wife's attempt to ruin her reputation. Mother would be scandalized by the former Miss Grantly's behavior, naturally, but she would also be upset if she knew Valance had slipped out of the ballroom with the intention of fornicating with a nameless stranger. He could easily imagine the disappointment that would flood her face. He had seen it before.

Mother's arrival ruined all of Valance's plans for the day. Instead of going to the club or spending time with his bride, he had to show his mother about the house, inquire about her journey, and listen to her complaints about the condition of the winter roads. Fortunately, her travels had so exhausted her that she went upstairs to take an afternoon nap, leaving Valance blessedly alone with his wife.

"I am so very sorry," he told her.

"For what?" Her lovely eyes widened.

Valanced wishing he knew her well enough to kiss her furrowed brow, to smooth away that frown. But he doubted she would welcome such intimacies from him, given that they were still near-strangers. He had been pushing his luck to put his arm around her earlier. He had only done so because she so obviously needed comfort.

Instead of kissing his wife's sorrows away, he merely shrugged. "Sorry for springing a family member on you. This is hardly a good time to have a house guest."

Most people would have known better than to intrude upon a newly married couple, particularly while they were still settling into their new home. Valance would have asked what his mother was thinking, but he was fairly sure he knew the answer. Mother wanted to investigate his new wife.

"I don't see how you are to blame for your mother showing up unexpectedly," Lady Valance said. "And you could hardly turn her away once she arrived. That would be rude."

"Yes, precisely." Valance relaxed, thinking the worst of the conversation was over.

"But I do have a few questions." She fixed him with her bright, clear eyes.

By now, he knew that Lady Valance *always* had a few questions. They were often difficult to answer, too.

"Yes, my lady?" he asked cautiously. "What would you like to know?"

"Why is your mother called *Mrs.* Valance rather than the Dowager Lady Valance?"

Oh, that one was easy enough. "Because my father died without ever inheriting the title. There is no courtesy title for a viscount's son, so he was only addressed as Mr. Valance."

"Oh! Did he die recently? Is that why your mother is in mourning?"

Valance sighed. "No. He died two months before I was born." He hated having to explain about the father he'd never known, but at least he was used to those questions.

Her eyes widened. "You never even met him? How sad!"

"Indeed." People always consoled Valance on his fatherless state, but the truth was, both Valance's grandfather and Sir John Carrington had done a good deal to make up for that lack. "My mother has mourned him ever since."

"She must have been deeply attached to him."

"Yes, I believe she was." But she also used her enduring grief as a tool. People would rush to the aid of an emotionally fragile widow, particularly one whose only child seemingly neglected her. Valance did *not* want to explain all of that to his wife. "Is there anything more you wish to know?"

Lady Valance studied him thoughtfully, that familiar line between her brows. "Why didn't you take me to your country house to meet your mother after we married? That might have been the politest thing to do. She seemed to be offended that she did not find out about the wedding until after we were married."

"Yes," Valance said dryly, "I believe she did take offense." He had probably not heard the last of it.

He did not quite know how to answer his wife's question. Under other circumstances, honeymooning at Dreadnaught Hall would have made more sense than having to house-hunt in such a hurry. It would, he thought wistfully, have been nice to show his wife his favorite things about his childhood home.

But his mother would have been there.

"I thought we would have more privacy in our own house," he explained. How wrong he had been! But how could he have known Mother would show up unannounced, demanding to be his house guest?

"Oh, I don't think that matters much. It is not as if we act like a married couple, anyway. We have nothing to conceal from a guest." She looked down at the rug, where Bishop Barkley napped. He had rather a loud snore for such a small dog; it was one of the many things about him that annoyed Valance.

Valance frowned. There was something about her tone of

voice that worried him. Had he imagined it? "I hope you have no complaint to make of my treatment of you."

Lady Valance met his gaze again and smiled, though he was not sure he trusted that smile. "Oh, no! I suppose I had some unreasonably romantic ideas about marriage. But of course, there is nothing in the least bit romantic about being forced to marry someone you do not know. You have been very kind to me, Lord Valance. I can have no complaints."

She stood up, as if to end the conversation, but Valance reached out and caught her hand. "Wait!" He knew he had not imagined the tone of distress in her voice. He needed to clarify what she meant.

But Bishop Barkley woke up in time to see Valance grab his wife's hand. Barkley took that to be a threat to the lady of the house. He leaped to his feet and rushed at Valance, barking shrilly.

"Oh, be quiet!" Valance snapped. The dog snatched up the tassel on Valance's boot and worried it. "Now you see why I hate that dog!" Barkley growled in response and attacked his other boot, to no avail.

Lady Valance chuckled. "Oh, did he attack you every time you touched your mistress? That must have been annoying."

It most certainly *had* been annoying, but Valance was horrified that she had remarked on it. A properly bred lady would never allude to her husband's amorous adventures prior to marriage.

"I am not going to discuss my mistress with my wife!" Overwhelmed with indignation, he let go of her hand.

"Why not? If I had had a lover, I would have told you about him." Her casual tone made this sound perfectly reasonable rather than horrifically scandalous.

"That is entirely different!" Valance protested.

If she had had a lover before him, they would never have gotten into this mess, because the Duke of Belmont would not have been trying to marry her. Though he might have offered her a *carte blanche*. Valance shook his head, refusing to speculate on that idea. Instead, he picked up the barking terrier and handed him to Lady Valance. As soon as she took Bishop Barkley in her arms, he stopped yapping.

"How is it different?" she asked. "I mean, I know people *think* it is more important for women to be chaste than it is for men, but why—"

But Valance could take no more of her questions. This one sounded precisely like the kind of question Abigail and her Bluestocking friends liked to debate. Had it been intended purely as an intellectual exercise, he might have been willing to discuss it, but he felt this conversation had gone on far too long, in far too personal of a direction. He did not want to discuss his past relations with other women.

"I need to go to my club for an important meeting," he announced. "But I will be back in time for dinner." He bolted out the door, leaving his wife alone with the dog he had bought for his mistress. The irony was not lost on him.

CHAPTER ELEVEN

IT DID NOT take long for Honora to learn what things would set Lord Valance off where his mother was concerned. Mrs. Valance had a way of widening her eyes, frowning, and saying "But, Oliver . . ." whenever she disliked something his lordship said.

Every time she did that, Lord Valance's whole body would stiffen. Not long after that, he would begin to massage his temples. Eventually, he would announce that he had a headache and leave the room. Honora could not tell if he was actually in pain or if he used his frequent headaches as an excuse for escaping his mother. Both seemed equally plausible.

Initially, Honora found Mrs. Valance easy to deal with. Mrs. Valance always behaved politely—even deferentially—to Honora, despite being a generation older. She told Honora stories about "Oliver's" boyhood, his prowess as a cricket player, and the high marks he'd earned at school.

But Honora noticed that when Mrs. Valance mentioned the Carrington family, she always scrunched up her face distastefully, as if she had just taken a sip of unsweetened lemonade. What was *that* about? Lord Valance seemed quite attached to Mr. and Miss Carrington. So far as she could tell, they were his closest personal friends. Miss Carrington was still visiting her family in Surrey, but Mr. Carrington frequently dined with them at Curzon Street.

When next he came to dinner, Mr. Carrington happily spent

an hour explaining to Honora why he had decided to set up his meteorite trap in the country rather than in London. Mrs. Valance frowned throughout most of the conversation, and shook her head expressively when the ladies and gentlemen separated. Honora, who found Mr. Carrington's astronomical magic fascinating, did not understand her mother-in-law's objection.

"It never seemed right to me that Sir John Carrington was appointed as Oliver's guardian," Mrs. Valance told Honora one day. "I understand why the testamentary guardian had to be a gentleman rather than a lady, and of course I was appointed as Oliver's caregiver. But we are not at all related to the Carringtons. It would have made more sense to appoint one of my brothers as guardian, don't you think? I can't imagine why my husband wrote his will that way."

"Perhaps he thought it would be helpful to have a guardian who lived close at hand." Given the late Mr. Valance's untimely death, it must have been convenient that the Carrington estate and the Valance estate bordered each other.

Mrs. Valance shook her head, looking as sour as she always did when discussing the Carringtons. "I am sure Sir John was a worthy man, but I could never approve of the way he and Lady Carrington raised their children. They let them do whatever they wanted! Climb trees, swim in the pond in the middle of winter, stay up late playing noisy parlor games, make fire balloons—"

"Fire balloons?" Honora had never heard of such a thing.

"Out of coated paper, I believe. Or was it silk? And a sponge soaked in spirits. Either way, it is a wonder they didn't burn down the whole forest. And they let Peregrine do all sorts of dangerous magical experiments." Mrs. Valance shook her head.

"That all sounds fun," Honora said wistfully. "My parents never let me climb trees." She had no idea how one made a fire balloon but she felt certain she would not have been allowed to do that, either.

"Well, of course not!" Mrs. Valance sounded scandalized by

the very idea. "Because your parents were raising you to be a young lady, and not a hoyden. But Lady Carrington let her daughters run just as wild as the boys, and now look at them! Both of them unconventional and very Blue. Miss Hannah is eighteen already, and the family have made no push to give her a Season or make a match for her."

"Lucky her." A sour taste filled Honora's mouth at the memory of the way her mother had urged her to encourage the Duke of Belmont's suit.

"Lucky?" Mrs. Valance's eyes widened with dismay. "My dear Lady Valance! Surely you don't mean that? Why, the poor girl will end up as peculiar as her older sister!" Her voice hushed as she added, "I believe that Miss Carrington doesn't even *attempt* to move in decent society anymore."

Honora's mouth fell open. It was the first time she'd seen that look of dismay directed at *her* rather than her husband. Some part of her wanted to immediately apologize for misspeaking, though she had done nothing more than state her honest opinion. Was this how Lord Valance felt when his mother turned her big brown eyes toward him and said "But Oliver . . .!"? No wonder the poor man spent all his afternoons at the club.

While Honora sympathized with her husband, she also thought it unfair that he so often abandoned her to deal with his mother while he went and did whatever it was men of leisure did all day. She never had a chance to tell him so, because she rarely had a chance to talk to him without his mother either present or likely to walk in on the conversation. It was really quite vexing.

True, Honora had plenty of her own tasks to keep her occupied. She had developed a regular routine for her mornings: walking the dog, a daily conference with the housekeeper, then reading and answering letters.

Letters were more important to Honora than ever before, though she received fewer of them. Her only source of information about her family now was her friend Verena, the daughter of the clergyman at Ashton Chipping. Thanks to Verena, she at least had the comfort of knowing her siblings were all in good health, though Verena reported that Dora seemed out of spirits. Honora could not begin to imagine how hard things must be for Dora.

She tried to keep her afternoons free for errands. Knowing Lady Grantly was not going to send her any of her possessions from home, Honora had more shopping to do. Most importantly, she finally replaced her spectacles so she could read and embroider without giving herself a headache. She purchased a pair that had been charmed to prevent the lens from breaking in a fall. They were attractive, made of silver frames with oval-shaped lenses, but their price took her aback.

After Honora came home with her new spectacles, she dug the leather purse out of the dresser drawer where she kept it hidden. She counted the remaining coins and realized, uneasily, that she had no idea how to manage her money, because she did not know how much she could spend. Lord Valance had never told her how much pin money she was to have. In the normal order of things, her allowance would have been spelled out clearly in the marriage contract, but they had never had such contracts drawn up.

She would need to talk to His Lordship about money. That was not a conversation she wanted to have in front of Mrs. Valance, which meant catching him sometime when they were alone. Which was never. She pondered the problem and decided her best option was to waylay Lord Valance right before he went to bed for the night. The master suite was the only place where she could be certain they wouldn't be interrupted.

That night, she cracked open the door between their bedchambers so she could hear when Lord Valance came in with his valet to undress. His valet was a quiet man who did not tend to engage in chit-chat, so she had to listen intently for the door shutting behind him.

Once Preston departed, she drew a deep breath, then tapped on the door leading into Lord Valance's room. He opened it at once, and her jaw dropped. She had imagined she would find him in a night shirt, maybe even a dressing gown, but that was not the case. He wore only his smalls, exposing more of the adult male body than Honora had ever seen before. It was rather a distracting sight.

"Yes, my lady? Was there something you wanted?"

"Um," Honora began. She had to forcibly remind herself that the rules of social interaction required one to make eye contact when speaking to another person. Dragging her eyes up to her husband's face took real effort. Lord Valance had a pleasant face, but she had seen it every day for a couple of weeks, whereas she'd had no prior opportunity to see him in a state of undress.

She could not help being intrigued by the sight. In addition to having body hair in places she had not expected, Lord Valance was more heavily muscled than she had realized. That must be the result of all those visits to Gentleman Jackson's. He was plump about the midsection, but she suspected there was hard muscle underneath that softness. She would have had to touch him to know for sure, though.

She clenched her hands, wishing she dared to touch him. Blood rushed to her face as she grappled with her unmaidenly desires.

A concerned wrinkle formed in Lord Valance's brow. "Is something wrong?"

The moment she opened her mouth, Honora began to babble. "I don't remember what I wanted. So, it probably wasn't important. So, I should go. Now. Yes, I should go now." Her blush deepened with every ridiculous word she uttered. She took a step back, thinking a retreat was the best way to end this horrific awkwardness.

"Wait," he said. "This might be a good time to talk."

Ah, right, that was what she had come here for. She had not come here to ogle her husband. "Yes, talk," she agreed. "Talking is good. I like to talk."

She was not sure whether she wished he would put his dressing gown on, so she would not be distracted, or keep it off, so she could keep admiring him. She longed to run her fingers through the hair on her chest, because she had no idea what the texture was like.

"Why don't you come in?" he suggested. "Rather than standing in the doorway."

"Oh, certainly. Of course." She followed him into his chamber, trying to walk and breathe and think normally, even though her heart was racing.

Her husband gestured to the pair of armchairs in front of the fireplace. "You will be warmer if we sit by the fire."

Where else *could* they sit? Honora wondered. Oh. He meant sitting here rather than on the bed. Right. Not only was there an undressed man in the room, there was also a bed. *Oh dear.* The blush that had died down began to burn her face again. This had clearly been a tactical error.

Lord Valance stared at her, looking increasingly worried. Any minute now, he was going to ask if something was wrong. She knew it.

"You must be colder than I am," she said, feeling she had to say something.

"Oh, right!" He seemed to finally realize he was significantly less clothed than in their previous interactions. "Let me grab my dressing gown."

She nodded and stared into the fire to compose herself. When she looked back at her husband, he wore a silk banyan tied tightly shut. The only reminder of his undressed state was the patch of bare skin she could see at the neckline.

That's better, she thought. Except she didn't just think it. She said it out loud. She clapped her hand over her mouth when she realized what she had done.

"I am very sorry." He sounded sincerely apologetic. "I did not mean to scandalize you, my lady. I ought to have put a dressing gown on before I opened the door."

"I was not scandalized," Honora explained, "merely distracted."

He stared blankly at her. He seemed to be doing a lot of that tonight. She must have said something ridiculous.

She tried to rectify the situation. "This is your bedroom. You can wear as little as you want in here." Unfortunately, that did nothing to improve the situation.

"So I can! All the same, I think I'd better keep my dressing gown on. I wouldn't want to distract you, my lady." He smiled at her. "Now, was there something you wanted?"

"Money." Honora finally remembered what it was she wanted to discuss. Lord Valance's banyan seemed to have improved her ability to think.

The confusion in his expression vanished as his face relaxed. "Oh, did you need more money? I should have thought of that. Would you prefer banknotes or coins?"

"No, no." She held up a hand to stop him from getting out of his chair. "I don't need more money yet. I just wanted to know what my quarterly allowance was to be."

He shrugged. "Do you need an allowance? You can simply direct your creditors to me. You need not fear that I will refuse to pay your bills."

"But how much can I spend?" She needed to know how much to budget, so she did not outrun the banker.

"As much as you want." It was surprising how matter-of-factly he spoke, given the ridiculousness of his words.

"No one can spend as much as they want," Honora insisted. Even the Prince Regent's coffers had limits.

"I suppose not." He shrugged. "But I have an income of some fifteen thousand pounds a year. Surely you won't want to spend more than that?"

"Fifteen thousand pounds *a year*?" Honora repeated, awed. Her family made do on five thousand a year. Most families in their social circle had much smaller incomes. Lord Valance's annual income would be considered a fortune by most people. He collected a small fortune *every year*. She could not wrap her mind around it.

"It might actually be closer to twenty thousand," he said apologetically. "But I don't remember off-hand. In any case, I doubt you'll run into dun territory."

"I quite agree." Honora shook her head, trying to imagine how anyone could spend that much money. Perhaps hardened gamblers might blow through that much in a year, but she could not imagine how else anyone with such an income could run into debt.

"Is there anything else you need?" he asked.

Honora bit her lip as she debated saying more. On the one hand, sitting by the fire in a comfortable chair had made her sleepy. The prospect of going back to her room and curling up in bed before the warming pan cooled tempted her. The night was only going to grow colder.

On the other hand, she seldom had a chance to converse with her husband alone. And he seemed to be in a good mood this evening. Not once had he rubbed his temples in pain the way he did when something annoyed him. Perhaps she ought to take advantage of the situation.

"There isn't anything else I *need, but* I do have a number of questions I wanted to ask." Was it her imagination, or did he cringe a little? No, she had not imagined it: his smile had faded.

"Yes?" he said warily. "What did you want to know?"

Honora wavered. Perhaps, after all, this was not the right time to ask questions. It might be better to bid her husband goodnight and return to her own chamber. She sighed, wondering when there ever *would* be a good time for her questions.

"Is something wrong, my lady?" Lord Valance prompted. "Whatever it is, you can tell me." He might have lost his smile, but his voice sounded warm and encouraging.

Very well, then. Honora took a deep breath and asked the question that had most plagued her. "I was wondering why you never come to my bed at night."

CHAPTER TWELVE

"YOU WONDERED WHAT?" Did she really say what he thought she said? Valance had expected another question about daily life or household expenses, not a question about his sexual habits.

"I wondered why you never come to my bed," Lady Valance repeated. "We are married, so I assumed we would share a bed. Was I wrong?"

Valance gazed into the dying fire, as if it could offer some wisdom to sustain him through this conversation. But though there were said to be soothsayers who could see visions in a burning flame, the fire offered him no magical insight. He was on his own.

"You were not wrong," he said at last. "As I told you, I do want an heir. Eventually. But although we are married, we are also strangers to each other. I did not think there was any need to rush into the physical side of marriage."

He had thought that went without saying, but apparently not. Perhaps he should have explained this earlier. But there never seemed to be a good time to talk to his wife now that his mother lived with them.

"I understand that," she said, in the voice of someone who believes they are being very patient, "but I don't understand why you feel that way when you were perfectly willing to go to bed with me the night of the masquerade."

Valance closed his eyes, knowing his head would start pounding any minute now. The questions were going to keep getting more complicated, weren't they? "The situations are entirely different."

He still felt ashamed of his behavior on Twelfth Night. What had he been thinking, following a stranger out of the ballroom merely because she was beautiful? The fact of the matter was that he had not been thinking at all. He had merely been lusting. And he did not want to admit that to the woman who was now his wife. In fact, he would rather never discuss that night again.

But he was not at all surprised when Lady Valance said: "Explain to me the difference."

Valance glanced wistfully at his soft, warm bed, with its blankets invitingly turned down. The warming pan would be cooling as they spoke. No doubt the blankets would be freezing by the time he crawled into bed. But he had told Lady Valance she could tell him whatever was bothering her. He owed it to her to talk about this, awkward thought it might be.

"There is much more at stake in a marriage than in an assignation that lasts a single night." Or a single hour, as the case might be.

"What do you mean *at stake?*" Lady Valance had already taken her hair down for the night; now she picked up a long strand and twisted it absently around her fingers.

As expected, his head began to throb. At least this time he had some of his usual pain medication close at hand on the dressing table. He opened the tin from George's and popped one of the lozenges into his mouth.

The cool mint was soothing, but what he really needed for this conversation was a snifter of brandy. If it were not so late, he would have rung for a servant to bring him one. But the whole household would be abed at this hour, and it seemed selfish to wake someone up merely because he craved liquid courage.

He put the tin away, cleared his throat, and continued his explanation. "Imagine, for a moment, that we had done what you wanted the night of the masquerade—and not gotten caught."

"That wouldn't have been what I wanted," she interrupted. "Getting caught was essential to my plan."

Valance gritted his teeth, thereby undoubtedly adding to his headache. He wanted to point out that the chances of them getting caught at precisely the right moment had never been high to begin with, making ruination an implausible solution to her problem. Moreover, since she had not divulged the reason for her seduction, Valance would have done anything in his power to minimize the damage to her reputation even if they had been caught. How could he have known she *wanted* to destroy her reputation?

But arguing that point would be a distraction from the real issue at hand. "Just imagine it," he insisted.

"Very well. But why—"

He hurried to speak before she could ask another question. He struggled enough to keep up with one query at a time; he would never be able to keep track of the conversation if she started interjecting additional questions.

"If we had, er, engaged in amorous congress in a spare bedroom at Belmont Court, afterward we would simply have gone our separate ways. We might never have seen each other again, except perhaps in passing. And what we had done would not have mattered in the least."

He knew this from experience. He still ran into Lady Morrow from time to time during the Season. When they met, they merely exchanged a few friendly words, as if they had never conducted a torrid *affaire* during a house party the summer after he left Oxford.

"It wouldn't?"

"Well, if you had actually been married, as you claimed to be, I suppose it might have damaged your relationship with your husband," he conceded. "Depending on what his expectations were, that is." A husband who had agreed in advance not to interfere with his wife's *amours* might not have cared what she did in back corridors at parties. "But it needn't have mattered to *us*. Whether the encounter was a pleasant interlude or an unmitigated disaster, we could have shrugged it off, walked away and been none the worse for it."

The line between her brows deepened. Valance held his breath, knowing she was going to ask something else. But what?

"How could it have been a disaster?"

"Never mind that!" He scrambled to retain control of the conversation. "My point is, there would have been no ongoing entanglement between us. Neither of us were trying to get up a long-term *affaire*, right? Whether we were good together in bed or not wouldn't have really mattered."

It would not have mattered how well they could communicate, how strongly they were attracted to each other, or whether their desires were at all compatible. Problems that might put a strain on a marriage would have been easy enough to shrug off during a one-time tryst.

"Oh." She frowned as she absorbed this. "And you think being married to each other makes that different?" She began to idly unwind the strand of hair wrapped around her finger. The sight was a little distracting, to be honest. It made Valance wonder what her silky hair would feel like in *his* hands.

"I am *certain* that it is different," he said, speaking as patiently as he could. It was not his wife's fault that she knew so little about this subject. Genteel young women were not allowed the sexual freedom wealthy young men enjoyed. They were expected to be innocent, if not outright ignorant. "We are not going to have a stitch once and never again. Whether things go well in bed or not, we are going to have to keep living with each other."

And sleeping with each other, at least until a son was born. After that they would be free to go their separate ways and find consolation, if such were needed, with other lovers. That was not the marriage Valance had envisioned in his younger and more romantic days, but under the circumstances, it would hardly be fair to expect his wife to stay with him forever.

He stared moodily into the fire again, pondering the dog's breakfast he'd made of his life. When he was younger, he'd assumed he would someday have a large family like Sir John and Lady Carrington's. The sort of family where the children fought and loved with equal ferocity—and either discovered important new magical formulas or set fire to the dining room, depending on the day of the week. But that no longer seemed like a reasonable desire.

"That was what I meant when I said there was more at stake now that we are married," he concluded. "And on top of all that, I was willing to, er, rendezvous with you in part because I was under the impression you knew what you were doing. I most certainly would not have followed you out of the ballroom if I had realized you were a virgin."

She blinked at him. "What difference does that make?"

"It makes a considerable difference." Valance spoke grimly; he did not have pleasant associations with this subject.

Most of his lovers had, of course, been experienced women. He was not a rake, and he was not in the habit of seducing virgins. Cherie had been the one exception, and their first coupling had gone so badly that he preferred never to think of it. There had been blood, pain, and tears. *So many tears.* Afterward, Cherie had dramatically informed him that she hated doing that, was never going to do it again, thought all men were beasts, and wanted to go home to her dear mother.

After that disaster, it had taken Valance weeks to convince Cherie to remain under his protection. He had to woo her all over again with jewelry, flowers, sweets, and a tiny terrier puppy wearing a diamond-encrusted collar. (She had been particularly charmed by that last gift, which might have tipped the scale in his favor.) Eventually, she welcomed Valance back into her bed, where things improved significantly. But in hindsight, he wished he'd simply given Cherie a fat purse and sent her back home. They would both have been happier in the long run.

"What on earth are you thinking about?" his wife asked. "You look like you are contemplating *The Death of Marat.*"

He laughed bitterly. "Something very like." He lifted his eyes to study her face, catching her in a yawn. "My lady, you should go to bed. So should I. If you wish to speak more on this, we can do so another day."

"But *will* you talk to me?" she asked bluntly. "Or will you run off to your club to get away from your mother?"

Valance winced. He had not realized it was so obvious why he left every afternoon. Could his mother tell, too? Or was Lady Valance particularly observant? He hoped his mother did not realize he left every day primarily to escape her.

"I will make time to talk to you," he promised. "Perhaps we ought to get in the habit of conversing before bed." He yawned, too. He had not been joking about needing sleep.

"Very well," she said. "Good night." And she left him alone.

As he'd suspected, the warming pan had gone cold during the conversation, and he shivered as he tucked the bedclothes about him. A traitorous angel whispered in his ear: *You would be warmer if you took your wife to bed with you.* He pulled a pillow over his head and refused to entertain that thought, appealing though it might be.

He had meant every word he said about his reasons for deferring such marital activities. Tonight's encounter had proven him correct. A woman who was shocked into incoherence by the mere sight of her husband in his drawers would be even more appalled by the process of consummating the marriage. Clearly it would take time before his wife became sufficiently accustomed to her new state in life.

Before he could drift off to sleep, a disturbing thought jarred him awake. For the first time, it occurred to him that although he must have spent hundreds of pounds on jewelry, flowers, and perfume when wooing Cherie Barbauld into a life of sin, he had not so much as given his wife a single rose.

He had not yet presented the new viscountess with any of the Valance family's heirloom jewels, nor had he given her any sort of wedding gift. He had, of course, given her money to replace her lost wardrobe and personal possessions, but he was not fool enough to think letting one's wife buy a new pair of spectacles was at all romantic.

What did husbands give their wives as gifts? Flowers? Jewelry? Promises they didn't intend to keep? Not for the first time, Valance wished his friend Markham were in town. Markham had gotten married about a year ago. If his sporadically written letters were to be believed, he was perfectly content living in rural Lancashire with his wife and child. He might have been able to advise Valance on how a newlywed husband ought to treat his wife.

Many of the members of the Cambion Club were married, but most of the married men were older than Valance, and he tended not to know them well; certainly not well enough to ask for marital advice. Poor Reverend Mr. Stephens wasn't married, since he could not afford a wife. Who else was? Thompson, perhaps? No, he was only engaged.

The only thing for it, Valance thought sleepily, was to write to Markham and hope he would respond more quickly than usual. He had a bad habit of letting letters languish unanswered for months. But Valance could think of no one else at all likely to advise him, so that would have to do.

CHAPTER THIRTEEN

THE NEXT DAY, Honora spent the morning in Russell Square, helping Mr. Carrington arrange the new furnishings in the dining room. He intended to display some of the household porcelain on a dresser, and he wanted a second opinion about how best to arrange things. They ended up moving furniture about quite a bit to give the room a more elegant appearance. At the end of the morning, Honora felt they had achieved a great deal.

"Would you say this room seems livable now?" Mr. Carrington asked anxiously. "My sister said she would not come back until it was livable."

They both studied the new furnishings: a drop-leaf table, made of a warm cherry that matched the shelves; verdant wallpaper printed with a subtle fern pattern; and ornaments over the mantel. The new mantelpiece ornaments were the only unusual part of the decor. One was an antique astrolabe, the other a fossilized seashell. Mr. Carrington insisted his sister would like these, and Honora took his word for it. They certainly seemed consistent with the scholarly tone of the household.

"Yes," Honora assured him. "I think it all looks very pretty." Miss Carrington and Miss Taylor would have to be very hard to please if they did not like so comfortable a room.

She took the carriage back to Curzon Street, feeling satisfied with her morning's work. But when she got back, she discovered that her mother-in-law viewed the matter differently.

"You went to Russell Square by yourself?" Mrs. Valance asked, her eyes wide. "Without a chaperone?"

Honora felt confused. "I do not need a chaperone, since I am a married woman now." Lord Valance had told her it was perfectly acceptable for married women to be seen in public with men who were not their husband.

"Oh, my dear." Mrs. Valance's tone instantly put Honora's hackles up. It was identical to the way she said "But Oliver . . ." just before Lord Valance developed one of his headaches. "People still gossip about married women, you know. You can never be too careful about your reputation. You represent the whole Valance family now, and it is your duty to uphold the family honor. I am sure you own mother would tell you as much if she were here."

Honora's lips tightened. Mrs. Valance frequently insisted that her advice to Honora was precisely what Lady Grantly would have said in her place. But how she could be certain of this, given that she had never met Lady Grantly, remained a mystery.

"I see. Thank you for warning me, Mrs. Valance." Privately, Honora resolved to ask Lord Valance whether he shared his mother's concern. She cared much more about *his* opinion.

She had not expected to have a chance to talk to her husband until bedtime. But, to her surprise, he returned from his errands earlier than usual and asked if she would like to go for a drive in Hyde Park.

"The crowd may be thin, since it is early in the Season," he warned her. "But it is a surprisingly warm day. I think if we dress snuggly, we can enjoy a comfortable ride." He hesitated for a moment, then added: "I should warn you not to expect a flashy pair of horses. My pair have perfectly matching strides, but they are not as handsome as what many people like for a curricle."

"I do not care about that." Honora had never had a chance to drive in Hyde Park; she had at most walked along the edge of the park. She was eager to see more of London. She would not have minded riding in a gig drawn by a mule.

She saw what Lord Valance meant when he brought his curricle around. His horses were dark bays, with a touch of rusty brown at their muzzles. They did not quite match: one of them had a lot of flash, with four white stockings and a white face, while the other appeared not to have a single white hair. They stood patiently, ears flicking back and forth, rather than dancing around as the high-spirited teams favored by whipsters were said to do.

It was a surprisingly temperate day for late January. For once, there were no dark clouds overhead and no chilly breeze nipping at noses. Lord Valance's expression matched the sunny weather, until he saw what Honora carried in her arms.

"Why on earth are you bringing that rodent?" Distaste dripped from his voice.

"I thought Bishop Barkley would like to see the park, too." Honora took the little dog for a walk every morning, and the footman walked him again in the afternoon, but she feared he might be bored of spending so much of his time indoors. Perhaps if he had more stimulation, he would stop chewing on the furniture.

"Do you mind?" she asked. From the disgust on His Lordship's face, she guessed he did mind. Her shoulders slumped. "Very well, I will leave him behind." She turned back towards the house. She would have to take Barkley to the park another day.

"No, no, you can bring him," he grudgingly allowed. "But mind you keep him from biting me."

"I am sure he will be a good boy. Won't you, Barkley?" The terrier wagged his tail and licked her hands.

Barkley did, in fact, seem to enjoy the carriage ride. He stood on Honora's lap, turning his head here, there, and everywhere. Every time a carriage passed them, he yapped.

"He's as good as a Dalmatian." Lord Valance sounded amused. "Who knew Yorkshire terriers made good carriage dogs?"

Honora smiled up at her husband. "Was there something you wished to talk about, my lord?"

"What?" He had been watching the road as he navigated into the park, but now he glanced down at her. "No, I just thought you might enjoy a ride in the park. With me, I mean."

"That was kindly thought." But rather surprising, too. Lord Valance had not exactly shown himself eager to spend time in her company. She had assumed the carriage drive was a ruse to get them away from his mother.

Despite the time of year, they still encountered people Lord Valance knew. Indeed, he seemed to know almost everyone by name. Several times, young men pulled up beside their carriage to chat with him. Each time, their eyes wandered over to Honora. Some of them were friendly. Some of them seemed curious. And some of them scrutinized her in the manner of housewives examining a joint in the butcher shop.

"My lord?" she whispered to her husband after one such encounter. "Is there something wrong with my appearance today?"

Perhaps her clothes were not appropriate for Hyde Park? She had worn a walking dress and a thick winter cloak. She did not yet have any carriage dresses, and she had not thought her pelisse would be warm enough. But now she worried she looked dowdy.

"Of course not!" He glanced down at her, surprised. "You show to advantage today, my lady."

"Then why does everyone keep staring at me?" Honora could not help feeling self-conscious. She sometimes committed social *faux pas* without realizing it, and she feared she might have done so today. There were so many rules about how a young lady must dress and act in different situations! She found it difficult to keep track of all of them.

"They are probably just staring at you because you are beautiful," Lord Valance suggested. "And you are unfamiliar, since you never had a London Season. Naturally, everyone is going to be curious about the new Lady Valance—and envious of me for having married you!" He smiled smugly.

Honora shook her head. She did not deny her beauty, but she did not believe it accounted for the attention she kept attracting.

"Well," he admitted, "you must realize we have been the subject of a good deal of gossip. People undoubtedly wonder about our sudden marriage. I have let it be known at the club that we met at a party, and I was, er, so smitten that I proposed almost immediately. It is a ridiculous story, but such things do happen." He shrugged his broad shoulders.

"I suppose that is the best explanation we can give." The real story was too sordid to reveal. She glanced up at Lord Valance doubtfully. "Will people really believe you to be so foolish, though?" He had never given the impression of being the sort of man who might fall madly in love at first sight.

He grinned. "Yes, that's the sticking point. The fellows at the club who know me best seem not to buy the story. But it will pass muster with the general public." To her surprise, he chuckled. "Perhaps you don't know it, but I have a reputation for being a bit of an absent-minded magician. And there's no denying that I lived in an unconventional household. Most of the *ton* assumes I am as eccentric as the Carringtons. My sudden marriage will be considered another one of my eccentricities."

"You don't seem the least bit absent-minded to me." Honora could not wrap her mind around the idea of Lord Valance being labelled eccentric. His helping her escape the party might have been a bit irregular—since, as he pointed out, it was not "the thing" for proper gentlemen to run off with well-bred young ladies—but to her, his behavior seemed perfectly rational, given the unusual circumstances.

He nodded to a passing acquaintance before turning to her again. "There are many people in high society who think anyone who prefers a night at home to a ball, a rout, or a card party is a bit peculiar. Particularly if one stays home to study magic."

"Oh, I see." Honora had heard such nonsense at home, too. A girl might be labeled a Bluestocking if she expressed a preference for reading rather than flirting. At least, so her mother had said. Mama had advised Honora to conceal the amount of reading she did when she talked to prospective suitors. But Lady Grantly had also told Honora she was lucky that the Duke of Belmont wanted to marry her. Honora no longer trusted her mother's advice.

"Damn," Valance growled.

Honora flinched, startled both by his profanity and the uncharacteristic anger in his voice. He stared ahead at a horseman approaching them. She squinted at the figure too. Speak of the devil! Belmont himself rode towards them.

"Turn around," she gasped. "Please." She had thought she would never have to see Belmont again, since she no longer lived near his principal seat. She'd forgotten that the duke came to London every year for the Parliamentary sessions.

"It is too late for that," Lord Valance replied. "And we would do well not to retreat. We don't want him to think we are scared of him."

But I am scared of him. Honora's stomach soured from the sheer weight of her dread. In her panic, she accidentally squeezed Barkley too tightly, forcing a whimper from him. She stroked his head by way of apology. She supposed it really was too late to retreat now. Belmont had already stopped his horse next to their carriage so he could greet them.

"Well met, Your Grace," Lord Valance said.

Honora glanced up at Lord Valance, puzzled by the change in his tone. The growl of a moment ago was gone. Instead, he drawled his words lazily, exaggerating his usual speech pattern into a caricature of a languid aristocrat.

"Indeed, Lord Valance." Belmont did not look at Valance. Instead, he studied Honora with eyes as cold as a basilisk's. "Miss Grantly, I am afraid you left my party under the weight of some misconception. I wish—"

Lord Valance interrupted. "I must ask you to address my viscountess by her proper title." He continued to speak in that listless drawl, but his eyes looked every bit as hard as the duke's.

Belmont flicked his eyes in Lord Valance's direction and nodded. Then he turned back to Honora. "My apologies, Lady Valance. I meant no disrespect. It is only that your marriage is so recent—and so very unexpected—that I keep forgetting you are Miss Grantly no more. I congratulate you on your nuptials, my dear."

Honora shuddered at the unwanted endearment. Then, to her surprise, Bishop Barkley growled at the duke.

"I am sorry! I do not know why my dog is behaving so. He is normally quite friendly." She tightened her grip on Barkley to keep him from jumping out of the carriage.

Belmont shrugged. "Animals take unusual dislikes. It is nothing you need apologize for."

"Animals often have excellent instincts when it comes to evaluating character," Lord Valance said. "Her Ladyship's pet usually shows good taste."

Honora's mouth fell ajar. Her husband's remark, delivered with such casual insolence, shocked her. Especially since Lord Valance did not even like Bishop Barkley.

"Perhaps the dog takes his manners from his master," the duke retorted. Then he inclined his head in farewell. "I hope to see you again, Lady Valance." He pointedly excluded her husband.

"Likewise." Lord Valance nodded and urged his horses to walk on.

Honora felt as if she had been battered over the head. The encounter with Belmont had frightened and confused her in equal measure. She stared up her husband, wondering who he really was. She had never heard him speak with such incivility. It surprised her all the more that he would speak that way to a man as important as the Duke of Belmont.

Lord Valance glanced down at her and frowned. "Is something wrong, my lady?"

So many things seemed wrong that Honora did not know where to begin. "Why did you speak to Belmont that way? He will be angry."

"Good. I want him to be angry. He must not be allowed to insult you." Lord Valance's expression had taken on what Honora privately thought of as his "grumpy bulldog look." His dark eyes, normally as soft as a puppy's, still looked cold and hard.

"But he is a dangerous man to cross." Why had she never thought about the possible consequences Lord Valance might face for having offended the duke? "He is one of the most powerful men in London, and—"

"And I am younger than him, stronger than him, and a better shot with a pistol," Lord Valance reminded her. "You need not worry about Belmont, my lady. The duke doesn't stand a chance against Bishop Barkley and me." He sounded almost cheerful now, as if he relished the prospect of a fight. Barkley, recognizing his own name, wagged his tail.

Honora shook her head, feeling she did not in the least understand the masculine mind. If they lived in patriarchal times, when men settled their disputes by clubbing their adversaries over the head with the jawbone of an ass, Lord Valance would undoubtedly be the victor in a confrontation with Belmont. But they lived in the nineteenth century, and disputes were seldom settled with donkey bones or brute violence. The duke's greater wealth and superior political connections might give him all the advantage he needed if it came to a fight.

But she did not feel up to an argument, so she contented herself with saying: "I don't want you to get into trouble on my behalf, my lord."

"It is my privilege to defend you, since you are my wife. But I will do my best not to get shot, arrested, or bankrupted in the process." He smiled down at her. His eyes had lost that cold look, and altogether he seemed much more like the man she thought she knew than like the dangerous stranger of a moment ago. "In any case, it is nothing you need worry about, my lady."

Honora scowled. It certainly seemed like something for her to worry about! But she did not have a chance to argue, because a pair of riders pulled up to greet them. Wonder of wonders, Honora knew one of them! It was Jane Crossly, a friend from her school days. To see a familiar face after so many strangers was a delightful surprise, and Honora returned home in much better spirits.

Even so, she very much hoped she would not run into the Duke of Belmont again.

CHAPTER FOURTEEN

January to February, 1817

VALANCE TOOK A perverse pleasure in being seen by Belmont with Lady Valance by his side. They saw a good deal of him, too, because it had dawned on Valance that a girl who had never before been to London would probably enjoy exploring the theater, the opera, and the occasional private party. Consequently, he began to squire his wife about town, which gave him the opportunity to spend time with her without his mother always on hand. It further served the purpose of showing the *ton* that the new Lady Valance had the manners and deportment of a true lady. Valance had nothing to be ashamed of, and he was quite happy to let the world know it.

He continued to take her on drives in Hyde Park. It really was the best place to meet people during daylight hours, and though Valance was not a renowned whipster, he was both fond of his horses and proud of his ability to navigate London traffic. If Lady Valance was impressed by his ability to drive, though, she never remarked on it.

He had, he realized, absolutely no idea what his wife thought about him. She might, for all he knew, hold him in the greatest dislike and merely be good at hiding her feelings. Some women were quite good at dissembling, and no wonder—society practically required it of them. Women were expected to build and maintain social connections, and doing so must often mean treating people they did not like as if they were good friends.

He hoped his wife was not dissembling when she cheerfully

told him that she liked driving in the park with him. By their third drive, Honora recognized some of the people they met, and others seemed eager to further their acquaintanceship with her. His curricle stopped to exchange greetings so often Valance thought they might be stuck in the park for hours.

Valance would not have minded this, except for the fact that a large percentage of those wanting to greet Honora were personable young men, some of them much better looking than himself. He rather enjoyed their occasional encounters with Belmont, because they gave Valance an excuse to be rude to someone. He could not insult perfectly decent men like William Biddleton or Lord Harvey, no matter how much he disliked the admiring looks they gave his wife. But every time they saw Belmont, Valance gave him the cut direct, driving past the duke as if he did not even recognize him. It was immensely satisfying.

"Are you always this popular?" he asked after one particularly busy afternoon at the park.

Honora laughed softly. "Only until people get to know me better. Then I either annoy them with improper questions or bore them by talking about books they haven't read. After that they usually stop paying so much attention to me." Her expression sobered. "Though that wasn't enough to drive Belmont away."

"You need not worry about him," Valance said confidently. "He cannot harm you now." And if he so much as tried, Valance would shoot him without the least compunction. He almost wished the duke *would* try something that would justify demanding satisfaction. Valance was not normally murderous by nature, but men like Belmont ought not be allowed to live.

HE GRADUALLY DISCOVERED that Lady Valance was not joking about the way people reacted to her questions and her extensive reading. She did have a habit of startling people with unexpected questions. But he also realized those aspects of her personality were related. Many of her questions stemmed not from ignorance or naivety, but from intelligence. She was intensely curious about the world and wanted to understand more of it. Had she been a man, she might have become a naturalist or a scholar.

Many people might have thought these traits were out of place in a woman, but Valance was used to living with people who were a little out of the ordinary. In her own way, Lady Valance was every bit as erudite as Abigail Carrington. She did not share Abigail's bent toward politics, and she showed no symptoms of wanting to write letters to newspaper editors or publish essays on human rights. Nor did she write poetry, as Susan Taylor did. But she read widely, thought about what she read, and asked questions. Quite often, Valance did not know enough about the subject to answer her questions.

One day, he took her to the British Museum, thinking she would like to explore the imperial treasures there. And she did. But she also asked rather pointed questions about the means by which the treasures had been acquired and whether their original owners had given them up voluntarily.

When they explored the Elgin Marbles, Lady Valance's comments ceased being questions and became outright condemnations. She shared Lord Byron's opinion that the marbles ought not have been removed from their rightful place in the Parthenon. Other museum goers who overhead their conversation began giving them strange looks.

"What would you have the Crown do?" Valance demanded. "Send the marbles all the way back? Do you really think the Ottomans would care for them this well?" He waved a hand at the famous display. "I am sure the British public appreciates this art the way it deserves."

"I don't know," Lady Valance said somberly. "But I do not think admiring an object gives one the right to take it." She scrunched up her face in disgust. "That is the way men like Belmont think."

Valance sighed. He felt more confident having an intellectual debate about art rather than discussing personal matters. As much as he would have dearly loved to thrash Belmont for the way he'd treated the former Miss Grantly, that would not heal her obvious emotional injuries. Valance had no idea what would heal them, and he feared saying or doing something that might make things worse.

"Marble cannot think or feel," he reminded his wife. "These statues and friezes do not mind being appropriated. It is not at all the same as human beings."

"But they were made by human beings," she retorted, "and there might have been people in Athens who cared deeply about them. I would hate it if someone came to Grantly Manor and stole our family portraits because they wanted to hang them on *their* own walls. Not that I will ever see Grantly Manor again." She dropped her gaze and her face took on a mournful cast. Belmont was not the only person who had hurt her.

Eager to distract her, Valance offered her what he knew most of London considered a treat. "Why don't we leave here and go to Gunter's?"

"It is too cold for ices today," she protested. "I had rather go home and have a cup of chocolate."

"Then by all means, let us do that, my dear." He offered her his arm, eager to get her away from all reminders of her distress.

UNFORTUNATELY, CHOCOLATE AND biscuits did little to help Lady Valance. She nibbled a biscuit, took a few sips of chocolate, and excused herself. Valance let her go, then wondered if he'd made a mistake. The look on her face worried him. After he drained the last of his own drink, he followed her upstairs.

He found her in her bedroom, sitting in a chair and staring at the wall. He approached cautiously. "My lady? Is something wrong?"

She looked up at him. "I was thinking about home. Grantly Manor, I mean. I wondered if the snowdrops were blooming in our south garden."

There were no tears in her eyes, and no sign she had wept. But her voice reeked of despair. Valance wished he had Lady Grantly before him so that he could give her a piece of his mind. He stepped closer to his wife and rested his hand on the back of the chair.

"I am so very sorry, darling. Is there any way I can help?" He could not imagine what might assuage such heartache.

"I don't think so." If she noticed the endearment he used, she gave no sign. She spoke in the same polite, formal voice she might have used with an acquaintance paying a morning call. "It is very kind of you to check on me, but there is nothing I need." She looked him in the face and made the saddest attempt at a smile he had ever seen.

The grief in her face wrung Valance's heart, and without thinking, he leaned down to kiss her on the forehead. "You have a home here now," he reminded her.

She rested her head against him for a too-brief moment before shifting away and smiling that cheerless smile that made his heart ache.

Valance knew her marriage to him could not replace Lady Valance's lost family. She had lost not merely her home, but her relationship with her three sisters and her brother, the young baronet. She was forbidden even to write to them! There was nothing Valance could do that would even begin to make up for such a loss.

But perhaps he should try, all the same.

CHAPTER FIFTEEN

HONORA DID NOT even blame her mother for shunning her. Lady Grantly always acted in what she thought was the best interest of the whole family, if not necessarily the best interest of any one individual member. She must have genuinely believed disowning Honora was the best way to protect the rest of the family.

For all Honora knew, her mother might be right. Honora certainly did not want her siblings to suffer. Jack deserved a chance to cultivate friendships that would be useful when he was grown. Her sisters deserved their own chance to make advantageous marriages, if they wanted to do so. Dora, in particular, had challenges enough in her life. Honora hated to think about the disgrace of her own elopement adding to Dora's hardships.

Perhaps it really was better for Honora to stay away from her siblings so they would not be associated with her disgrace. But *was* it a disgrace to marry a young, handsome viscount? Why? If anything, she'd thought marrying Lord Valance would raise her standing in society. She had not realized eloping and marrying by special license would taint her reputation so much. It wasn't as if they had gone off to Gretna Green!

Fortunately, most of Lord Valance's acquaintances behaved perfectly politely to the newly married couple. The Valances had begun receiving invitations for parties, routs, and balls, though they only accepted a few. So far as Honora knew, no one had cut

Lord Valance because of his elopement. But perhaps, as with so many things, the scandal of eloping attached more to the lady in question than to the gentleman.

She sighed, feeling she would never fully understand the complicated rules of society, try as she might. She would do better to stop moping and get ready for dinner. She got to her feet and rang for Clack.

"My lady," Clack said as she arranged her hair, "you could use some jewelry. Some pretty earrings, perhaps, or some brilliants for your hair."

"I do not need jewels," Honora said absently. She had never been in the habit of wearing much jewelry. All she had now were the pearl eardrops she had worn the night of the masquerade.

But Clack did not drop the subject. "Does the Valance family not have any heirloom jewels? You would look very well with sapphires or emeralds, if you don't mind my saying so."

"I do not know what jewels the Valance family may own," Honora admitted. She supposed she *ought* to know that. In the normal order of things, Lord Valance would have presented her with whatever he wanted her to wear from the family jewelry collection. Showing off the family's wealth was one of the roles of an aristocratic wife.

Perhaps he did not want Honora to wear the Valance jewels. He had been more attentive to her lately, but that did not change the fact that this was an unwanted marriage for both of them. Nothing could change that.

"You will get lines on your face if you keep frowning," Clack scolded. "Try to cultivate a cheerful expression."

Honora snorted. That was precisely what her mother used to tell her! But perhaps Clack was right. She resolved to push her unhappiness away, so she pasted a smile on her face before going down to dinner.

She kept up her cheerful façade throughout the meal, and during their time in the drawing room with Mrs. Valance, but she let it drop when it was time for bed. Not that she turned in right away. Over the last week or two, she and Lord Valance had fallen into the habit of meeting in his room every night to talk after retiring from the drawing room. It was their chance to check in with each other away from listening ears. His Lordship would ask if there was anything Honora needed, and she would ask if there was anything she could do to assist him. There never was, though. He did not ever seem to need her help. She supposed he had not really needed a wife at all.

Lord Valance kept a decanter of cherry brandy—the only kind Honora liked—on his dressing table. He offered to pour a snifter of it for her now. They often had a drink together by the fire while chatting about the day, or their plans for the week, or what they had been reading. It had become one of the most pleasant parts of the evening.

Tonight, though, she shook her head. "I am tired," she told him, though that was not quite the right word. "Glum" or "melancholy" might be more accurate. Would she ever be able to think of her childhood home without heartache?

"Are you unwell?" he asked her.

"No. It has been a long day, that is all."

Lines of concern formed on his face as he studied her. "You will tell me, won't you, if there is anything I can do to make things easier for you?"

Love me, Honora thought. With her family cut off, there was no one in her life who loved her, and no one whom she could love back. No wonder she felt like moping tonight. But she could not ask Lord Valance to love her. She understood perfectly well that theirs was merely a marriage of convenience.

"There is nothing you can do," she told her husband.

THE DAY AFTER that, she came up to dress for dinner and discovered an unfamiliar jewelry box on her dressing table. She opened it to reveal a set of blue-green jewels. Not turquoises, though: these were translucent gems. Some kind of sapphire? Or something else? Clack entered the dressing room and peered over Honora's shoulder.

"Aquamarines!" Approval warmed Clack's voice. "Perfect for you. And the setting is very fashionable. They must be new, or newly-set." The maid smiled. "You must have talked to His Lordship about jewelry last night."

"No." Honora shook her head. "I did not say anything about that conversation to him." The jewels had been his idea entirely.

The case contained a necklace, a bracelet, a brooch, earrings, and a hair ornament. If Lord Valance had purchased this specifically for her, it must have cost a small fortune. A little of the pain in her heart eased up as she admired the parure.

"You should wear them tonight, my lady," Clack suggested. "To see how they look, at least."

And, Honora thought, so Lord Valance could see that she appreciated his gift. She would not normally wear jewelry when dining *en famille*, but tonight she would make an exception. Tonight, the smile on her face at dinner was real. She looked forward to their next social engagement, when she could show her new finery to the world.

Her chance came soon enough. At the beginning of February, Abigail Carrington and Susan Taylor returned to London, having apparently reconciled their quarrel with Mr. Carrington. Miss Carrington sent a note asking if Lord and Lady Valance would like to accompany them to a musical production of *Twelfth Night* playing at The White Rose, one of London's unlicensed theaters.

"Would you like to go?" Lord Valance asked over breakfast. "I have never visited this theater, but the manager has been in the business for years. He probably knows what he's doing."

"But Oliver," his mother interjected. "Wouldn't you prefer to patronize the legitimate drama rather than one of these little mushroom theaters? The quality of the acting cannot be good. No one *I* know ever goes there."

Lord Valance sat still for a moment, as if he were choosing his words carefully. "Miss Taylor is well acquainted with the theatrical world, and if she thinks this is likely to be a good performance, she is probably right. As a matter of fact, her cousin is playing the role of Viola."

For some reason, his mother's expression soured.

"Miss Taylor's cousin is an actress?" Honora put her fork down in surprise. She did not know anyone who had ever been on the stage, apart from amateur theatricals.

"Her own mother was *on the stage*." Mrs. Valance dropped her voice when she uttered the last three words, as if they were too scandalous to be said out loud.

"How interesting! Was her father an actor too?" That seemed rather an odd background for a genteel lady's companion, but the Carrington family did not always play by the usual rules.

Lord Valance laughed. "No, Mr. Taylor is a respectable barrister. The younger son of a baron, in fact. It was quite the scandalous marriage in its time—a barrister from a noble family marrying a girl right off the stage! But they seem to have made it work."

"I cannot understand why they have kept up the connection with her mother's family, though," Mrs. Valance fretted. "It is one thing to marry a girl from a disreputable background. It is another thing entirely to consort with her family!"

Lord Valance ignored his mother and addressed Honora directly. "Would you like to go?"

Honora nodded. "I should like to meet Miss Carrington and Miss Taylor. And I like Shakespeare, although I prefer *Measure for Measure* to *Twelfth Night*."

"No one likes *Measure for Measure*!" her husband protested.

"I do." She had always liked Isabella, and she liked the way the play exposed hypocrisy. "But I like to assume Isabella does not marry the duke at the end."

"Why wouldn't she want to marry the duke? Any young lady would be happy to become a duchess," Mrs. Valance insisted.

Honora cringed, thinking this question treaded entirely too close to the reason for her elopement. Perhaps Lord Valance noticed, because he quickly changed the subject, and they said no more about Shakespeare or the theater.

But now she had new acquaintances and a good play to look forward to.

CHAPTER SIXTEEN

A S IT TURNED out, the performance of *Twelfth Night* at the White Rose *was* quite good. Whoever had written the songs that broke up the spoken drama had a gift for wordplay, though many of the jokes bordered on the bawdy. But then, so did much of Shakespeare, so one could hardly complain of that. And Lady Valance did not seem shocked by any of the humor.

Valance wondered, though, whether his wife even understood all the jokes. How much did she know about sexual congress? When she had propositioned him at the Masquerade, had she even understood what she offered him?

He wondered if he should ask his mother to talk to Honora about marital relations. But that would mean admitting to his mother that he had not yet consummated the marriage, despite having been married a month. No man wanted to admit that! At the same time, he did not relish the prospect of having to explain the marriage bed to his wife.

Because, he thought as he watched her laugh at the play, he really had no excuse to put that conversation off forever. Nor did he particularly enjoy living in a celibate marriage. On the contrary, one of the unanticipated effects of spending more time with his wife was that he had grown increasingly frustrated with the distance between them. He was tired of bidding her good night and going to his cold bed alone. They were married, after all. Perhaps they ought to start acting like it. But he had no idea how to begin bridging the distance.

He had not thought it right to ask to share his wife's bed when they had been strangers. But they had been living together for a month, and they knew each other much better now—better, in some ways, than many couples knew each other when they became betrothed.

Living in the same house as they did, Lord and Lady Valance could have few illusions about each other's faults. He knew she often felt cranky and withdrawn in the morning, preferring to avoid breakfast table chit chat. She probably knew at least half the things that triggered his headaches. She could have told a stranger which brandies he liked, and he could have informed the same stranger that his wife had a fondness for both vermouth and cream sherry, but did not like port.

More importantly, they could read each other's expressions and reactions. For example, he could tell that she'd been relieved that the Duke of Belmont was not present. Lady Valance sat in the front of their box, next to Susan, who pointed out cast members she knew. Because Valance sat right behind her, he clearly saw his wife scanning the audience at the beginning of the play, and he noticed how she relaxed when she realized the duke was not there.

Would she ever feel safe in society, given that she was bound to meet Belmont year after year?

Before Valance could worry too much about that, Abigail Carrington leaned closer to him and tapped him on the shoulder with her fan. He twisted around in his chair to face her.

"Oliver," she whispered, "do you always ogle your wife this much when you are in public? Really, I am quite embarrassed to be seen with the two of you. It is positively disgraceful." Her eyes danced and her lips curled up, so he knew she spoke in jest.

"I am not ogling my wife," he said, trying to reply with dignity. "But I cannot help staring at her. She is the most beautiful woman in England, after all." Possibly in Great Britain. He could not vouch for the whole of the United Kingdom, though. He had never been to Ireland.

Lady Valance looked particularly well tonight. She wore a dress of a silvery-blue shot silk. And she wore the set of aquamarines he had purchased for her. They were not *quite* the same color as her eyes, but they came closer to matching them than any other jewels he'd seen. No wonder so many other theatergoers took a second glance at her when they scanned the audience.

Abigail's eyes widened. She opened her fan and covered her mouth with it, probably to hide her laughter. "You really believe that, don't you? Goodness, Oliver, you must be absolutely smitten."

"What? No! I am merely stating the truth." But a blush rose on his cheeks. He darted his eyes away to avoid seeing one of his oldest friends laughing at him.

He did not think he'd said anything ridiculous. On the contrary, it felt like an obvious law of nature. The sun rose in the east and set in the west, spring always blossomed into summer, and the Viscountess Valance was the most beautiful woman in England. *Facts!*

Abigail chuckled and poked him with her fan again. "I am very happy for you, old friend. But perhaps I will wait to come to the theater with you again until the honeymoon is over. Couples in the first glow of love often nauseate other people with their happiness."

Valance snorted. "You would know all about that, wouldn't you?"

He remembered very clearly how Abigail had behaved when she and Susan fell in love. So much whispering. So many bashful glances, followed by so many blushes. So many accidental brushes of hands together. They probably thought they were being subtle, discreet, and cautious. But even Peregrine had noticed.

"Touché," she said, apparently willing to own up to it. "It is because I remember what it is like to fall head over heels in love that I recognize it now. Well, I wish you a long and happy life together, and I hope you consider us as possible godparents when the first baby is born."

"Oh, be quiet," Valance grumbled.

"And if you want my advice," Abigail added, "you will send your mother back to Surrey where she belongs. No couple needs in-laws on hand all the time."

"Says the woman who lives with her younger brother?" He cocked one eyebrow at her.

She shrugged. "Peregrine knows better than to interfere with us."

That was true, Valance supposed, unless one counted his magical experiments as interference. But Peregrine never *meant* to cause trouble to his housemates. He merely forgot that other people valued dining room tables more than shooting stars. Apart from such occasional accidents, he was good company.

In truth, Valance had preferred living with the Carringtons to living with his mother. He always had. As a child of six or seven, he had even made the mistake—an absolutely dreadful blunder, he now understood—of telling his mother he wished he had been born a Carrington rather than a Valance. She had not taken this revelation well, and she never forgave the Carrington family for alienating her son's affections.

But to Valance, his wish had seemed only natural. At Dreadnaught Hall, there were no other children to play with. Nor was he allowed to slide down the banister, track mud into the nursery, teach his dog to eat off a plate at the dinner table, or play with magic unless his tutor was present. If he made too much noise, he was told he gave his mother a headache.

At Carrington Abbey, if Abigail handed musical instruments to her younger brothers and announced they were going to pretend to be a military band, her mother simply warned her to make sure she didn't wake the baby. If Peregrine tried to fly a kite with magic instead of wind and string, his father only told him "For God's sake, do it on solid ground next time and not on the roof!" lest he break his neck.

And when Valance ran over from his own house and interrupted breakfast at the Abbey by shouting that he had discovered an entirely new way to work sorcery with pen and paper, the whole household celebrated. To be precise, Sir John and Lady Carrington praised him, Roderick smiled, Abigail clapped, Peregrine and Cosmo cheered, and Hannah shrieked with inarticulate toddler joy. He could hardly help preferring their reaction to his mother's disinterested "That's nice, dear."

After that announcement, Lady Carrington had fixed him a plate of crumpets and marmalade, without suggesting that he "really did not need to eat so much, Oliver dear." On the contrary, Lady Carrington always let Valance eat as much as he was hungry for, never once suggesting he might, perhaps, be getting a little stout. Nor did she force Peregrine (always a picky eater) to try foods he did not like. She allowed him to stick to bread and butter if that was all he wanted. As a child, Valance had appreciated that very much, even if he could not articulate why he so much preferred it to his own mother's approach to food.

Was it any wonder Valance had longed to be part of that household? That, too, seemed like some clear and inarguable law of nature. Fire burned, ice chilled, and the Carringtons were the happiest family in the world. *Facts!*

Given that history of life-long friendship, Valance spent the last act of the play considering the possibility that maybe, just maybe, Abigail Carrington was right. She usually *was* right, though he did not always like to admit it. Perhaps he had become infatuated with his wife. Just a little. It was only natural, wasn't it, that if you put a healthy young man in a house with the most beautiful woman in England, he might become a tiny bit smitten? It could happen to anyone! (Well, almost anyone. Probably not Cosmo Carrington.)

Valance kept pondering this new idea as he handed Lady Valance into the carriage after the play. Perhaps that was why he sat beside her, close enough that his arm brushed against hers, instead of sitting in his usual seat across from her.

"Oh, sorry!" She scooted away from him.

His heart sank. "You need not apologize. I am the one who sat here. Do you mind? Would you rather I move to the other seat?"

"Why would I mind? It is your carriage." She spoke lightly, as if the subject were of no importance.

Valance had no idea how to respond. Ownership of the carriage had nothing to do with it. He was asking if his physical proximity was acceptable to her. Did she not understand?

"Miss Carrington calls you 'Oliver,'" she remarked, apropos of nothing. "But her brother calls you "Valance." Why is that?"

Valance shrugged. "I grew up next door to her, and we were in and out of each other's homes all the time. We have never stood on ceremony with each other. Her brother only stopped calling me "Oliver" when we went to school together. At school, boys are always called by their surnames."

"But which do you prefer?" she persisted. "Valance, as Mr. Carrington addresses you? Or Oliver?"

He frowned, though she probably couldn't read his expression in the dark carriage. "It depends on who is addressing me." That answer sounded pedantic, even to him. "Most of my friends call me Valance. But I do not mind the Carringtons calling me by my given name. Sir John was my guardian until I turned twenty-one, you know. So it was—"

"Almost as if you were one of the family," she suggested. Unlike his mother, she did not seem to think that was objectionable.

"Yes, precisely." Sir John had essentially stood in the place of a father to him, and the Carrington children were the closest thing he had to siblings.

"I am part of your family now," Lady Valance pointed out.

Valance smiled. "You most certainly are." He cautiously reached to find her hand. They both had gloves on, so he could not feel her bare skin. But he lifted her hand and held it lightly in his, hoping she would not pull it away from him.

"Do you want me to call you Oliver? Or would you prefer that I address you formally? I know many wives do not call their husbands by their given name."

Valance wished the carriage were bright enough for him to see his wife's face, because he could not quite interpret her tone. Of course, he could have whipped out a scrap of paper and scribbled his light spell. But that would have meant letting go of her hand.

"You may address me however you see fit."

"Indeed? Should I call you my *caro sposo*, like Mrs. Elton did in *Emma*? Or ought I always address you as 'my lord,' as if I lived in awe of your great dignity?"

He did not need to see her face to recognize the playfulness in her voice. "I don't believe you have ever been the least bit in awe of me."

"I suppose not. Though you can be rather frightening when you are angry, you know." Her voice lost its playful edge.

Valance frowned. Frightening? That surprised him. He thought he had good control of his temper.

She clarified: "When we met the duke in the park that first time, you seemed like an entirely different person."

He squeezed her hand, hoping to reassure her. He thought he knew what she meant. "When I meet the duke, I must speak his language. He will not respond to good humor and reason. I must address him in terms he will understand: threats and insults. Like the way Bishop Barkley does not understand when you lecture him for soiling the rug, but he *does* understand if you give him biscuits every time he relieves himself outside." He enjoyed comparing the Duke of Belmont to a spoiled lapdog.

"Bishop Barkley is making excellent progress," she said happily. "I almost think he can be trusted in a room alone now, don't you?"

"No, I do *not*. I think the moment your back is turned, he will chew on the furniture again."

"*But, Oliver—*" she protested, doing a very good imitation of his mother.

He burst into surprised laughter. "You may *not* call me Oliver if you are going to say it like that!"

"Very well, my lord." Her meek voice did not fool him. She was still teasing him. "I believe I will call you Valentine. That's very Shakespearean, isn't it?"

"No," he said, in between gasps of laughter, "you will *not!*"

He wanted to pull her onto his lap and kiss the nonsense out of her. He reached out intending to do that. But he remembered in the nick of time that what made her run away from Belmont Court—what made her willing to seduce a random stranger to escape her fate—had been the duke kissing her. Perhaps she would no more welcome Valance's kisses than she had Belmont's.

She seemed not to notice he had stopped laughing. "But what should I call you?"

"I think, my lady, you ought to call me Valance, as most of my friends do." That is, when they did not shorten it to "Val." He was not sure how he felt about her using that nickname.

"I reserve the right to call you Valentine when we are alone together," she teased.

He swallowed nervously. She had given him the perfect segue to the subject that had occupied his mind all evening. "Lady Valance—"

"*Honora,*" she corrected him. "If I am to dispense with your title, you must dispense with mine."

"Honora." It did not sound quite right, but he was not sure why.

"Yes?"

"I want to kiss you," he blurted out.

CHAPTER SEVENTEEN

THE MOMENT THE words were out of his mouth, Valance panicked. He hadn't meant to say that! Bloody hell! How was he going to fix this?

"I mean, I don't want to kiss you," he babbled, trying to correct course. "That would not be respectful. And I do respect you. Very respectfully." He longed to sink beneath the carriage and be crushed by the horses' hooves. That might prevent him from saying anything more ridiculous.

"You can only kiss women you disrespect?" Doubt and confusion colored Honora's voice.

"No, that's not what I meant!" She must think him a fool. *I am the biggest idiot in England,* he thought—but he didn't just think it. He said it out loud. He groaned and buried his face in his hands. When would this god-awful carriage ride end?

"I do not think you are an idiot," she said politely, "but I *am* having trouble understanding you. What are you trying to say?"

"Right now, I am trying *not* to say anything, since I apparently do not know how to use words."

"But do you want to kiss me, or not?" The carriage came to a slow, gentle stop just as she finished speaking.

"Oh, good, we're home." He tried to speak cheerfully. "It is very late, so I think we ought to go straight to bed, don't you?" Perhaps a good night's sleep would enable him to speak sensibly again.

"But are you going to kiss me, or not?"

"No! I would never do that!" *Never?* What in God's green earth was he even saying? How could he have made such an utter mess of this conversation? It had been going so well, too. Up until he mentioned kissing.

"Well," she said, "I wish you *would.*"

Valance was rendered speechless for a long, awkward moment. He finally gathered his wits sufficiently to ask, "Er, you do?"

Before she could answer, the groom opened the door of the carriage and lowered the steps.

"Yes, I do," Honora replied. Then she stepped down from the carriage.

Valance remained in the carriage, staring after his wife. His brain seemed to be working more slowly than usual tonight. Had she actually said what he thought she said, or was that some delusion born of his own desire?

"My lord?" the groom asked him. "Is something wrong?"

"No." Valance scrambled out of the carriage and trotted after his wife. He caught up with her inside the house, just as she started to ascend the stairs. "My lady—"

She looked back over her shoulder and raised her eyebrows.

"Honora," he corrected, though the name still did not sound quite right.

"Yes?"

She stood on the first step, which brought her head closer to his level, though she was so much shorter than him that even the stair did not quite close the height gap between them. Valance cautiously reached out to stroke her cheek. Then he stepped forward and kissed the most beautiful woman in England on the lips.

He kept the touch of his mouth against hers light and brief, not being at all certain how she would react.

She reacted by frowning, and his heart sank again. He was right to worry, wasn't he? He drew in a deep breath, preparing to apologize for his forwardness, when she said, "I really think you can do better than *that*, Valance."

"I beg your pardon?"

She drew a wavering smile. "That really isn't all there is to kissing, is it?"

Valance gaped like a fish desperate for water. Then he shut his mouth and loosened his cravat, finding it rather hard to breathe. "I most certainly *can* do better than that, and if you are going to throw down the gauntlet, I *will*."

Her smile widened at this, so he wrapped his arm around her waist and drew her closer to him. Then he commenced kissing in earnest. He could tell she did not know how to respond, but what she lacked in experience, she made up for in enthusiasm. When he paused to verbally check in with her, she put an arm around his neck and pulled him back to her.

After that, things got so intense that he reached out and grabbed the banister with one hand, because he was half afraid they were going to topple over. Honora seemed to be learning very quickly, and she showed no sign of tiring of their occupation. On the contrary, she pressed her body against his in a way that gave at least one part of his anatomy very firm ideas about what ought to happen next.

He had no idea how much time had passed before he heard a gentle, unobtrusive cough. He reluctantly drew away from his wife and looked for the source of the sound. Preston stood at the top of the stairs, wearing his most wooden expression.

"My lord," Preston said, "I merely wondered if you required my services undressing tonight?"

Valance had been taught that a gentleman never yelled at his servants, but for once he felt tempted to break that rule. A well-trained valet should know better than to disturb an employer who was occupied the way Valance had been occupied!

"No, Preston, your services are not needed. I will undress myself tonight." Unless Honora undressed him—but no, he should not ask that of her. He clearly remembered how mortified she had been at the sight of him in his smallclothes. There was no need to rush things, no matter how randy he might feel at the moment.

"Very good, sir." Preston discreetly retreated, leaving Valance alone with his wife again.

But she now stood a foot away from him, looking down at the floor. Valance sighed. Clearly, the moment had been ruined. And who knew when a moment like that might come again?

"I am sorry about that."

"You have nothing to apologize for," Honora said quickly.

He wished she would at least look him in the eyes. The way she kept pleating her dress suggested she felt anxious. Maybe this had been a huge mistake.

"I suppose we had better go to bed now." He tried to conceal his disappointment, but regret seeped into his voice.

She cleared her throat, as if about to speak, but said nothing.

"Yes?" he prompted.

"Are you going to go to bed by yourself," she asked, still staring down at the floor, "or with me?"

"Um." Valance had no idea how to answer her. Because he could not clearly see her face, he could not tell which answer she wanted to hear. "Whichever makes you happier?"

She finally lifted her chin. "I would like to go to bed with you."

"Oh." His heart thumped. So did something that wasn't his heart.

"If you don't mind," she added politely.

Valance struggled not to laugh at the idea that he would mind. He succeeded in turning his chuckle into a cough. At least, he thought he succeeded, until Honora smiled bashfully back, blushing very prettily.

"How could I mind an invitation from so beautiful a woman? I would like to go to bed with you." Possibly the understatement of the year, given that he'd been thinking about it half the evening. "But are you certain?"

"Oh, yes," she said, her face alight with interest. "I have so many questions!"

"Questions?" This time, it was panic rather than lust that made Valance's heart skip a beat. He had entirely forgotten his earlier concerns about her understanding of marital relations. What if she didn't know what she was agreeing to?

"Yes." She nodded her head briskly, not seeming to realize the impact of her words. "No one tells girls anything, you know."

Damnation! She probably had no idea what to expect. What was he supposed to say? Valance ran a hand through his hair, ruining what had been left of Preston's coiffure.

Why didn't they make books for this sort of thing? This would be so much easier if he could simply hand her a book! Instead, the marriage bed was traditionally explained by mother to daughter, sometimes not until right before the wedding. If Lady Carrington had been in London, Valance would have asked her for help. But she rarely came to town.

That left only one option.

Valance rubbed his temples. He did not have a headache yet, but he expected one to crop up any minute now. "I suppose you had better talk to my mother about it tomorrow. She will be able to answer any of your questions, I am sure. And we can wait—"

Honora frowned and shook her head. "I had rather talk to *you*. I trust you more than your mother."

Valance drew a deep breath. He really did not want to have to explain the facts of life to his wife. He felt certain this would be the most painfully awkward conversation in the history of language. Hadn't he already played the fool enough for one night?

But he found it touching that she trusted him so much. And perhaps it was better not to involve anyone else in so intimate a matter.

"Very well," he reluctantly agreed. "Why don't we sit down by the fire, have a drink, and talk this over properly?"

She nodded. "Yes, please. You *will* explain things to me,

won't you?" She fixed him with keen, critical eyes.

Valance would have liked to dodge that sharp gaze, but he kept his eyes steadily locked with hers. "Yes, I will," he promised. "I will tell you whatever you want to know. But I am going to need brandy for this conversation." Probably a good deal of it.

CHAPTER EIGHTEEN

BEFORE MARRYING VALANCE, Honora had not been in the habit of drinking hard liquor, or even fortified wines. She had never even tried port till she came to Carrington House. But neither Valance nor Mr. Carrington thought it at all strange that she wanted to try the drinks they enjoyed. She discovered she did not care for whisky or port, but she did like cherry brandy. Valance poured a snifter of it now and handed it to her without her asking.

Her husband lounged in his chair, resting his feet on a low ottoman while he rubbed his temples. Honora sat more primly, her feet flat on the floor. She could not relax. A few sips of the brandy spread a pleasant warmth throughout her body, but it did little to quiet her buzzing nerves.

"Does your head hurt terribly?" If she was the one who'd given him that headache, she felt sorry for that, but she did not know what she could have done differently.

He shook his head. "It's not so bad. I have some paregoric lozenges on hand if I need them." He took a sip of his brandy. "So. What, precisely, do you want to know?" He looked a little more relaxed now. Maybe the brandy worked more effectively for him.

Everything, Honora thought. She wanted to know everything. The buzzing in her veins seemed to be equal parts excitement and nerves. Her mouth had gone dry, so she took another sip of brandy before answering him.

"I know so very little," she began. "I know men and women can lie together, and sometimes it gets the woman with child. I know people enjoy doing it. Especially men." She stared down into her brandy as she tried to sort the few scraps of information she had collected over the years. "People usually take their clothes off to do it. And I think it has something to do with, ah, genitals. That is about all I know."

He nodded. "That is all right as far as it goes, but it does not nearly go far enough."

Honora looked at him expectantly, waiting for him to elaborate.

"Well, I don't really know where to start." He swirled the brandy around in his glass, staring at it much the way Honora kept staring at *her* drink. "I suppose we should start with the body parts."

Valance gave her a brief and somewhat confusing explanation about cocks and cunnies (a word she had never heard before), rutting and spending. His frequent pauses to clear his throat and the way he kept averting his eyes suggested that he found this topic difficult to discuss. Even so, he answered all of her questions, from "Will that hurt me?" ("Maybe the first time") to "Is this something *you* enjoy doing?" (Answered with a sound suspiciously like a smothered laugh, followed by a flat "Yes.")

He drained the last of the brandy in his glass and looked thoughtfully at the decanter. But he seemed to decide against drinking more. Instead, he set his glass down. "Does that explanation satisfy you? Or do you want step-by-step instructions?" The corners of his mouth curled up with amusement.

"Yes, the latter." Honora nodded her head briskly.

"I was joking!" His face fell into the familiar grumpy bulldog lines.

"I know," Honora admitted. "But it was a good idea. Why don't you tell me exactly what will happen when we go to bed?"

He leaned his head on his hand and studied her thoughtfully.

"You are not going to give me any peace until I explain everything in minute detail, are you?"

"No, I am not." Honora felt relieved he understood that much about her.

"Would you rather I tell you? Or"—he hesitated for only a moment—"Had you rather I show you?"

Honora swallowed nervously. She did very much want to find out what it was like to go to bed with a man. And she specifically wanted to know how her husband would treat her in bed. But she had assumed, based on Valance's obvious dislike of the conversation, that they would once again put that off for another night. She hadn't expected him to offer a choice.

"Whichever is easier for you," she said politely.

He chuckled ruefully. "It would be easiest for me to go to bed and pretend we never had this conversation. But I don't think you want that, do you?"

Honora shook her head. "If you need an heir, we are going to have to do this eventually." He could not go his whole life without consummating their marriage—could he? Did he really find it so distasteful a prospect? He said he enjoyed bedding women, but that did not mean he wanted to bed *her*. Her stomach sank at that thought.

"I suppose if you don't find me desirable, then we could . . ." Could what? There was no way to get out of the marriage now. Was there? No, there was! She brightened. "I could get caught committing adultery, so you could sue for divorce. Would that be best?" It seemed a lot of trouble to go through, but if it was the only way of freeing Valance from an unwanted duty, so be it.

Valance's eyes widened. "What are you even talking about?" He sounded absolutely horrified. "Get caught committing adultery? Have you taken leave of your senses? The whole point of this marriage was to preserve your reputation!"

"Oh, right. But I couldn't think of another way to release you from this marriage." She twirled a lock of hair around her finger as she thought. "What if I faked my own death?"

How would one go about that? Could she find a corpse that resembled her? Or would it be possible to enchant a corpse so it looked like her? Probably Valance could do that with one of those notes he imbued with his magic. But there was still a problem. . .

"Do you know where I can obtain a dead body?" Honora asked.

She had thought Valance's eyes were opened as wide as possible, but she was wrong, because they widened even further.

"My God, you are even more outrageous than Peregrine." He sounded almost awed. "I had not thought such a thing was possible, but in all the years I have known him, he has never once asked me to help him find a dead body."

"Since he is your best friend, I will take that as a compliment." Honora lifted her chin boldly, feeling she had scored a hit.

He grinned back at her. "Point to you. But you are talking utter nonsense, you know. Why would I want to get out of this marriage? I like you."

"Oh." Honora once again found it necessary to stare into the depths of the empty brandy snifter in her hand. "I thought perhaps you regretted marrying me."

"Regret marrying the most beautiful woman in England? I think not!" he scoffed.

She jerked her head up, startled. She expected to see him grinning at his own joke. But though a faint smile lingered about his lips, he did not look amused. He looked as if he was admiring her Honora's heart skipped a beat, and the weight in her stomach lightened. Perhaps she had misunderstood the situation.

"Well, my lady, what would you have us do? Do you wish to sit here talking all night? Or had you rather go get ready for bed, and wait for me to come to your room?"

Honora narrowed her eyes suspiciously. "Will you actually visit me tonight?" She could not help remembering their wedding night, when she had stayed up for hours waiting for him. In hindsight, she probably ought to have asked him about his intentions rather than making assumptions.

"If you wish me to, yes," he promised. "But there is no need to rush anything—"

"It could hardly be rushing, given that we have been married over a month." Perhaps she spoke a little tartly, though she had not meant it as a criticism.

Lord Valance flinched. "Do you feel I have neglected you?"

Honora studied her empty glass again as she searched for the right words. It was rather a difficult question. "Maybe at first. A little."

She thought about the morning after the wedding, when her husband left her alone at Carrington House without a word of explanation, though she had been scared and confused at the rapid changes in her life. At the time, she had not even realized how frightened she was. She had left her old life behind and embraced a new one in the span of less than twenty-four hours. Looking back, it seemed like a feverish dream.

"But you have not neglected me lately," she acknowledged.

Over the last few weeks, Lord Valance had shown her a good deal of attention. Not only had he carved time out to speak with her alone, he had escorted her about town. She had no idea what had caused this change, but she had no complaints. On the contrary, she had discovered she enjoyed his company.

"I like you too, you know," she shyly added.

He stood up so he could bow to her, though he did not drop the grin on his face. "I am glad to hear that, my lady. But if you will excuse me, I ought to ready myself for bed. I will see you in, say, half an hour?"

"Yes," she agreed, and headed to her room.

CHAPTER NINETEEN

IN TRUTH, HONORA found it difficult to focus on her bedtime routine. It was hard to sit still long enough to brush out her hair. She wanted to pace the room. She wanted to walk back into Valance's room and ask him more questions, because she still did not feel he had adequately prepared her. And, because it was late and it had been a rather eventful day, she occasionally found herself thinking longingly about her pillow.

She wasted so much time pacing back and forth that when Valance did knock at the door between their rooms, she had not finished with her hair. But she put the brush down and opened the door.

He wore his dressing gown, which was a little disappointing. But that might be for the best, given that Honora had been reduced to incoherent babbling the only time she'd seen him (mostly) unclothed.

She had no idea what one ought to say to one's husband in this situation. If there existed a script for it, no one had taught Honora her lines. So, she simply waited for him to speak.

"There's something we should talk about first," Valance said without preamble. "I did not think to ask you if you wished to avoid conception." He opened his palm to reveal a heavy signet ring.

From the outside, the ring looked perfectly normal. But when Honora picked it up, her fingertips hummed with magic. She turned it over in her hand, looking for the charm that might cause that buzz of power. She did not find any words or sigils creating the spell, but she did find a hinge.

"Does this open up?"

"Yes. There's a trick to it." He took the ring and popped open the lid, revealing a small hollow space beneath the bezel. "It's a renaissance poison ring. I can put spell papers inside, as long as my writing is small enough."

Honora peered at the tiny scrap of paper inside the ring. Her ability to see magic told her that this was medical magic, though it was not a spell she had seen before. "Are you saying that is a contraception charm?"

"Yes. Had a devil of a time writing that small." He grimaced as he snapped the compartment shut. "In any case, the spell works. If I wear the ring, the spell will keep you from getting with child. Do you want me to do that?"

She studied his face, but could not tell from his expression what he preferred. "I thought you needed an heir?"

He shrugged. "Someday, yes. That does not mean we need to conceive one tonight."

"I see no reason to avoid it," Honora told him.

After all, she could not help being curious about pregnancy and childbirth, too. Some of her mother's friends seemed to hate pregnancy, griping about the backaches, swollen ankles, and other symptoms. But others were delighted when they found themselves with child. She wondered which sort she would be.

"Very well." He dropped the ring into the pocket of his dressing gown.

"What do we do now?" Honora asked straightforwardly. Did they have to get undressed first? Should she have put on a nightgown instead of keeping on her shift? Should she go lie down on the bed? Should she have been in bed already when her husband came to her room? She frowned just thinking of all the possibilities.

"You look like you are about to take some rigorous examination in school." Valance brushed a strand of her hair away from her face. "I promise, I will not grade your performance. Nor will there be a test afterward."

"I know that." Heat rushed into her face. She had not realized how clearly her thoughts were written on her face.

"You have a charming blush," Valance told her. "But I want you to feel comfortable with me." He tipped her chin up with one finger and brushed his mouth against hers.

Honora returned his kiss. Then she was in his arms, one arm around his neck, while they exchanged slow, lingering kisses.

Valance pulled away for a moment to finally answer her question: "This is what we do first. I intend to kiss you until you beg for more than kisses."

Honora would have asked him what exactly he meant by "more than kisses," but her mouth was already otherwise occupied, because he had resumed kissing her. Valance moved forward, slowly walking her backwards towards the bed. When her legs hit the mattress, he let go of her so he could disrobe.

His dressing gown fell to the floor. He wore nothing underneath but his drawers, but Honora did not have much of a chance to either study or admire his body, because he sat down and pulled her onto his lap.

"Is this too much?" he murmured in her ear. "I do not want to rush you or frighten you. But I do want you, very much. I have wanted you since the moment our eyes met across that damn ballroom on Twelfth Night."

"You did?" Honora had drunk only a little brandy, but she felt strangely tipsy. Was that the effect of her proximity to her husband? His body was warm against hers. Was that why she felt so flushed? She reached out to stroke his chest, as she had longed to do the other night. Unreal though this moment might be, Valance at least felt reassuringly solid.

"Why do you think I was willing to sneak off with you down an empty corridor? I don't normally do that sort of thing." He nuzzled her neck right beneath her ear, sending shivers all the way down to her toes. They were pleasant shivers, though. "Tell me, darling, why did you pick *me*?"

Honora found it difficult to talk, because Valance was now stroking one of her nipples through the thin cloth of her shift. She had not expected it to harden under contact the way it did. Why did it do that? And why did her husband ask her questions and then do things that made it so very difficult to answer him? That seemed unfair.

"Um, I don't really know why it was you. I couldn't take my eyes off of you for some reason. Maybe it was your unusual magic?" That was the only explanation she'd ever come up with.

"Oh, I'll show you magic, all right." His voice rasped right in her ear, and Honora broke out into goosebumps. He moved his hand to her other breast. That started a new series of physical reactions, some of which she did not recognize.

"Valance," she asked, "why is there a pulsing sensation between my legs?"

He paused his kissing to answer her. "Probably because you desire me." He sounded pleased. "Would you like me to do more than kiss you now?"

"Yes. But what do we do next?" she asked practically.

"I would like to pleasure you." Honora drew a breath, intending to ask him to clarify ("pleasure" not being a very specific word), but he continued without her asking. "Tell me, do you ever touch yourself between the legs?"

"Not now, but sometimes when I was child. It felt good." She had quit doing it when her mother told her "self-pollution" could cause illness or insanity.

"Exactly," he agreed. "I would like to touch you there, with either my hand or my mouth. May I do that?"

Did that mean being touched there did not cause insanity? Had her mother misled her? Or was it only injurious if one did it to oneself? It must be all right, she reasoned. Valance would not do something that might harm her.

"Yes," she told him.

He responded by pulling off her shift and laying her down on the bed. Her heart hammered in her chest. Some of that was undoubtedly due to nerves, but most of it was due to Valance's attentions.

"My God, but you're beautiful." It was not the first time Valance had called Honora "beautiful," but the word took on a different significance tonight. He did not mean merely that her appearance fit Society's standard of feminine beauty. He meant he desired her.

He stroked her cheek, then let his hand wander further down her body. "If I do anything that makes you uncomfortable, you must tell me at once."

"I will," she promised. Though "comfortable" did not really seem like a word that fit any of her current sensations. She felt nervous, thrilled, and flushed. Parts of her body that normally seemed to slumber were awake and making demands she had no idea how to satisfy. None of that felt bad, but it did not feel comfortable, either.

Valance moved further down the bed, dropping kisses on her body along the way. Each kiss seemed to wake her nerves up more, and she found herself breathing heavily even before he reached the soft folds between her legs. He nudged her legs apart and put his mouth on her and—

"Oh my God," she gasped. It was not blasphemy, but reverence. She had no idea her body had been made for sensations like that.

Valance reached up to take hold of her hand. She clung to it tightly as he continued to tease, lick, and suck. This was what her body had been demanding. How did he know what she needed when she had not known?

In some dim corner of her mind, Honora thought it was deeply unfair that people had concealed the possibility of such pleasure from her. If her mother had known this was what the marriage bed was like, why had she not told her daughters that? She had, on the contrary, implied that being bedded by one's husband was an important, albeit sometimes unpleasant, duty.

This did not feel at all like a duty to Honora, and it was not in the least unpleasant.

The heat and tension between her legs kept building. It was agony and ecstasy all at once. She simultaneously wanted it to stop—because it felt like sweet torture—and to last forever. But it did not last forever. Instead, shivers of sharp sensation swept over her body.

"Oh, I *like* that," she gasped. Then muscles deep within her pulsed, and she was taken beyond words. She could only moan as waves of powerful sensation rolled over her.

When the paroxysm of pleasure ended, Valance lifted his head, wiped his mouth, and smiled at her. "How was that, darling?"

"So good." Her body, thoroughly spent, seemed to sink into the mattress. She was not sure she was capable of moving. "But too short." The climax had ended almost as soon as she understood what was happening.

Valance chuckled. "I would be happy to please you again later, if you are not satisfied. But if you don't mind, I would like to take my turn first."

"Yes, of course." At this point, Honora would probably have agreed to anything he asked. "What do we do next?"

He crawled up the bed to rest beside her. "We have options. If you would like to be in control, I can lie down and put you on top of me. Then you would be able to move however you wanted—as fast, as slow, as deep, as hard. Would you prefer that?"

"No!" Honora felt certain of that. "I would have no idea what I was doing. I want you to show me what to do."

He chuckled. "Yes, I know." He kissed her on the forehead. "I could simply take you like this, lying beside you. That might be most comfortable for you." He hesitated for a moment and added: "I am so much larger than you. You may think I am too heavy to lie on top of you."

Honora ran a hand through his hair, fascinated by the texture. He kept it shorter than was fashionable, perhaps because it had a tendency to curl. But she had always liked his curls. Just now, she found them very distracting.

"Well?" he prompted.

She forced herself to focus. "I want you to do whatever you like best. I know so little about this. But I am sure you are not too heavy. I like how you are both soft and strong at the same time." She ran a hand along his upper arm, feeling the muscle underneath the surface. He was hers to touch, she thought wonderingly. Her husband.

"All right." He reached down to nudge her legs open a little wider. Then he settled between her legs, propping himself up on his elbows as he rested above her. This gave her a good view of his face, which she liked. She stroked his cheek, exploring the texture of his stubble.

Now she felt him gently nudging his way into her—cunny? Was that the word? For some reason, her mother had never taught her words for those parts of her body. Whatever it was called, she felt as if it were being stretched beyond capacity. There was a faint sting. Then there was just Valance, slowly sinking deeper into her body.

She buried her fingers in his hair again. "Is there something *I* should be doing?"

He lowered his head to kiss her before answering. "You can do whatever you want, darling. When I start moving, you can move with me, if you wish. *I* would like that. But you need not do anything you do not like."

She wanted to ask what he meant by "moving," but she did not have the opportunity, because he kissed her again, more deeply this time. Now Valance surrounded her. His tongue explored her mouth, his scent filled her lungs, his body rested above hers, and his firm shaft slowly slid in and out of her.

So that was what he meant by "moving." She tried to move with him. It would have been hard not to, because he seemed to be everywhere. The very air she breathed was flavored with his presence. This total immersion might have terrified her if she'd known and liked her husband any less. All at once, she felt very glad they had been interrupted before they could complete that Twelfth Night tryst, just as she felt grateful that Valance, of all people, had been the one to run away with her.

Meanwhile, Valance kissed her eyes, her cheek, her ear, her neck. "Nora," he murmured. "Sweet Nora."

She shivered and clung to him more tightly. No one ever called her "Nora." Her parents had always disliked that nickname. Perhaps she would not have liked it if anyone else had called her "Nora." But when Valance said it? Yes, she liked that very much.

He paused in his loving. "Talk to me, darling. How does this feel?"

"Good. It feels good." She did not refer to only the sensations between her legs, pleasant though those were. She liked all of this: the warmth, the closeness, the kisses. Even his scent. She sighed happily and kissed the place where his neck met his chest.

"I am glad to hear that," he murmured. "And perhaps you will like this, too." He turned onto his side, pulling her with him. Then he slid one hand in between their bodies so he could stroke the sensitive spot between her folds.

Honora gasped. "Oh, that's clever!" She had not realized he could please her at the same time as he pleased himself.

Valance chuckled, a deep belly laugh she could feel as well as hear. "I must confess I have never been called clever in bed."

"I meant it as a compliment!"

"I know that," he assured her. "But you flatter me." He returned to kissing her, but he kept up the motion of his hand, ratcheting up the tension higher and higher.

Please, Honora thought silently, *please I need. . .* Before she could recall the right words to describe what she needed, there it was again: the shivers of pleasure, the pulsing muscles, the relief afterwards as the tension left her body.

When her climax ended, Valance rolled them back into their

original position. He began thrusting in earnest, with deep, hard strokes. His rhythm changed. Then he buried his face in her hair and grunted as he finished.

They lay together limply, bodies still entangled. Honora's pounding heart began to slow, just as her sweaty body began to cool.

Valance broke the silence. "That went much better than I expected."

Honora wondered what, exactly, he had expected. But for once, she was not interested in asking questions. She felt happy, satisfied, and thoroughly exhausted.

Valance moved away, coming to rest beside her. He turned on his side so he could face Honora. "Are you all right? Any discomfort?" He stroked her cheek with a feather-light touch.

"No discomfort," she assured him. "*I* thought it was perfect. But I want to sleep now."

He smiled. "Sleep sounds like a good idea. Do you want me to go back to my room?"

"No," Honora replied. "I want you by my side." So, they slept side by side together, like a proper married couple. She drifted to sleep with a smile still on her face.

CHAPTER TWENTY

V ALANCE HAD SPOKEN nothing but the truth when he told
Honora he liked her. Over the end of January and the
beginning of February, he had done his best to get to know her,
and he had discovered her to be excellent company. Their tastes
overlapped enough that it was not difficult to agree on which
entertainments to attend. Neither of them liked squeezes at
which the entire *ton* tried to cram itself into a couple of too-small
reception rooms. Both of them liked the theater. Honora liked
the opera more than Valance did, but he did not mind accompa-
nying her.

And, to his very great relief, she seemed to like casual dinners
or card games at Carrington House with his friends. He had no
idea how he would have coped with a wife who disliked the
Carringtons, and he was glad he did not have to find out.

On nights when they did not go out (which happened more
often than not), Honora would join him in his room for a glass of
brandy. They sat by the fire and talked, sometimes for a few
minutes, sometimes for hours, about all sorts of things: their
childhoods, books, the latest gossip, or Valance's challenges
developing his system of runes.

Sir Isaac Grantly had been a moderately powerful sorcerer,
and although Honora could not work magic, her father had
taught her far more about the history and theory of magic than
most non-magicians ever learned (or wanted to learn). Conse-

quently, Valance could talk to her about his magical work the way he might have talked to one of the magicians from his club.

Except he had never in his life wanted to do with his friends the things he liked doing with Honora in bed. And she, thank God, seemed to enjoy them too. He would not have delayed consummating the marriage so long if he'd known how good things could be between them. In marrying Honora, he had, by some miracle, found a good friend who was also an enthusiastic bedmate. He had never expected that combination.

On some level, though, Valance feared his happiness might melt away with the changing of the seasons. In his admittedly limited experience, infatuations ended in either heartbreak or disgust. If two people weren't torn apart by circumstances, they eventually wearied of each other. He knew perfectly well that there were people who remained contented partners until parted by death, but he might as well ask for the moon. All he could reasonably hope for was to enjoy things as long as they lasted. He resolved to gather his rosebuds while he could.

So, when the twelfth of February proved to be an unusually temperate day, he took Honora for another drive in the park. Hyde Park had gotten more crowded. Those noblemen who took their parliamentary duties seriously were in town now, and some of them had brought their families. It took even longer than usual to exchange greetings with everyone.

When they returned to the house on Curzon Street, their butler announced, "There is a young person waiting for my lady in the morning room."

"A young person?" Valance repeated, mystified. Weller's use of the word "person" rather than "gentleman" signified someone of dubious social standing. But Weller should not have allowed any unsavory callers into the house. Part of a butler's job was turning away undesirable visitors.

"The person in question insisted that her ladyship would wish to see him. He identified himself as Mr. *Rossini*." Weller wrinkled his nose over the very un-English surname.

Valance's frown deepened. He knew no one by the name of Rossini.

But Honora gasped. "Rossini? What was the first name?"

"I believe it was Theodore, or possibly Theophilus? I am afraid I do not recall, ma'am. He carried no calling cards." If possible, Weller's distaste grew stronger, as if a stranger without calling cards must belong to the lowest dregs of society.

"Dora!" Honora shook her head, but a faint smile tugged at the corners of her mouth. She fairly ran on her way to the morning room.

"I suppose you did well to let Mr. Rossini in," Valance said doubtfully. "Her ladyship appears to know him."

"So it seems." Weller took Valance's coat and hat, and Valance followed his wife, curious about this Mr. Rossini.

When he walked into the morning room, he found Honora embracing a slender young man who stood a few inches taller than she did. The stranger had black, curly hair that spilled over his forehead into his eyes. He greeted Valance with a cheeky dimpled grin.

"Er, how do you do?" Valance glanced from his wife to the stranger whom she apparently knew quite well.

"Oh, very well, thank you," the stranger piped.

"Valance, this is my sister Dora." Honora wrinkled her nose in disgust. "She does not always dress this way."

Dora glanced down at her clothing and shrugged. "These clothes are far more practical for travel than a walking dress, and people are less likely to notice a boy traveling alone." She pulled a face. "The only problem is one of the passengers on the stage thought I was a truant school boy. I had to make up a cover story on the fly."

"Oh." Valance did not know what to say about this staggering revelation. His first impulse was to question the relationship, given that the two siblings looked nothing alike.

But as he examined Dora more carefully, he saw that Dora's eyes were a shade between blue and green—not quite the same color as Honora's eyes, but close. There was a similarity about the shape of their cheek bones, too, though Dora had a strong, cleft chin and a straight nose. If Valance imagined her dressed as a young lady (admittedly a difficult task), he supposed Dora must be nearly as pretty as Honora, but in a different style of beauty.

"But what are you doing here, Dora?" Honora asked.

Valance thought that was a very good question. He looked at Dora expectantly.

"Oh, I ran away from home. That's all." Dora grinned, as if this were something to be proud of. "It's been quite an adventure, Honora. I see now why you ran away too. I wish I had thought to do this years ago!"

Honora did not look pleased. "I ran away because I had to." She shook her head reproachfully. "And I am of age, so there was nothing wrong with my leaving home if I wished. But you are a minor. Mother will probably send someone after you, to take you home."

Dora dropped her smile. "No, she will not. I am not going back to Grantly Manor, and you can't make me."

The stubborn tilt of Dora's chin reminded Valance forcibly of her sister. He suspected they were in for a long discussion.

"I wonder if anyone would care for some refreshments?" He glanced at Honora and raised his eyebrows.

Honora nodded. "Oh, yes, some sherry would be most welcome."

"I would like brandy," Dora suggested.

"No!" Valance and Honora spoke as one.

"You are too young for brandy," Honora explained. "You may have ratafia or sherry."

Dora's grimace suggested she did not care for these traditionally feminine beverages. But Valance agreed with his wife. If this was how Dora behaved when sober, he had no desire to see her drunk.

He rang for Weller and ordered the drinks. Then he sat down and rubbed his forehead. He did not have a headache yet, but he thought it very likely he would have one soon.

"So, um . . ." Valance had no idea what the etiquette for such a situation was. Ought he address the young person as Mr. Rossini, since that was the name Dora had given Weller? Or would it be better to call Dora "Miss Grantly," since she was Honora's sister? Was "Rossini" even Dora's real surname, or was it an alias? Her first name was the only thing he knew for certain. "Dora, if I may?"

"Of course, you may call me Dora," Dora said happily. "You are my brother-in-law now. I mean, except for the fact that I am illegitimate. By law I am no relation to Honora at all."

"Oh, I see."

At that moment, Weller entered with a tray of drinks and a solemn expression. Was it too much to hope that Weller hadn't overhead Dora's most recent words? Given the slight widening of Weller's eyes, it probably was. Soon everyone in the servant's hall would be talking about Lady Valance's illegitimate sister who ran around the country in trousers.

Valance decided the most courteous thing to do would be to pretend this was all perfectly normal, as if he met his wife's runaway natural siblings every day. He gestured to Dora to take a seat. Then he took a large gulp of brandy to fortify himself for the rest of the conversation.

"So, what brings you to London, Dora?" He was proud of how casual his voice sounded, despite how much the unexpected visitor had startled him.

"The same thing that brought Honora here. I had to escape dire peril." For someone in dire peril, Dora sounded surprisingly cheerful. To look at her, one would think she was on holiday.

"What dire peril?" The line between Honora's eyes showed she took the claim more seriously than Valance did.

"Your mother was going to send me into service," Dora explained. "She was about to ship me off to work as the stillroom maid at Hetherage Hall."

"A servant?" Honora sounded horrified. "You? She would

have done better to send you to finishing school!"

Valance could not picture Dora at finishing school. Did a school capable of "finishing" Dora even exist? Doubtful!

But something else troubled Valance more. "Hetherage Hall belongs to the Duke of Belmont," he announced. It was one of the duke's smaller properties, located in the Lake district.

"Oh no," Honora gasped. "That cannot be a coincidence."

"I agree." He finished off the last of his brandy and set the glass down. He had better stay sober for this conversation. "But why would the Duke of Belmont want Dora as his maid?"

"To punish me for running away from him." Honora spoke in a small voice, averting her eyes. "I made the mistake of telling him that Dora was my best friend in all the world."

"What a wretched man." Really, it was most unfortunate that Valance had not shot Belmont when the duke called at Russell Square.

"The duke isn't the only one to blame. Lady Grantly agreed to the plan, after all." Dora scrunched up her face. "In any case, going to Hetherage Hall was out of the question. If the duke is so dangerous that Honora ran away rather than marry him, I thought I ought not to work at his property."

"Very likely right." Valance did not like to guess at the duke's motives, but they could not be good. Honora was probably right that he meant to punish her by hurting her sister.

"But why are you dressed that way?" Honora asked.

Dora's grin returned. "To prevent myself from being recognized, of course! I got the idea from you."

"From me?" Honora sounded startled.

Dora nodded. "In your letter to me, you said you were glamoured to look like a man to get away from Belmont Court. I thought that was a good idea, so I wanted to do the same. But I didn't know any disguise spells, so I borrowed this outfit from Tom Roble. He helped me cut my hair, too."

When put like that, it did seem logical. Perhaps Dora was more sensible than Valance's first impression. She had, after all, been successful in her escape attempt.

"But it must not have been a good disguise, because you recognized me right away, didn't you, Honora?"

Honora rolled her eyes. "Of course, I recognized you! I know you too well. I could identify you by your aura, no matter what disguise you wore."

"Oh, right. But most magicians cannot read auras, so maybe it is a good disguise after all!" Dora's face brightened again.

"I hope you brought other clothes with you, though." Honora shook her head as she studied Dora's garments. "Those do seem to fit you nicely, but I don't see how I can introduce you to my mother-in-law dressed like that."

All the blood drained from Valance's face. He had completely forgotten about his mother. She must be dressing now, but she would, of course, dine with them shortly. And she would have to be introduced to Dora.

His stomach churned as he imagined how that meeting might go. Valance's mother had many prejudices and Dora would offend several of them at once. Mother did not like foreigners, she did not think gentlemen's by-blows should be allowed to circulate in polite society, and she thought a woman dressing like a man was an abomination unto the Lord.

"I wonder," Valance suggested as tactfully as he could, "If Dora might feel more comfortable staying at a hotel?"

"Oh, that might be fun," Dora said.

But Honora turned her elegant frown towards Valance. "Why can't my sister stay here? Is she not welcome at our house?" Her grip on her wine glass tightened.

Damnation. "Of course, she is welcome here!" No other answer was possible. He could no more turn away his wife's sister than he could turn away his own mother. But how on earth could both those people be accommodated in the same house? Such a conjunction might bring about the end of the world.

"I did bring some gowns. In fact, this is the only boy's outfit I have with me. I can change into a dinner dress if you like." Dora studied her garments, looking wistful. "I did think this waistcoat rather charming. Such a pretty color! But I suppose trousers are not at all the thing when dining with new acquaintances."

Valance relaxed slightly. "Good idea. I think that would make introductions a little easier." He would still need to speak to Mother in advance, to prevent her from saying anything she shouldn't.

"But Dora, what about your hair?" Honora asked. "You have cut it so short!"

Dora ran a hand through her curly crop. "Yes, isn't it divine? I like it much better this way. So much more comfortable, and it will be easier to care for! I think I shall wear it like this all the time."

Honora looked unconvinced. "I liked it the way you used to wear it. You had such lovely ringlets! But I suppose it is your hair, not mine."

"My lady," Valance suggested, "perhaps you would like to show your sister to the Rose Room?" This being a small house, that was the only empty guest room they had. "I had better speak to my mother."

"Oh yes," Honora agreed. "Dora, you will want a chance to freshen up."

The moment the sisters were gone, Valance buried his face in his hands. He allowed himself only a moment to despair. Then he got up to go change into evening clothes. Most likely, Mother would be finished dressing soon, and he would have a chance to speak to her—assuming he could figure out the right thing to say.

CHAPTER TWENTY-ONE

O NCE THE DOOR to the guest room clicked shut behind them, Dora turned toward Honora. "Tell me everything! Are you having fun in London? Do you like Lord Valance? Do you think he is handsome? Does he treat you properly? Because if he doesn't, I think you ought to run away with me and we can open up a girl's school together."

Honora blinked, not certain which questions ought to be answered and which ought to be ignored. "Dora, where would we get the money to start a school? I still do not have access to my fortune. And neither do you."

Whatever his flaws as a husband and father, Sir Isaac Grantly had tried to do right by his illegitimate daughter. His will bequeathed the same small fortune to Dora as to his legitimate daughters. But her money, like Honora's, was held in trust. Uncle Robert was unlikely to thwart Lady Grantly's schemes.

"Oh, right. I suppose that won't work." Dora sighed.

It was a bad idea anyway, in Honora's opinion. True, running a school was one of the few ways gentlewomen could earn a living. But since neither of them had any teaching experience, Honora suspected any school they ran would fail sooner rather than later.

"Anyway," Honora said, "You need not worry about me. I quite like living with Lord Valance." Especially over the last week, during which he had generously helped educate her in bed.

She blushed at the memories.

Dora did not miss the blush. She grinned. "Oh, are you sweet on him? That's good. I am glad you married him instead of Belmont. I was very worried when you did not come back from Belmont Court after the masquerade. I thought perhaps Belmont had kidnapped you."

Honora laughed, but it was a hollow laugh. Surely even Belmont wouldn't stoop to kidnapping? Or would he? If it was true that he'd pushed his first wife down the stairs, he might be willing to do anything.

"I was perfectly safe. Lord Valance helped me escape."

"And then you fell in love with him?" Dora suggested. "So romantic!"

"I suppose it is romantic," Honora granted. But she was not sure "falling in love" adequately explained her relationship to Valance.

Her prior experiences with romantic love had all involved hopeless infatuations with unsuitable young men: a second son who could not afford to marry, a curate who did not intend to take a wife until he found a living, and a university scholar who seemed fond of her but could not marry anyone, because it would mean giving up his fellowship. That had been a pity, as he was not only one of the most intelligent men she had ever met, but also had the most beautiful hazel eyes. Why did the universities deprive the young ladies of England by forbidding fellows to marry?

None of those past infatuations had amounted to more than a little flirtation at assemblies and dinner parties, a few compliments on her beauty, and a pinch of heartache. Compared to those past beaux, Valance seemed less like the object of an infatuation and more like a trustworthy friend—a friend who happened to be attractive and very good in bed. Honora did not know a word for that, even if she had been willing to discuss her feelings.

Time to change the subject. "I am afraid I must go dress for dinner. I will send my maid in to help you after I dress."

Valance came in while Honora's maid finished arranging her hair. He leaned against her dressing table and waited to speak until Clack left the room.

"I have spoken to Mother about Dora. She has promised to behave civilly, and I trust her promise."

"Thank you." A little of the tension in Honora's shoulders dissipated. Dora had already experienced ostracism and judgment for things beyond her control. Honora could not have borne it if her sister were insulted in Honora's own home.

"You once told me your mother had leverage over you," Valance continued. "Is Dora that leverage?"

Honora nodded. "Mama threatened to send Dora away if I discouraged Belmont's attentions." Her lip trembled, remembering. "But I never thought she would send her into service to Belmont!"

She picked up one of the scent bottles on the dressing table and pretended to be fascinated by it. "You are probably wondering how it comes about that I have an illegitimate half-sister." She did not look up at her husband. She was afraid she might see condemnation there. Valance had clearly been taken aback by Dora's arrival.

Valance shook his head. "I believe I can guess. I assume she is your father's child, not your mother's?"

"Yes. Her own mother died when she was still a baby. She has lived with us ever since. The story Father gave out was that Dora was his cousin's daughter. He always referred to her as his ward."

In theory, only the Grantly family was supposed to know the truth about Dora's parentage. But most people in the neighborhood had likely guessed it. Dora had inherited not only Sir Isaac's eye color, but also his distinctive cleft chin, making it hard to conceal her relationship.

"In reality, her mother was a concert singer," Honora continued. That was putting it politely. The words her mother used to describe the late Miss Rossini did not bear repeating.

"Ah." That single syllable spoke volumes.

Honora supposed she did not have to explain to Valance that wealthy gentlemen often employed actresses, singers, and dancers as their mistresses. Very likely he had done the same, though she hated thinking about it.

"I hope you do not have any illegitimate children," she blurted out. How dreadful it would be if he had children whom he neglected!

He sucked in a sharp breath. "Not so far as I know. I have always taken precautions to avoid that. I realize no contraceptive spell is one hundred percent reliable. But most of my lovers have been, er, professionals who would know how to deal with the consequences of an unwanted pregnancy."

She glanced up and caught him blushing. She had embarrassed him. But maybe he *ought* to be embarrassed by his past behavior. Why had Valance been allowed to seek pleasure among women of easy virtue, when Honora had been forbidden to even be alone in a room with an unmarried man?

"By 'professionals' you mean prostitutes or courtesans," she said. "And by dealing with the consequences, you mean—"

"Never mind what I meant," Valance interrupted. He crossed his arms over his chest truculently. "This entire conversation is most improper. A gentleman does not discuss his relations with women prior to marriage with his wife! Suffice it to say, I do not believe I fathered any children out of wedlock, but if I did, I would take care of them. I would most certainly *not* send them into service at any property owned by the Duke of Belmont."

"I cannot believe my mother would let him punish me by hurting Dora." Honora had been reluctant to face the awfulness of that, but there could be no other reason for sending Dora into service. The terms of their father's will made it clear his illegitimate daughter was to be raised and educated as a gentlewoman. Could Lady Grantly legally even send Dora out to work? Perhaps Honora ought to consult a solicitor on her sister's behalf.

"Don't take this the wrong way, but I suspect I would be

happier if I never met your mother."

Honora sighed. "It does not matter. Mama wants nothing to do with me anymore, anyway. She will probably be glad to get rid of Dora, too. She never liked having her about the place."

Dora's presence at Grantly Manor must have been a constant reminder of Sir Isaac's infidelity. Honora could sympathize with her mother's situation as a wronged wife, but she did not think it excused Lady Grantly's coldness. Dora had always been given the harshest punishments for even minor infractions.

A happier thought occurred to Honora. "Can Dora live with us now?" She sent Valance her most pleading look.

To her disappointment, Valance slowly shook his head. "If it were safe for her to do so, yes. But you said she is a minor. Won't her guardians try to find her? Nora, they will look here first. Especially since the two of you are so close."

"I suppose that is true." Honora stared at her own reflection in the mirror. If her mother were here, she would remind Honora that frowns put wrinkles on one's face. But Honora could not help scowling into the glass. "What should we do, then? Consult a lawyer? I think my mother may be violating the terms of my father's will. He would *never* have wanted Dora to be a servant!"

"I wondered about that." Valance played with one of the cornsilk-colored ringlets Clack had labored so hard to produce, idly winding her hair around his finger. "We probably ought to talk to my solicitor. Mr. Watson might have some ideas about what legal action we could pursue. In the meantime, I think we ought to hide Dora somewhere safe."

"Where would she be safe?" The Duke of Belmont had a long reach.

"What would you say if I took her to Carrington Abbey?" Valance suggested.

Honora raised her eyebrows in surprise. "Not Dreadnaught Hall?"

He shook his head. "The Hall is empty of anyone but servants. There would be no one there to keep an eye on Dora or to protect her if someone showed up looking for her. And that would be the second place they would look for her, wouldn't it? Since it belongs to me? But it might take a while for anyone to think to check the Abbey. And most of the Carringtons are magicians. They are better equipped to protect someone than the staff at the Hall."

"She could travel there in disguise," Honora said slowly. "To make doubly certain of her safety, you could cast a glamour over her, like you did for me. And we would have to change her name."

Rossini was far too distinctive of a surname. Could they call her Dora Smith, or would that be too obvious? Would they have to change her name from "Dora" to something else? Laura? Cora? Flora? Honora wrinkled her brow as she considered the matter.

"Hiding her at the abbey is only a short-term solution," Valance warned. "But that might buy us a little time to take legal action."

"I wish she could stay here with us." Wistfulness leaked into Honora's voice.

Leaving Dora behind had been the absolute worst thing about running away with Valance. Since her father's death, Honora had served as a buffer between her mother and her unwanted natural sister. When she ran off with Valance, she'd worried about Dora's happiness in her absence. But she had thought Dora would be safe from any serious harm. She had not realized her mother was so vengeful.

"Why is she called Dora, anyway?" Valance asked. "To rhyme with your name?"

Honora crinkled her nose. "Yes. My father had distinctive taste in names." By "distinctive," she meant "dreadful," but she did not want to openly insult her father. "Her full name is Theodora. And my younger sisters are Belinda and Clarinda."

Valance said nothing, but the face he pulled made Honora giggle. Clearly, he did not approve of the rhyming names.

"Whoever named *you* had more sense," she told him. No one

need be ashamed of the name "Oliver."

Valance gave her an odd look. "My mother chose the name. But it was my father's name first."

"Oh, so it is a family name. When we have a son, will you want to name him Oliver, too?" Honora asked idly.

But the hand that had been playing with a lock of her hair stilled. "One Oliver at a time is enough for any family." The reflection of his face in the mirror looked uneasy. "You will tell me, won't you, if your courses are late?"

"Naturally." She cleared her throat. "I expect them in a day or two, in fact. I will tell you if I am late."

"Good. Not that there is any rush." He lowered his head so he could kiss her cheek. "We are both quite young. We have plenty of time in which to produce an heir."

Honora returned his kiss with interest. Then Valance lifted her up to sit on top of the dressing table. He cradled her head with one hand as he kissed her thoroughly. She opened her legs to make room for him, and he pressed close to her. Her body heated with desire.

But when he lifted up her skirt, she reluctantly interrupted him. "We are supposed to go down to dinner. Right now, in fact." They might already be late.

"Oh. Right." He sighed, but obediently stepped away from her. "Dinner. Yes. We have a guest, so we'd better not keep them waiting." A faint blush colored his cheeks.

"It has been an eventful day," Honora pointed out. "Perhaps you will be exhausted by the time dinner ends and have to go to bed early. And perhaps I, being a loving wife, will go up to check on you, and somehow fail to return to the drawing room."

No doubt it would be very wrong to abandon her sister to the company of Mrs. Valance, but people who chose to visit newlyweds ought to expect such abandonment.

Valance grinned back and kissed her on the forehead. "That seems like an extremely plausible scenario. I am glad I married such an ingenious woman." With that, they went down to the drawing room.

Mrs. Valance probably had many questions about Dora's background, the reason for her sudden visit, and the reason for her just-as-sudden departure, planned for the very next day. But, to Honora's relief, Valance's mother kept these questions to herself. She made polite conversation as if Dora were any normal, perfectly respectable debutante rather than the daughter of a concert singer. But, Honora reasoned, Valance might not have told his mother the whole story.

In any case, Dora looked about ten times more respectable when dressed in a sprigged muslin gown. She had only come out of the schoolroom last spring, but she could display good manners when she chose to do so, and she chose to do so tonight. She made unexceptionable conversation about social life in rural Kent, her adventurous journey to London (Honora suspected she left out many details), and the weather.

Honora relaxed, realizing she need not fear social disaster for her most rambunctious sister. She could see Valance felt relieved as well. He must have been even more anxious than she was about how Dora and his mother would interact.

VALANCE AND DORA left for Carrington Abbey before breakfast the next day. Dora donned her boys' clothes again, and to make doubly sure of her concealment, Valance cast a glamour over her, disguising her as a tow-headed youth. Today she answered to the name Theo Hart.

"Why Hart?" Honora asked. The "Theo" part needed no explanation.

Dora grinned. "I wanted to be Theo Doe—like Jane Doe, you know—but I thought that would be too obvious. Almost as bad as Smith, right? But 'hart' is another word for deer. It would have made more sense to be Theo Hind, but I didn't think that rolled off the tongue as easily, did you?"

"I suppose not," Honora granted.

"And when I get to the Abbey and change out of these clothes, I will be Cora Hart, and I think that sounds good, too. I will tell everyone I am from Tunbridge Wells. I think I remember it well enough to lie about it."

They had gone to Tunbridge Wells on holiday several times, most recently being last spring.

"Keep your lies to a minimum," Valance advised. "The more falsehoods you weave, the easier it is to get caught."

"Oh, I know that," Dora cheerfully replied. "I have a good deal of experience lying, you know."

Valance blenched. He turned pleading eyes towards Honora.

Feeling obligated to play the part of a responsible older sister, Honora said, "Dora, I hope you are going to behave properly at Carrington Abbey. Please do not get into any trouble."

"When have I ever gotten into trouble?" Dora asked.

Honora thought that was a question best left unanswered. She merely followed Valance and Dora to the waiting carriage.

Everyone had agreed that Honora should stay in London, keeping Mrs. Valance company. If Dora were seen traveling with her sister, people might figure out her identity, despite the disguise. Valance thought it better, therefore, for only him to accompany the runaway on the short journey to Carrington Abbey.

Honora might have agreed to this arrangement, but that didn't mean she liked it. She shook Dora's hand (hugging seemed inadvisable, given Dora's disguise), and kissed Valance good-bye.

"Travel safely." She wanted to add, "come back soon," but worried it would sound too needy. Valance had business of his own at Dreadnaught Hall, and he might need to stay for a few days to make sure Dora was safe and comfortable at Carrington Abbey.

Valance seemed to guess her unspoken request, though, because he touched his forehead to hers and promised: "I will be back before you know it."

Honora waited until the carriage pulled away to walk into the house. She hoped the next few days flew by.

CHAPTER TWENTY-TWO

I T TOOK LESS than a day to get from London to Carrington Abbey. Valance's initial plan had been to stop at Dreadnaught Hall first. He could deposit Dora at the Hall and walk or ride over to the Abbey to speak to Sir Roderick and Lady Carrington (both Lady Carringtons, in fact) about the unexpected visitor.

But halfway there, it occurred to him that taking Dora to Dreadnaught Hall might be a mistake. The fewer people who knew about his association with her, the better. When they stopped to change horses, therefore, he told the coachman to go straight to Carrington Abbey.

He would not have liked to show up at anyone else's house with an unexpected guest, particularly one with so complicated a backstory as "Theo Hart." But Valance felt sure of his welcome at the Abbey.

The front door was opened by the butler who had served the Carringtons for nearly twenty years. His face lit up at the sight of Valance.

"Master Oliver!" Then Morris corrected himself: "I mean, my lord." He gave Dora a quizzical glance.

"Master Oliver will do," Valance told him. "Is the family at home, Morris? I have a guest I wish to introduce."

"Sir Roderick is out, and young Lady Carrington is indisposed, but the dowager lady and Miss Hannah are in the morning room, along with Master Peregrine."

"Peregrine? I thought he was in London." Peregrine had not told Valance he was going to Surrey. But Valance did not see him nearly as often since his marriage.

"He arrived yesterday, my lord," Morris explained. "I believe his visit has something to do with preparing for a spell he will work here in April."

"Oh, right! I had forgotten about that."

Peregrine had decided to work his meteorite spell from the safety of an empty field on the Carrington estate. Valance wholeheartedly supported this change of plan, and he suspected that Abigail did, too. After the dining room debacle, Abigail was understandably eager to avoid having the spell cast anywhere near her townhouse.

Morris led them to the morning room, though Valance knew the way by heart. The decor here was all left over from a previous generation, displaying more flourishes and scrolling than was popular now. The furniture had been arranged not for parties, but for the use of the family, with sofas, armchairs, and a *chaise longue* grouped closer together than was common, to allow for general conversation. As a result, the room felt cozy rather than ostentatious.

"Oliver!" The dowager Lady Carrington had been lying down on the *chaise longue,* but she got to her feet to greet him. "What a pleasant surprise."

"Good afternoon, ma'am. You are looking very well today." Valance dutifully kissed her cheek.

She did look well. Her hair, a true golden blonde, was lightly touched with white. She stood much shorter than Valance—no taller than Honora, he guessed. Hannah, who had been sitting nearby, got up to greet Valance too. She was the only sibling to have inherited her mother's golden hair and her plump figure, though she stood an inch or two taller than Lady Carrington.

Peregrine rose from his chair, too, but he cocked his head to one side and frowned rather than offering to shake hands. "Valance, why is the young lady traveling with you glamoured to look like a young man? This seems to have become a habit with you, and I must say it is a strange habit."

Valance sent a speaking glance in Peregrine's direction, but otherwise ignored the question in order to make the necessary formal introduction.

"My lady, Hannah, Peregrine, may I present Theo Hart? Or Cora Hart, whichever the case may be?" He glanced over his shoulder at Dora and arched a single eyebrow, not knowing how she preferred to be addressed.

"I suppose now that I am here, it might as well be Cora. Most of the time I behave like a young lady. In theory, anyway." Dora took the spell-paper out of her pocket and tossed it into the waste paper basket, breaking the glamour that had disguised her. Then she curtseyed as gracefully as her trousers allowed.

"I am pleased to meet you. I am one of Lady Valance's school friends." She spoke confidently, and, Valance thought, convincingly.

But Peregrine snorted. "That sounds like a pack of lies. Who are you really?" His wide eyes looked both guileless and curious.

Valance glared at Peregrine, then looked to Lady Carrington for help. At least, he hoped his expression conveyed his appeal for assistance.

"Peregrine, Hannah, I would love it if the two of you would go out to the garden and see if there are any flowers blooming for the dinner table," Lady Carrington announced.

Hannah took the hint at once. "I believe I saw some primroses in the south side of the garden."

"Why do you need two people to pick primroses?" Peregrine asked, evidently not taking the hint. "If you want me to leave the room, you could just say so." He looked reproachfully at Lady Carrington.

His mother sighed. "I am sorry, Peregrine. You are not a child to be fobbed off with excuses. Yes, I do want a chance to speak privately with Oliver and Miss Hart."

Peregrine nodded to his mother, bowed to Dora, and left the

room.

Lady Carrington turned towards Dora. "Now, why don't you have a seat, my dear, and tell me what this is all about."

Dora did as requested, beginning with her real name and her relation to Honora. Then she explained the reason for her flight from home. When her story became convoluted, Valance stepped in and clarified matters as best he could, but for the most part, he let Dora do the talking.

As Dora spoke, the lines on Lady Carrington's forehead grew deeper. By the time Dora finished, the dowager's usually cheerful face looked distinctly unsettled.

"You are welcome to stay here as long as necessary," she assured Dora. "And we will call you whatever name you wish. We have plenty of extra bedrooms. I believe we will put you in Abigail's old room, in fact, as no one is using it. Er, are you a magician?"

"Oh, yes, I am a sorceress," Dora chirped. "But only a moderately powerful one, I am afraid."

"Excellent. We have a laboratory on the third floor if you need it, and half of the library is devoted to works of magic. You are welcome to make use of either. But for now, I wonder if you would like to refresh yourself? I can have one of the maids take you up to your room." Lady Carrington tugged the bell pull to summon a servant.

"Are you trying to get rid of me so you can talk to Lord Valance alone?" Dora asked bluntly.

Lady Carrington smiled ruefully. "Yes," she admitted. "Please give me a moment alone with your brother-in-law, Miss Hart?"

"As you wish." Dora left, though the longing glance she cast over her shoulder suggested she did so reluctantly.

Lady Carrington waited to speak until Dora was out of earshot. Then her smile faded. "Oliver, what is *really* going on here? Why would Belmont mistreat your sister-in-law? Surely he doesn't blame her for Honora's elopement?"

"I doubt he blames Dora," Valance agreed. "But I know he

was angry about Honora getting away from him. I suspect he is used to getting his own way."

Lady Carrington nodded. Though she rarely visited London, she undoubtedly knew the duke by reputation.

"I am not sure what Belmont intended to do with Miss, er, Hart, but I think whatever it is had better be avoided." Valance ran a hand through his hair, feeling suddenly tired. He wished he had thought to nap on the journey.

"You are probably right about that. Such a man may not give up the hunt easily," Lady Carrington warned.

"I know." Valance sighed. "Believe me, I know." He considered telling Lady Carrington about Belmont's visit to Russell Square but decided against it. He had told no one about that conversation or the threats that had been exchanged. "I may very well have to confront him in order to resolve this." If it *could* be resolved.

Lady Carrington's somber expression deepened into a frown. "I hope you do not do anything foolish, Oliver." She fidgeted with her rings for a moment. "Really, this whole business of eloping and marrying so hastily seems most unlike you."

"Yes, I know." None of Valance's behavior on Twelfth Night had been in character. "So far it has turned out well, though." A smile tugged at the corners of his mouth.

Last night, Honora's plan to escape their guests had worked perfectly. Valance had pled exhaustion and retired early, Honora had come up to check on him a short time later, and he had loved her so thoroughly, she shouted his name at the height of her passion. He still felt proud of that.

"I am glad to hear that," Lady Carrington said.

Her entirely too-knowing expression made him wonder if she could guess why he smiled. Embarrassing, but what could he do? Hiding anything from someone who had known him all his life was well-nigh impossible. In some ways, Lady Carrington understood Valance better than his own mother did.

Lady Carrington's frown subtly shifted shape. "But why

didn't you bring your wife with you, Oliver? I want to meet Lady Valance."

Valance recognized that look. He was in trouble. He automatically sat up straighter. "For strategic reasons, ma'am."

He explained their concerns about people identifying Dora. There was enough similarity between the two sisters that someone who saw them together might guess their relationship. "I expect we will come down to Dreadnaught Hall this summer, when the Season is over. Hopefully, you will meet Lady Valance then."

"You had better do so," Lady Carrington said. "As it is, I am quite disappointed in your correspondence, Oliver. You have told me absolutely nothing! Do you realize *Peregrine* has written more about Lady Valance than you have?" She shook her head. It was a blighting incitement, given that Carrington was notoriously bad at responding to his family's letters.

"I will strive to do better, ma'am."

To make up for his supposed neglect, Valance spent the next fifteen minutes describing Honora to Lady Carrington. It was a pleasant topic of conversation, and he did not mind repeating some of it after dinner, when Sir Roderick and his wife asked about the new Lady Valance, too. There were few things he'd rather think about than his wife.

He kept an eye on Dora during the after-dinner hours, worried that she might reveal too much about her true identity. But she seemed not to have exaggerated when she claimed to be skilled at lying. Any time the topic of conversation veered towards something that might expose her identity, she subtly steered the talk in a different direction. This seemed like a rather disturbing talent for a girl just out of the schoolroom, but Valance could not deny that it was useful.

Valance intended to tell Sir Roderick the truth about "Miss Hart," he being the head of the household, but he saw no reason for it to be known among the whole family. This meant evading pointed questions from Peregrine, who had not been fooled by their rather thin cover story.

When Peregrine could get no information from Valance, he crossed the room to sit next to Dora. Valance ignored their conversation until he overheard Peregrine telling Dora that the blue-green waistcoat she'd been wearing when she arrived brought out the color of her eyes. That sent a chill down Valance's back.

Valance tuned out Sir Roderick's story about a recent case he tried as magistrate. Instead, he stared across the room at Dora and Peregrine, trying to overhear their conversation. If any other man had made the remark about the waistcoat, Valance would have assumed him to be flirting with Dora. But Valance had never known Peregrine to flirt.

So far as Valance knew, Peregrine confined his relations to the fairer sex to weekly visits to a high-class brothel. He treated the women of his own class with either friendship (as in the case of Susan, Honora, or a few of Abigail's friends) or indifferent courtesy (as in the case of almost everyone else). He had certainly never engaged in anything like a courtship with a marriageable young lady before. The idea of Peregrine striking up a flirtation with Dora was both inconceivable and alarming.

Sir Roderick finally noticed that Valance had ceased listening to him. "Is something wrong?" he asked. "If you are concerned about Miss Hart, you need not be. My sister will be glad of her company. Hannah finds the country rather dull right now, since my wife is indisposed and we are not able to entertain often."

Valance turned back to his host and forced a smile. "I am glad to hear that. We much appreciate your hospitality."

In truth, Valance was not at all worried about how Dora would get along with Hannah, who was one of the more sensible members of the family. In fact, he hoped Hannah would be a good influence on Dora. But it would not be good for Dora to enter into some kind of flirtation or dalliance with Peregrine. That could only spell trouble, because Peregrine could not possibly intend to marry her. Could he?

Valance spoke with Roderick for a few minutes, then glanced over at Dora again. She was in the middle of telling Peregrine that the next time she came to London, she planned to don her boy's clothing so she could go watch a dogfight or cockfight. Valance's eyes widened.

"I must advise against that. Those events are very cruel to animals," Peregrine told Dora. Valance relaxed, until his friend added: "If you like, I will take you to a boxing match instead. There is just as much bloodshed, but everyone agrees to be injured, so it is more ethical."

"Oh, that would be lovely," Dora replied. "But first I will have to get a hat that fits properly and a pair of men's boots. I don't think my outfit looked quite right with half boots. I would like a pair of Hessian boots."

She wistfully studied her present footwear. She wore plain leather slippers rather than boots. They were perfectly suitable for a casual dinner, but her expression suggested she found them lacking.

"If you like, I can introduce you to my bootmaker when next you are in town." Peregrine sounded as if he were neither joking nor humoring her, but genuinely trying to help. "You would look smashing in Hessian boots."

"Wouldn't I just!" Dora displayed her mischievous dimpled grin, and Peregrine smiled back.

Valance's heart sank. It was not his imagination. *They were flirting together*. Or at least, Dora was flirting with Peregrine. But he certainly seemed to be flirting back. *Good Lord!* To Valance, the two of them seemed like fire and oil: throw them together and a mighty conflagration could occur. Bringing Dora to the Abbey might have been a terrible mistake.

CHAPTER TWENTY-THREE

February 14, 1817

T HE DAY AFTER Valance left, Honora moped about the house, not knowing what to do. She felt so tired she lay down on the *chaise longue* to rest, instead of paying the morning calls she had planned. She assumed her fatigue was due to staying up too late last night reading, until she discovered her courses had begun. After that, she asked for a hot compress and took to the chaise with a book. Where her monthly bleeding was, cramping and backaches would soon follow.

This was never her favorite time of the month, but it felt particularly bittersweet this time. She'd secretly hoped she might be with child, if only so she could learn what pregnancy was like. Discovering otherwise was a greater disappointment than she expected.

What, she wondered, could she and Valance do differently next month? She did not think it possible to go to bed together more often, given that they had not missed a single night since the first time. Should she get a fertility charm from a midwife? Perhaps one of her married friends from school would have advice for her. Didn't Jane Crossly have a baby now? Maybe she would know what Honora could do to be more successful.

Honora got up from her comfortable place on the *chaise longue* to write a quick note inviting Jane to call next week. It would be good to talk to another young wife about marriage, even if she was not brave enough to ask for advice on conceiving. Probably there was no tried-and-true method, or else there wouldn't be so many couples who wanted children and could not have them. Still, Jane might have something to recommend.

When she'd finished the note, she went to the front hall to put it with the outgoing mail. Had Valance been home, she would have asked him to frank it for her, but she saw no reason to delay sending it till his return. When she reached the hall, though, she discovered a commotion in progress. Weller was arguing with someone at the door.

"Lord and Lady Valance are both out, and even if they were at home, you could not see them. You had best be off. If you are in need of money, you must speak to His Lordship's man of business." Weller, having had years of experience turning away unwanted visitors, had perfectly mastered the necessary calm-but-firm tone of dismissal.

"I do not want money," an angry voice answered. "I want my dog back!"

Dog? Surprised, Honora drifted closer to the door. "Weller, who is it?"

The butler looked over his shoulder and shook his head slightly. "Nothing you need concern yourself about, my lady." He began to close the door.

"You cannot turn me away like this, after two years in his protection! At least give me my dog!" the woman yelled. *"Trou du cul!"*

Honora frowned. What dog was she talking about? Bishop Barkley? Then that must mean . . . she gasped. She had assumed that Illegible Scribble was gone from her husband's life forever. Apparently, she'd been mistaken.

She drew herself to her full height. "Weller, let the woman in. I would like to speak to her."

Weller's eyes almost imperceptibly widened. "My lady!" he protested. "I am very sure His Lordship would not like that."

"His lordship would tell you to do as I say. Please open the door and let her in, that I may speak with her."

With visible reluctance, Weller opened the door and ushered

in the visitor.

The stranger swept into the room with a rustle of silk petticoats. "Thank you, my lady."

A cold, sick weight filled Honora's stomach. If this was Illegible Scribble, she could see why Lord Valance had kept her for two years. She was a beauty of a very different style from Honora: tall, voluptuous, rosy-cheeked, dark-haired and dark-eyed. In nearly every way, she looked Honora's opposite. All they had in common, so far as she could tell, was their youth. (Well, she supposed they both did have broad, curvy hips. But Illegible Scribble had a more impressive bosom.)

"Can I help you, ma'am?" Honora strove to speak calmly, despite her roiling emotions. "I heard you mention a dog. Have you lost a pet?"

"Not lost." The woman sniffed, as if she had a cold. Or had been crying. "I . . . well, I sent my dog to Lord Valance to keep him for me while I was away from town, and now I want him back. He is *my* dog. His Lordship gave him to me." She faced Honora with her chin lifted and her shoulders set squarely, prepared for a challenge. Her aura showed no signs of magical abilities, but its strong, vibrant colors suggested a powerful personality.

"Describe the dog for me, please," Honora suggested.

Before the woman could do so, Bishop Barkley trotted out of the morning room to see what all the hubbub was about. The moment he glimpsed the stranger, his ears perked up. He galloped towards her. He flung himself at her feet, jumping up and down in an attempt to properly greet her. Illegible Scribble reached down and picked him up, and he began to wash her face.

Honora's eyes blurred as she blinked back tears. So. This woman really *was* Illegible Scribble. This was the mistress Lord Valance had dismissed in order to marry Honora. This must be the style of beauty he really favored. And she could not possibly look more different from Honora.

"I see that Bishop Barkley does know you, ma'am." There

was no point in denying the dog's identity. He had made it clear that he belonged with Illegible Scribble.

"Of course, he knows me. Lord Valance gave him to me two years ago this very day, as a Valentine's Day gift." The former mistress glared at Honora. "You may find it hard to believe, my lady, but there was a time when His Lordship adored me. He worshipped the ground I walked on, wrote poetry in my honor, and showered me with gifts." She sounded simultaneously proud and bitter. "But men are fickle, as I am sure you will learn, and—"

"My lady," Weller interjected, "I really think—"

"Weller, please leave us. I wish to have some speech with Miss . . ." Honora faltered as she realized she could not address the stranger as Illegible Scribble. What was she to call her, then?

Weller frowned, but he retreated, as she had requested.

"I am Miss Barbauld," the woman supplied. "And I need no introduction to you, my lady." She scanned Honora from head to toe in much the same way Honora had studied her. "I wish you joy of His Lordship. Heaven knows I couldn't have put up with such an oaf much longer myself. He never was quite to my taste, you know."

Honora gritted her teeth. "I will not listen to insults aimed at my husband. I merely wished to know if you needed any assistance." She wished she'd listened to Weller. Speaking to Miss Barbauld had been a mistake.

"So very charitable of you, my lady. But no. I will take my dog, and that will be all."

Barkley seemed to be in a rare state of bliss. His tongue lolled out of his mouth and his tail kept lazily wagging. Honora's angry heart softened at the sight. Perhaps he had missed Illegible Scribble all this time.

"I am sure you have missed him. The dog, I mean," she added hastily, seeing a smirk on Miss Barbauld's face.

"Yes, I have missed my baby." Miss Barbauld kissed Barkley on the nose. He wagged his tail enthusiastically.

Little traitor! Earlier that day, he'd snuggled on Honora's lap as if he belonged there. She had found his presence comforting in Valance's absence. Now even that comfort was to be taken away from her.

Miss Barbauld caught Honora's eye and hesitated for a moment. "I hope you realize it is all worthless," she said softly. "Nothing but dust and ashes."

"Really, madam, I have no idea what you mean." Honora drew in a deep breath, intending to send Miss Barbauld on her way. There was no need for her to linger now that she'd gotten what she came for.

"I mean men's affections," Miss Barbauld clarified. "Every endearment he whispers in your ear, he once whispered to me. Oh, the things he said to me to lure me down the primrose path!" She shook her head. "He would show up in the green room after my performances, bearing the most expensive bouquets and the most extravagant compliments. I was young, naïve, unused to such attention . . . naturally, my head was turned."

A lump formed in Honora's throat, and her eyes prickled. She did not want to hear any of this!

Miss Barbauld twisted her mouth into a bitter smirk. "He lured me away from the safety of a loving family, promised to care for me, and took my virtue, only to turn me out once he decided it was time to reform."

"I am very sorry for any injury that may have been done to you, but really, I believe you have said enough." Honora's voice trembled. She could not bear to stand here another minute, hearing how her husband treated other women.

Miss Barbauld shrugged her shoulders gracefully. Was that her theatrical training showing? "Thank you for allowing me to take my dog. I have missed him. But as for Oliver? You may keep him, and much good may it do you. I hope you realize he will tire of you, too, sooner or later. And then he will no doubt haunt the green room at some other theater, tempting some other respectable girl to her ruin."

"I think you had better go." Honora used the firmest voice

she could muster, though the ground beneath her seemed unsteady. No, that was her own body shaking with emotion. "Good day, Miss Barbauld. I must ask you never to come here again." She hoped her trembling wasn't visible.

"There is nothing else here that I want." Miss Barbauld turned on her heel and walked out the door with Bishop Barkley in her arms.

Honora lingered in the front hall, half expecting the visitor to return with more damning last words. When it became clear she was really gone, Honora dragged herself up the stairs to her bedroom. She let herself into the room, locked the door behind her, and collapsed on the bed.

Barkley was gone. She would never take him for another walk in the park. Nor would she spend another morning training him. He had learned to sit and lie down on command, and they were working on "stay." But he would never learn that. Illegible Scribble—or rather, Miss Barbauld—had obviously made no effort to train the dog during the two years she'd owned him. She would probably not start training him now.

That must be why she felt like crying, Honora told herself. There could be no other reason for tears. It was not as if she'd learned anything about her husband she had not already known. She had known he kept a mistress since the day she met him. Goodness, she had even told him he need not dismiss Miss Barbauld! She tried to smile at the irony, but her lips would not cooperate.

In any case, she could have no reason for being angry with Valance. In seducing, deflowering, and then dismissing an innocent girl from the lower orders, he had done no more than other young aristocrats. It ought not have surprised her.

Perhaps Honora had built up a false image of Valance. He had rescued her from an unhappy marriage to the Duke of Belmont, so she'd come to view him as some sort of hero. As if he were better than other men. How very childish of her! Knights in shining armor no longer rode about rescuing fair maidens.

Honora was a woman grown, so she forced herself to face the facts. Valance was no hero. It had been very good of him to marry her, but after all, he had gained things from their marriage, too. She knew he hated the marriage mart and the elaborate system of courtship through which men of his class were supposed to find their brides. In marrying her, he had happily circumvented all of that. Perhaps he had seen her in the light of a fortunate windfall. Fate had dumped an eligible bride right onto his lap; all he had to do was reach out and take her.

Moreover, he needed an heir. With no younger brothers who could inherit after him, Valance must feel that need rather urgently. But once Honora provided the heir he wanted, he would have no more use for her. He'd made it very clear when he proposed that their marriage would be a temporary arrangement. When there was no longer a reason to share bed and board, they would go their separate ways.

So even if Miss Barbauld was right about Valance soon moving on to his next lover, that did not matter one bit. He had promised Honora she could have as many lovers as she wanted once they'd produced a son. No doubt he would do the same.

Having known all that since the beginning of their marriage, Honora had been a fool to grow attached to her husband. But she had. She'd realized it yesterday, when the evening stretched before her with nothing to do but chat with her mother-in-law or read a book.

Once, she would have been happy enough to read a book beside a comfortable fire all evening. But without Valance sitting by her side, with a book of his own in hand and a brandy glass on the side table, the night seemed long, empty, and boring. Honora was so deeply smitten with her husband that she missed not only his conversation, but also his silence. *Lord, what fools these mortals be!*

Last night, her bed had felt colder without him lying next to her, just as it seemed cold and comfortless now. He would come home soon, of course. Maybe even tomorrow. She would have his conversation, his companionable silences, and his presence in bed again, at least for a little while longer. She had no right to ask for more than that. She had no right to ask for anything at all from him, given the great favor he had done in marrying her.

None of this, Honora reminded herself, was new information. There could be no reason for her to cry over today's conversation. Therefore, the tears trickling down her cheeks must all be due to losing Bishop Barkley. And how foolish that was, too! Imagine growing fond of a spoiled lapdog that had belonged to her husband's mistress! She really ought to have had more pride. Obviously, the dog preferred his previous owner to Honora. She ought to say good riddance. Apparently, she was too sentimental to do so.

Strangely, what kept echoing in her mind was Miss Barbauld saying, "But as for Oliver? You may keep him." Why, Honora wondered, had Lord Valance asked his wife to address him as "Valance," when he had allowed his mistress to call him "Oliver?"

That was probably the sort of question that should never be asked. Inquisitive though Honora might be, even *she* knew such questions existed. Even so, she cried a little harder. Though, of course, every tear was for Barkley. She had nothing else to cry about.

CHAPTER TWENTY-FOUR

WITH EVERY DAY that passed, Valance missed Honora more. He missed her cheerful conversation and her habit of listening to him thoughtfully even when he rambled too long. He missed her many questions and the suspense of not knowing what she would ask next. He missed her quiet presence by his side while he read or worked on his runes.

He began to consider that he might, just possibly, be more than a *little* infatuated with his wife. Lovely thought that might be in some ways, in other ways it seemed unfortunate. He had promised Honora her freedom once he had an heir. Given that promise, falling deeply in love with her might only set him up for heartbreak.

But he could not help missing her, longing for her, and thinking ahead to his return. If he could, he would have left as soon as Dora was comfortably settled at the Abbey. But he had promised his mother he would meet with his steward while he was in the country. His steward told Valance that some of his tenants wished to speak to him too. It had been so long since his last visit that he felt he owed them some of his time. Their requests for repairs and improvements were all quite reasonable, but it took time to listen to them, come to an agreement, and pass his instructions on.

Next, it turned out that the boundary fence between Carrington land and the Valance estate needed to be repaired. The actual repairs could be safely left to the stewards to manage, but Sir Roderick suggested Valance might like to ride the property line with him, inspecting the fence and keeping an eye out for any trees that ought to be felled or stiles that needed to be repaired. How could Valance refuse such a reasonable request?

The weather cooperated, giving the two landowners a fine day for an afternoon ride. They had a pleasant conversation about recent innovations in agriculture (a subject on which Sir Roderick was much better informed than Valance), and startled several foxes, prompting Sir Roderick to discuss the need to hunt the land more often. Having lost his father to a hunting accident, Valance did not care for the sport, but he understood the need to protect local henhouses from the vulpine population.

All this time, Valance did his best to keep a watchful eye on Dora. He did not trust her to stay out of trouble. But if he had imagined she would don men's clothing and go galloping off to the nearest boxing match the moment his back was turned, he was mistaken. Instead, she capably acted the part of a dutiful, well-mannered young lady of genteel birth. Only the mischievous twinkle he sometimes saw in her eyes suggested otherwise.

He also apprehensively watched Dora interact with Peregrine. She was as curious about the meteorite spell as Honora had been, and being a sorcerer, she could be of practical assistance fine-tuning the formulas.

Valance had no objection to his best friend working magic with Honora's sister. He knew perfectly well that Peregrine had always wanted the help of a sorcerer with this particular project. He would've offered to help Peregrine himself if not for clear memories of past failed collaborations. But the way Peregrine and Dora smiled and laughed together after dinner each night suggested their interest in each other might go beyond collegiality.

He tried talking to his friend about it. "You will behave properly around Miss Hart, won't you?"

"Of course," Peregrine said cheerfully. "When have I not

behaved properly?"

"I mean," Valance clarified, "you won't let her get into any trouble while she's here?" Valance could not forget Peregrine's offer to take her to a boxing match, or his suggestion that he could help her buy a pair of Hessian boots. Oil on fire! Surely Dora did not need such encouragement.

Carrington chuckled. "What kind of trouble do you think she will get into right under my mother's nose? She seems like a well-behaved young lady, and I would guess her to be quite intelligent. And I rather like her haircut. So very practical, isn't it?"

That did nothing to assuage Valance's concerns. "I think," he said sourly, "you should remember that she is—" he had been about to say 'my sister-in-law' until he remembered that only Lady Carrington and Sir Roderick were supposed to know Dora's identity.

"That she is what?" Peregrine waited, a look of expectant curiosity on his face.

"Just out of the schoolroom," Valance finished. "I believe she is only eighteen or nineteen." Peregrine must be a good four years older than her.

"Well, you need not worry. I will keep an eye on her for you. I shall take care not to let her run up any gambling debts or elope with any scoundrels. Not that there *are* any scoundrels hereabouts. Really, Valance, I can't imagine what trouble you think she could get into in so sleepy a corner of the country." Peregrine's smile looked positively benevolent.

But Valance still worried. He tried talking to the dowager Lady Carrington about Dora. She, too, chuckled at him.

"Oliver, I have already raised five children. Five quarrelsome and adventurous children, as you very well know! I am sure I can handle Miss Hart. She is just Hannah's age, you know. But I like seeing what a responsible man you have grown into. Sir John would be very proud of you."

"That's neither here nor there," Valance said hastily.

He did not want to become maudlin about his guardian's

untimely death. In his opinion, Lady Carrington's tendency to become sentimental about her late husband was one of her few flaws. It was certainly understandable that she still missed the husband she had loved so much. But Valance did not want to become teary-eyed over a man who would have affectionately teased them for being mawkish.

"I suppose," Valance admitted, "you are used to dealing with unconventional young women."

So far as he could remember, Abigail had never worn, but she had organized a reading group to discuss the work of Elizabeth Montagu and Mary Wollstonecraft. The local gentry had become so appalled by what their daughters began repeating from these meetings that they sent the vicar to Carrington Abbey to protest. No one knew what Sir John said to the vicar, but he never called at the Abbey again.

"I most certainly *am* used to it." Lady Carrington smiled, and Valance wondered if she, too, was thinking of Abigail's youth. "I believe your sister-in-law will do very well here, Oliver. You have nothing to worry about."

Valance cleared his throat. "And—forgive me for speaking plainly, madam—you won't let her spend too much time alone with Peregrine?"

Lady Carrington raised her eyebrows. "I cannot imagine what harm you think *Peregrine* would do her!" Her usually warm voice plummeted at least twenty degrees in an instant. "My son is a gentleman, and he knows how to treat a young lady with respect." She paused and narrowed her eyes. "Or do you mean to imply that the son of a baronet is not good enough to court your sister-in-law? Because I must say, Oliver, I did not expect you to treat your childhood friend—"

"You mistake me! I meant no such thing." He was not sure what horrified him more: the fact that he had offended Lady Carrington or the fact that she seemed to view a match between Dora and Peregrine as both possible and acceptable. "If anything, it would be Miss, er, Hart who would not be suitable, given her background."

"It is not her fault she is illegitimate." The steely glance Lady Carrington directed at Valance indicated she had yet to forgive him. "In any case, I have nothing to say to the matter. Peregrine has his own fortune and can marry—or not—to suit his own tastes."

Valance sighed. "Miss Hart is quite young. It will be at least two years before she comes of age, and there is no saying whether her legal guardian would approve a marriage before then." Dora's current estrangement from her guardians might prevent her from marrying even the most respectable suitor.

"That is an important consideration," Lady Carrington granted. "But, of course, she could always petition Chancery for permission to marry. I believe it is the court's responsibility to handle such situations."

His eyes widened. Goodness, she was taking this seriously! He could think of nothing more to say, so when she changed the subject, he let her do so. But he kept worrying.

VALANCE ENDED UP staying at the Abbey for an entire week. That was longer than he'd planned, but new things kept popping up to demand his attention, and then Lady Carrington (the younger, not the elder) asked him to stay for her dinner party. The day after the dinner party he set out for London, quite relieved to be on his way back to his wife.

He spent the drive making notes for a new set of runes he wanted to experiment with. Between one thing and another, he had not had the time he liked to devote to his magic. He had temporarily abandoned his attempt to perfect a rune for fire. Instead, he was working on a general cancellation spell, one that could be used to undo different types of magic. He was still working on the new rune when the carriage pulled up in front of his townhouse.

Valance closed his notebook and sprang down from the carriage with a renewed step. He was going to see his wife again after a week's absence. He wondered if she had missed him even half as much as he missed her.

He found the ladies of the house at home. His mother sat in her favorite easy chair, knitting and chatting. Honora lay on the *chaise longue*, her head propped up on a pillow while she turned the pages of a book. The moment he walked into the morning room, though, both women's faces brightened with a flattering delight.

And the moment his eyes met Honora's, his heart fluttered in his chest in a most alarming way.

"Oliver!" his mother exclaimed. "Back so soon? What a pleasant surprise!"

"It did not seem soon to me! I feel like I've been gone for a month." He nodded at his mother, but he went straight to Honora to greet her first.

She rose to her feet and held her hand out in greeting. He ignored her hand, instead taking her face in both his hands and kissing her lightly.

"It seemed a long time to me, too." Honora smiled up at him.

But then she lowered her eyes. Had it happened a few weeks ago, he would have thought she felt bashful. But all shyness between them had long since disappeared. Hadn't it?

Valance sat on the *chaise longue* and tugged on Honora's hand to get her to sit by his side. Although his mother was watching and no doubt judging, he wrapped his arm around his wife's waist and brushed a kiss against her cheek. He wished his mother would take a hint and find some excuse to leave, so he could kiss Honora the way he wanted. Instead, Mother kept asking cheerful questions about how everyone at the Hall fared, how Dora was settling in at the Abbey, and about the health of the younger Lady Carrington.

"Amelia is in the family way again," Valance said, regarding the latter question. "And having a rather rough time of it, I believe." Sir Roderick's wife had spent much of her time in her own chambers, made miserable by morning sickness.

"Well, I hope for their sake it is a boy," his mother said. "Sir Roderick is a patient man and an affectionate father, but I am sure he is disappointed to have only girl children."

Valance shook his head. "I am not so sure about that. Roderick adores his daughters. And he has two younger brothers, so he need not worry about the succession." Unlike Valance.

The issue of the succession had become a tricky one. Valance did not want his title and estates to pass to some distant cousin who did not understand the land or its tenants, or who might quarrel with his neighbors. He had never wanted that. But, on the other hand, he did not particularly want to have a son right away. Once his heir was born, there would be nothing to keep Honora by his side.

"But what good does it do to have two brothers, if they have no intention of setting up their own nurseries? I doubt Peregrine will ever marry." His mother made a moue of distaste and shook her head. "And doesn't Cosmo plan to compete for a fellowship at Cambridge? If he becomes a permanent fellow, he will not be able to marry, either."

"That is a good point about Cosmo." He was as dedicated to mathematics as Peregrine was to magic, but unlike Peregrine, Cosmo wanted an academic career, which would indeed prevent him from marrying. Fellows were generally not allowed to have wives. This had never bothered Cosmo, who seemed supremely uninterested in women—or men, for that matter.

"Why wouldn't Peregrine marry?" Honora turned questioning eyes towards Valance. "He is a handsome enough young man, and doesn't he have an independence? It is not as if good-looking bachelors with fortunes are ten-a-penny, even in London."

"Yes," Mother said dryly, "but I don't believe he has ever looked at a woman. Has he, Valance?"

"Ah, well, I don't know about that." Valance bit his lip to keep from laughing. Since he was the one who had introduced Peregrine to his favorite brothel, Valance knew perfectly well that his friend sometimes did more than *look* at women. But that was not the sort of detail Valance could share with his mother. She had never really understood either Peregrine or Cosmo.

He confined himself to saying: "I believe Peregrine likes a pretty girl as much as any man." Particularly, it seemed, girls with dimples who wore their hair cropped short. But he could not say *that*, either.

Honora narrowed her eyes as she watched him. Valance hurried to control his expression before she asked why he was grinning foolishly. At some point, he would have to share his suspicions about Peregrine and Dora with his wife, but now did not seem the right time.

"So," he said, eager to change the subject, "what happened while I was gone?"

His mother replied with tidbits of gossip she had heard during her morning calls. Honora talked about going to Hatchard's to rebuild her collection of books. She had also gone riding in the park with one of her old school friends, on a borrowed hack.

Then his mother casually said, "And we finally got rid of that annoying dog. No more soiled rugs. I am so glad! I never did like house-pets."

"What?" Shocked, Valance looked at Honora. She stared down at the floor, her hands tightly clasped on her lap. "Why would you do that? You loved that dog!" He could imagine no reason why his wife would send Bishop Barkley away.

Honora cleared her throat, but did not lift her gaze from the floor. "His owner came to get him."

Valance frowned. "What do you mean? *You* are his owner!"

"I mean his original owner." She kept her eyes averted as she spoke. "Miss Barbauld."

Never before had Valance known what it meant for someone's blood to run cold, but that was the only way he could describe the chill he felt. For Cherie to come to his home was a gross breach of etiquette and an insult to his wife.

"Miss Barbauld came *here*?" he whispered hoarsely. "And took the dog?"

"Yes."

"I am so very sorry." He did not know what else to say. Honora had already lost so much in the last two months. Must she lose her pet, too? "I will get you a new dog."

The moment the words were out of his mouth, he knew he'd made a mistake. He felt Honora stiffen underneath his arm.

"No, thank you," she said politely. "That will not be necessary. I am happy Barkley is reunited with someone he loves so much."

"I don't know about that." Valance felt miserable on her behalf. "He certainly seemed fond of you. He might not have wanted to return to his original owner."

"Oh no!" When she looked him in the face, he saw that her bleak expression contradicted the forced cheerfulness of her voice. "He was quite thrilled to meet her again. I never saw him so happy as when he was in her arms. I am sure he was glad to go back."

The dismay Valance had experienced when he first learned Cherie had been here was nothing compared to his horror at hearing Honora herself had seen Cherie. He'd been hoping that Weller had handled the situation discreetly. A good butler should know better than to allow his employer's cast-off mistress to meet the lady of the house!

"You met her, then?" The words nearly stuck in his throat.

"Yes. She seemed fond of the dog, so I saw no reason to stop her from taking him." The trembling of Honora's lower lip suggested she was close to tears.

"I am so very, very sorry," Valance repeated numbly.

He was no longer thinking of that blasted dog, though. His former mistress and his wife had met in Lady Valance's own home. He could imagine few domestic disasters worse than this. How could he possibly make things right?

CHAPTER TWENTY-FIVE

HONORA FELT RELIEVED when the conversation shifted away from Bishop Barkley's absence, and even more relieved when it was time to dress for dinner. Valance came in to speak to her, but because Clack was arranging her hair, he could say nothing personal, for which she was grateful. She had no idea what to say to him about Miss Barbauld's visit. On the whole, she had rather not speak of it at all. Better to let the nastiness she'd heard stay buried at the bottom of her mind.

After dinner, Valance settled into the leather armchair by the fire, stretched his legs out, and ostentatiously yawned.

"Oliver, you must be fatigued from travel," his mother said. "Perhaps you should retire early."

"Perhaps I should. I believe I *am* rather tired." When he caught Honora's eye, the corner of his mouth quirked up.

Honora could not mistake his meaning. He wanted her to follow him upstairs so they could go to bed together. She nodded her agreement. Even Valance's return had not entirely lifted her low spirits. But she had certainly missed him over the last week, and it would be good to spend time with him alone.

When she turned in for the night, she found Valance waiting in her room, a book in his hand.

"*Finally*," he said, as if he had waited long and hopeless centuries for her.

He caught her in his arms and kissed her. She kissed him

back, wondering why her heart still ached even when she was in his arms.

"Oh, I have missed you so much, Nora." His husky voice sent a pleasant shiver down her spine—and, for some reason, brought a lump to her throat.

"I missed you too." She leaned her head against his shoulder, hoping to find consolation.

He felt like a living wall: strong enough to support her, warm enough to comfort her, and solid enough to last forever. But even walls could crumble and fall. She was not the first woman who had leaned on Valance for protection, and she would probably not be the last. She closed her eyes, praying she did not break into tears.

Valance had begun pulling out her hairpins, but he paused halfway through. "Darling, are you all right? I am so very sorry about Bishop Barkley."

"It makes no difference." It did make a difference, but what could she say about it? "He belonged to Miss Barbauld in the first place, and if she wanted him back, there was nothing else to do but return him." She shrugged, hoping she sounded nonchalant rather than heartbroken.

Valance hugged her to his chest again. "I am sorry, too, that she had the effrontery to come here and confront you. You do not deserve such an insult."

"She felt she had been wronged." Honora had rather not talk about Miss Barbauld at all. But she did not particularly feel inclined for bedsport, either. Perhaps she ought simply to turn in for the night. She might wake up feeling more herself in the morning.

"Wronged?!" Valance stared at her in surprise. "How did I wrong her? I treated her most generously while she was in my protection, and I left her with adequate support when we parted. She will not go hungry." He shook his head. "I am shocked by her audacity."

Was that all that mattered? Was it adequate to merely ensure a former dependent did not starve? Even if the dependent in question had also been one's lover? Honora fidgeted with her wedding ring. A ring Miss Barbauld never had the chance to wear.

Suddenly, she needed to know something. "Valance," she said hesitantly, "Was it true Miss Barbauld was a respectable woman before she met you?"

"Respectable woman?" he repeated, still sounding appalled. "Of course not! She was an actress. Her whole family were on the stage, and she had been brought up to that life."

Honora cleared her throat and spoke more plainly. "But is it true you took her virtue?"

Valance refused to meet her gaze, which was answer enough. "I was her first lover, if that's what you mean. What of it? I know perfectly well that I will not be her last. She has probably already chosen a new protector by now."

His indignation sounded like sulkiness now. Honora swallowed heavily and clasped her hands together, not sure how to explain her reaction.

"I am very sorry if her words hurt you, but darling, Cherie has nothing to do with you." Valance caught her hand and rubbing his thumb soothingly across hers. "She was once my mistress, but you are my *wife*. I have nothing more to do with her. And there will be no other mistresses. So long as we live under one roof, I will keep faith with you."

So long as we live under one roof. But how long would that be? Honora closed her eyes, wishing she could shut her mind to the impermanent nature of their arrangement. But that was not the only thing bothering her, and maybe not the most important thing.

"If I had come from a family like hers," she whispered, "would I still be your wife? Or merely your next mistress?"

"What are you talking about? Your father was a baronet!" Valance dropped her hand and lifted her chin up, forcing her to look him in the eye. "How could you be on the stage?" His face wrinkled in concern. "I don't understand what you are getting at, Honora."

"I suppose what I mean," Honora explained, "is that you married me only because I am a gentleman's daughter. If I had been a girl of the lower orders, or even the middle classes, you would not have married me to protect my good name. You would at most have taken me as a lover. Wouldn't you?" She began fidgeting with her ring again.

His scowl made him resemble a grumpy bulldog more than ever. "Are you asking if I would have married an uneducated girl with neither manners nor connections to recommend her? Then you are right. I would not have done so. But what of that?"

Though this was what Honora expected, she felt sick at heart. "It seems to me you are worse than Belmont. He at least wanted to marry me, despite being so far above my station." Dukes generally married the daughters of other upper aristocrats, creating new alliances. They rarely married the daughters of mere baronets. That was why Honora's mother had been so thrilled when Belmont asked for permission to pay his addresses.

"*Worse than Belmont?*" Valance backed away from her, moving one step at a time toward the connecting door. "You think I am worse than a murderer and a rapist?" He shook his head in disbelief.

"No." Honora struggled to clear her tightening throat. "Of course not. I ought not have said that." She had no idea how to explain her disillusionment. "You are just, perhaps, a little too aware of your superiority. Or a little too snobbish in your treatment of those beneath you."

Her words did not have the desired effect.

"So, you think what, exactly?" He crossed his arms in front of his chest and glared at her. "Are you suggesting I did wrong to keep a mistress? That I am a scoundrel because I bedded an actress? Are you angry with me for doing as other men do?"

She cringed at the scorn in his voice. The lump in her throat made it hard to force her words out. "Not angry. Disappointed."

He had taken advantage of a woman far beneath him in fortune and station, only to cast her aside when he no longer wanted her. He had treated Miss Barbauld differently from Honora merely because she was not a lady. Because he thought she was beneath him. Honora could not approve of that.

"I am sorry to have disappointed you, my lady." He bit off each word.

Honora shivered at the coldness in her husband's voice. He had never spoken to her this way before. She wrapped her arms about herself.

He stared at the wall rather than looking her in the face. "I think I had better take myself out of your presence, lest I disappoint you further."

"I am sorry," Honora whispered, though she did not know what she was apologizing for. Valance stood still for a moment, so he must have heard her, but instead of responding, he walked into his room and shut the door.

Honora waited a few minutes to see if he changed his mind. When it became clear that he was not coming back, she got ready for bed. She did not ring for Clack, but undressed herself, brushed her teeth, and brushed her hair. She avoided looking at her face in the mirror. She suspected she would see red, puffy eyes and a shiny nose.

She snuffed out her candle and crawled into bed. Some tiny part of her still hoped Valance would come to her room and accept her apology. But he did not, and she slept alone.

IN THE MORNING, Valance spoke to her politely at breakfast. Naturally, they could not continue last night's conversation while his mother sat at the table. When Mrs. Valance left the room, Honora hoped to have a chance to smooth things over with Valance. She could see she had hurt him deeply. She ought not have said anything about Miss Barbauld. It was not Valance's fault Honora's illusions about his character had been shattered. After all, he had never pretended to be perfect.

But Valance did not give her a chance to apologize. Before his mother had finished her morning coffee, Valanced announced he had to meet a friend at the club. "I will be back by dinner time," he promised, steadily looking away from Honora.

When errands took Mrs. Valance out of the house, too, Honora was left alone in the morning room. She listlessly turned the pages of a book, wondering what to do with herself.

She stared unseeingly at the print for what might have been only a few minutes or an entire hour. Then Weller entered the room, bearing a calling card.

"A Lady Grantly to see you, my lady. Will you receive her, or shall I say that you are not at home?"

"Lady Grantly?" Honora took the card, though she did not need to read it. Her mother's cards had not changed in years. She cleared her voice, feeling suddenly nervous. "Ah, yes. You had better show her in."

If Honora's mother was here, the day was about to get worse.

CHAPTER TWENTY-SIX

VALANCE DID NOT, in fact, go to his club. He did not feel like sitting around chatting with his friends or reading the papers. He would much rather go shoot something, or kick something, or punch something. Should he go to Gentleman Jackson's? He had not dropped in there for a couple of weeks and would be out of shape, so he would be more likely to find himself on the receiving end of someone else's punch. Manton's, perhaps? But that would mean going home to get his pistols. He was not ready to go back home.

Instead, he simply strode up and down the streets of Mayfair, going nowhere in particular. He prayed he would not run into any of his friends. He did not want to make polite chit chat with anyone. He felt far too angry.

He was not sure who he was angrier with: Cherie or Honora. He was furious with Cherie for daring to visit Honora, and for whatever she'd said to blacken Valance's name. She ought to have known better than to behave like that. Didn't Cherie realize how gossip spread? If other men learned how volatile and unpredictable her behavior was, she might alienate possible protectors. No man wanted a mistress who caused strife at home.

But Valance was equally angry with Honora for believing Cherie. Maybe angrier. What right did Honora have to judge him for things he had done before he met her? She'd married him knowing perfectly well what kind of man he was.

Not that he was any worse than other men, of course. Better than many, in fact. He had dismissed his mistress right away once he determined to marry. Many men would have kept their mistresses despite their wedding vows.

And when had he ever treated Honora with anything but respect and affection? How could she possibly compare him to *Belmont,* of all people? He had rescued her from Belmont! She had been a total stranger to Valance, but he had gotten her away from the man she feared, protected her reputation as best he could, luxuriously provided for her, and lavished affection on her. Few men in his situation would have done as much.

What, then, did his wife expect from him? Was he supposed to go back in time to live his life over again as a monk? He scoffed at the very idea. Honora certainly seemed to appreciate his skill in bed. How, exactly, did she think he'd developed those skills?

And yet, as Valance argued his case against an imaginary opponent, some part of him knew all of this was beside the point. What had upset Honora was not the fact that Valance had bedded other women before her, but that he had seduced a virtuous girl.

He told himself that doing so did not make him a rake. Many actresses sought wealthy protectors who could support them. They enjoyed a much better style of living than they could hope to earn with acting alone. It was more like a system of patronage than prostitution, when all was said and done.

Besides, he had not been the only man interested in young Cherie Barbauld. If he had not pursued her, someone else would have taken her as a mistress. Very likely she would have ended up with some unpleasant older man seeking to amuse himself because of his wife's indifference. Or she might have taken a lover who could not support her as Valance could. Cherie had certainly enjoyed buying clothing, perfume, and sweets with his money. She had willingly entered into their arrangement. If she'd had any complaints about her treatment, she had not aired them to Valance.

However, there was one thing Valance could not argue with.

Honora was right that he would not have married the former Miss Grantly if she had been, say, the daughter of a laborer. Or even a grocer's daughter. He had proposed to Honora because a gentleman simply could not run away with a genteel young lady and then refuse to marry her. But if she had been anything else, if her father had not been a gentleman, Valance would not have felt obligated to offer for her. He might have helped her escape an unfortunate situation; he might have offered her temporary shelter; but he would not have extended to her the protection of his name.

But what was wrong with that? A man needed more from his wife than a partner in bed. He needed her help making social connections, hosting entertainments, managing the household, and rearing his children. Because Honora had been raised in a genteel household, she had the necessary manners, skills, and knowledge. A woman raised in a different environment would not.

Valance felt very consoled by all of this sound reasoning. As his anger cooled, he thought he might go to his club after all. He looked around to see where he was. He'd wandered far from Curzon Street, and it took a moment to get his bearings. But the sight of a confectioner's shop he'd sometimes visited with the Carringtons helped steer him in the right direction.

He remembered his first visit to that shop very well, because it occurred shortly after Susan had joined the house as Abigail's new companion. (This was before they had fallen in love, of course.) Susan had initially seemed to be a quiet little mouse of a girl, and the visit at the confectioner's was the first time Valance ever heard her say more than three words in a row.

Valance stopped in his tracks when he remembered what Susan had discussed as they lounged in the carriage eating ices. She had spoken very frankly about her mother's thespian family, including relatives who still worked in various theaters around London. And she had talked about how her father had come to marry an actress.

A quarter of a century ago, Estelle Landon had taken the stage by storm with her first speaking role. Wealthy men about town had showered her with gifts, compliments, and offers of comfortable establishments.

Mr. Taylor, a younger son starting his career as a barrister, could not compete with those offers. So instead of offering Miss Landon jewels or carriages, he had offered what none of the rich young lordlings were willing to give her: his hand in marriage. She had accepted him, and from Susan's account, they had lived happily, though perhaps not quite respectably, ever since. Mr. Taylor's legal career had probably suffered from the *mésalliance*, but he apparently had no regrets.

So, there were some gentlemen willing to marry beneath their station. Valance had to admit that. Estelle Landon had obviously been a superior woman, and young Mr. Taylor had had both the wisdom to recognize that and the courage to act on his realization. No doubt he should be commended. But that had nothing to do with Valance. No one in their right mind would have expected him to marry Cherie Barbauld rather than set her up as his mistress.

He shuddered at the very idea. Marry Cherie? As if he would ever have wanted to do so! Even at the height of Valance's infatuation, there had been nothing binding him to her but physical desire and doting fondness. At the end, he had hardly been able to stand her company for more than an hour at a time—and only for that long if they were doing something other than talking. Cherie seemed no fonder of Valance than he was of her. Witness the amount of time she spent with Thomas Sowerby!

A marriage required more than physical attraction to work. Little as Valance knew about matrimony, he knew that much. Infatuation did not last, and physical appearance changed over time. The happiest couples he knew were the ones who were bound together by friendship as well as attraction. Like Sir John and Lady Carrington, or like Valance's own grandparents, who had been able to make each other laugh even after decades of marriage. They had been so close that Grandmother had passed away one month after Grandfather's death.

Why couldn't Valance have had that kind of marriage, too? Not that he would want Honora to die of a broken heart. He would rather she live and be happy, even if it were without him. And yet, he had made her very unhappy, hadn't he? At breakfast, he'd noticed shadows under her eyes, as if she'd had a rough night.

Valance came to a halt and stood stock-still. Last night, Honora had tried to apologize to him, and he had not listened. He ought to have done her the courtesy of hearing her out. Honora had been hurt by her encounter with Cherie, and instead of listening to or comforting his wife, he had blamed her for daring to judge him. As if he were somehow beyond reproach!

The last of Valance's righteous indignation crumbled and fell to the ground. He sighed, knowing there would be no visit to the Cambion Club today, no Manton's, and no Gentleman Jackson's. He needed to go home to talk to his wife.

Valance looked around to get his bearings once again, and laughed ruefully. He stood on Curzon Street, a few dozen yards from his own home. By some serendipity, his feet had carried him here without his knowledge. Clearly, this was where he ought to be.

A heavy traveling coach stood in front of his house. He glanced at it, puzzled, as he climbed the steps to the front door. He did not recognize the coat of arms on the side. It might be difficult to speak to Honora if she were receiving callers. But morning calls did not last long. After this visitor left, he could tell Weller they were not at home to any additional callers. Then he and Honora could have the conversation they should have had last night.

Once inside the house, he heard angry voices coming from the morning room. He hurried down the corridor and thew open the door. Honora sat rigidly upright, her hands clenched into fists and her face as cold as marble. A book lay next to her on the striped cushion of the sofa, as if someone had interrupted her while reading. In fact, she still wore her reading glasses.

Across from her sat a slender woman whose fair hair was lightly touched with silver. People often described women of her age as displaying "the remains of great beauty." But Valance saw nothing beautiful about the angry expression on the stranger's face.

"I wish I had dragged you home and locked you in your bedroom before you could ruin the family name, you ungrateful child!" the woman spat. "How dare you defy your own mother this way! If you do not tell me where your sister is, I will have the law on you."

Valance clenched his hands into fists. "Excuse me." His words cracked into the room. Both women turned to face him. Honora got to her feet at once and came to stand by his side.

"Mother," she said politely, "May I present Lord Valance to you?"

Lady Grantly rose to her feet and curtseyed somewhat stiffly. Valance inclined his head in acknowledgment, though he would rather have tossed her out on her ear. He did not care who she was or how she was related to Honora. No one could be allowed to speak to his wife that way.

But this situation called for finesse, not forcefulness. He paused to take a few deep breaths before he spoke. "I am sorry to interrupt, ladies," he drawled. Honora's eyes flicked towards his face, as if surprised by the change in his tone. "I seem to have walked in at an inopportune time. I am, of course, very pleased to meet you, Lady Grantly. But I should make one thing clear: you must treat my wife with respect, or you will no longer be welcome here."

He watched Lady Grantly's expression change as she shifted her gaze back and forth between Valance and Honora. She now looked uneasy rather than angry.

She turned to her daughter and spoke in a much quieter

voice. "You will have to forgive my strong words, Honora. I spoke out of an excess of concern for your sister. Your father left her in my care, so I am naturally very worried about her. Can you at least tell me if you have seen Dora?"

"My man of law is currently investigating some questions regarding the late Sir Isaac's will." Valance used his most lofty voice and looked down his nose at Lady Grantly in a manner calculated to ruffle feathers.

Lady Grantly pursed her lips, but she held her tongue while Valance continued.

"I am afraid we cannot discuss Miss Rossini's situation at present, as the case may go to court." Valance had no idea whether they had a legal leg to stand on, but this all sounded very grand. "Is there anything else I can help you with before you go on your way, madam?"

Lady Grantly glanced at Honora and anxiously licked her lips. "Honora, you have no idea how much trouble you have caused for me." Her voice shook with some strong emotion.

"How?" Honora spoke fiercely, though her voice trembled. "You wanted me to marry well. I did so. You always said your greatest desire was for me to have a comfortable home. I have one. Why can't you be glad that I am happy?"

If she *was* happy. Valance could not help wondering about that, given last night's argument. He put an arm around Honora's waist and gently tugged her closer to him. She leaned a fraction of her weight against him, and some of his worry eased.

"Happy!" Her mother shook her head, and her frown lines deepened. "*You* may be happy, but what about your family? Don't you realize the Duke of Belmont holds the mortgage to Grantly Manor?"

Ah, the missing piece to the puzzle! Valance had wondered why Honora's mother was so desperate to marry her daughter off to Belmont, and why she seemed so angry about Honora escaping the unwanted marriage. But if Belmont held the Grantly family's debts, he must also hold considerable power over them.

"You ought to have told us that sooner." Valance infused as much rebuke as possible into his voice. "Naturally, I will buy the mortgage from him and make a present of it to you. I would have done so already if you had informed me earlier."

"Belmont will never sell to you!" Honora protested.

He tightened his hold around her waist, hoping to reassure her. "He will sell to me, given the right pressure." Valance spoke as confidently as he could, though he was internally panicking about how he could possibly force Belmont's hand. "I will have my man of business see to the matter at once. Good day, Lady Grantly. It was a pleasure to meet you."

Lady Grantly bit her lip, as if she did not know how to respond. Then she bowed her head, accepting his dismissal. "Good day, my lord. It was a pleasure to meet you as well. You must forgive me for berating my daughter. I have only her happiness in mind."

Bullshit, Valance thought. She had the main chance in mind. But he did not let his smile falter until the woman left the room. Then Honora turned to face him fully. He held his arms out and she collapsed against him.

Valance held her tightly for a moment before speaking. "If you wish, I will tell Weller never to admit Lady Grantly again."

"I don't know." Honora spoke into his shoulder, muffling her voice. "She is still my mother. Your mother annoys you, but you don't send *her* away."

"My mother has never tried to arrange a marriage between me and a murderer for financial gain!" At least, he didn't think any of the young ladies Mother had introduced to him had been murderers. But how would he know? No doubt many murders went undetected.

A new idea presented itself to Valance. It might be too late to act on it. But it might not. He would have to do some investigation in areas far outside his wheelhouse, but Mr. Watson might be able to help him get started. For now, though, there were other things he and his wife ought to talk about.

CHAPTER TWENTY-SEVEN

HONORA FELT SAFE and loved in her husband's arms. She would have been happy to rest there forever. But she could not do that. There were so many things she needed to say. She decided to start with the easiest one.

She stepped out of his embrace so she could see his face as she spoke. "Valance, generous as you are, you can't *really* buy the mortgage from Belmont. He will not sell it."

Even if Belmont would sell, she did not think it right for her husband to spend so much money on her family. He would have to sell out of the Funds, wouldn't he? Or sell one of his smaller properties? She had no idea how much money the Grantly family owed on the mortgage, but she doubted Valance kept so much capital sitting around.

"I had rather not discuss that right now, if you please," he grumbled. "I have other things to say."

"Yes?"

He sheepishly stared down at the toes of his boots. "You were right that I married you only because you were a gentleman's daughter. You would not be Lady Valance now if you had been born any lower. There are some men wise enough to recognize worth wherever they find it, but I would not have been one of them." He sighed, then looked her in the eyes as he concluded: "I would have missed having the most beautiful woman in England as my wife merely because of my prejudices."

Honora stepped forward and leaned against him again, thinking he had said enough. Valance wrapped his arms around her tightly and dropped a kiss on the top of her head.

But he was not done speaking. "You were also right that I treated Cherie—Miss Barbauld, I mean—differently than you because she was an actress rather than the daughter of a gentleman. If any man had seduced you, I would have thought him the worst of rakes. But when I seduced Miss Barbauld, I thought I was behaving like an honorable *gentleman* because I amply provided for her." He spat out the word "gentleman." "I suppose that makes me an arrogant ass, doesn't it?"

"Typical English aristocrat," Honora agreed. But she said it without rancor. He might not be better than others of his rank, but he was not worse. "You ought to do better in the future."

"I will try." He squeezed her more tightly.

"But Valance," she whispered. "You are *not* worse than Belmont. I ought not have said that." He had done nothing to deserve such an insult.

"I ought to have listened to your apology last night," he told her. "I know very well that I am not as good a husband as I ought to be. I will try to do better on that front, too."

He tipped her chin up and kissed her forehead, then her eyelids, and finally her mouth. Each kiss was like a drop of sweetness counteracting the bitterness of last night's quarrel. She kissed him back on his chin, his cheek, and his mouth, feeling as if a little more warmth seeped into her bones with each touch.

"Better now?" he asked.

"Better." But it was only partly true. All the lingering sourness of their argument had been washed away, but her heart still ached over some of the things Miss Barbauld had said.

She did not fool Valance. He frowned. "Something still troubles you?"

Honora leaned her head against his shoulder. "I hope you don't tire of me in a couple of years." Probably he would, though. People did not typically stay in love long, did they?

"What?" The incredulity in his voice comforted her a little. "Why would you think that?"

She could not admit that Miss Barbauld had suggested it; she did not want to bring Valance's former mistress back into the conversation. She struggled to articulate her concern in other terms.

"When you proposed to me, you said we would go our separate ways after you had an heir. You know. Keep separate households. Take lovers." Stop living like a married couple, in short. "It will probably not take us long to conceive a child, will it? And if it is a boy, there will be no need for us to keep living together." Her voice wavered over the last words.

Valance tightened his arms around her. "Bullshit. I will always need you. And if we have children, they will need both of us."

"But you said—"

He interrupted her. "I know that when I proposed, I suggested a temporary arrangement. But I only said that because I didn't want you to feel trapped. You had just run away from one unwanted marriage. I didn't want you to feel you were bound to me forever merely because I compromised you."

"Oh." Honora was too busy absorbing that idea to say anything more. But the ache in her heart slowly died. A warm, sweet spark began to glow in its place.

"And," he added, "I believe I was a fool to say that, anyway. As I recall, we vowed before God to love, honor, and comfort each other as long as we both should live. I don't remember any loopholes in the marriage service."

Honora smiled. "You are not a fool. It was kind of you to offer me my freedom. But I thought you did so because *you* did not want to stay with me." He had no more wanted to marry her than she had wanted to marry him, after all.

He nuzzled her hair. "I *do* want to stay with you. I want this to be a real marriage, no matter how it started. I don't intend to run away if things get hard." His voice dropped to a low rumble as he added, "And I certainly hope you feel the same way."

"Yes," Honora whispered into his shoulder. She was not even sure he would hear. But he must have heard, because he picked her up, carried her to the sofa, and proceeded to kiss her thoroughly.

Most unfortunately, Valance's mother chose this precise moment to walk into the morning room. "Really, Oliver!" she said, sounding scandalized. "There are proper times and places for that, you know."

"This is my house!" Valance protested. "And I reserve the right to kiss my wife in any room in the house, at any time of day. If you dislike that, you are welcome to return to Surrey. Really, Mother, what did you *expect* to see when you moved in with a newly married couple?"

Honora bit her lower lip, trying to hold in an unexpected bubble of laughter. She knew better than to laugh at her mother-in-law, but her shoulders shook with the effort of restraining herself.

"There is no need to be rude!" Mrs. Valance stalked out of the room, letting the door slam shut behind her.

Once she heard the footsteps walking away, Honora released her laughter. She laughed, in fact, in rather undignified hoops. After a moment, Valance chuckled too, though he did not lose control the way she did.

"It is not really funny," Honora admitted once she had finally gotten herself under control. "But it has already been a long day." Perhaps her tiredness made her giggly.

"It certainly has. You must need an afternoon nap, after so tense a confrontation."

"That might be a good idea." Honora did not normally take naps, but last night's troubled sleep seemed to be catching up to her.

"I probably ought to join you in bed. I am sure you will sleep better with me by your side." Valance gently bit her ear, making his meaning clear.

Honora's heart pounded. "I think I am extremely unlikely to fall asleep if you are in bed with me, but you are welcome to join me." Her voice dropped to a whisper as she added, "I have missed you."

"I intend to make up for lost time," Valance said.

And he did. They were both hungry for each other, and their first coupling was hard, fast, and desperate. Afterwards, they did indeed nap. In fact, they slept so long that Honora's maid came to remind her that it was time to dress for dinner. Never had Honora been so grateful for the curtains on her bed, which provided a modicum of privacy.

"We are not dining downstairs tonight," Valance announced. "Please ask the cook to send up a tray with sandwiches and fruit. And inform Mrs. Valance that she will be dining alone tonight."

"Don't forget the wine," Honora suggested. "A sweet white wine, perhaps?"

If Clack considered this an unorthodox request, she refrained from commenting. The cook went above and beyond, sending up a tray with a cold meat pie, sandwiches, pickles, grapes, fresh strawberries, and two kinds of wine.

Where, Honora wondered, had the cook even gotten strawberries from this season? They must have come from a hothouse somewhere, and they were probably frightfully expensive. She did not ask any questions, though. She simply enjoyed the picnic dinner. After Valance's week-long absence, it was most pleasant to lounge in bed and chat with him while they ate.

He told her more about his visit to the Abbey. "Lady Carrington wishes to meet you. Would you mind if we spent part of the summer in Surrey? Hopefully by then we could have Dora with us, too."

"I would not mind." She would be very happy to see her sister again. She and Dora were closer in age to each other than Honora was to any of her full siblings. They had always been fast friends. "I would like to see Dreadnaught Hall. And you must have work to do there."

"Yes, I have been rather neglecting the estate since I came of age. I ought to do better." He stroked her cheek with an idle finger. "I suppose it is time enough for me to play the role of responsible landlord."

"And politician?" she suggested hopefully.

Valance rarely bothered to attend Parliamentary meetings, despite spending most of the year in London. Honora believed he ought to use his political power as a peer for the betterment of the country, rather than sparring at Gentleman Jackson's or shooting at Manton's all day.

Valance rolled his eyes. "Don't remind me! My mother already nags me about my responsibilities. I don't need to hear it from you, too." But the kiss he gave her suggested he did not bear her any grudges.

Honora caught his lower lip in hers, teasing it. He turned on his side and pulled her closer.

"Did I mention that I missed you?" he murmured.

"Yes, several times." Amusement rippled in her voice. By now, he'd made it abundantly clear how glad he was to be reunited with her.

"Let me tell you without words." He tugged on the tie of her dressing gown.

"I like that idea." He was not the only one happy about his return.

Fortunately, she wore nothing beneath her dressing gown. Once Valance untied it, she wriggled free and pressed her body against his, savoring the closeness. For the longest time, they simply lay like that, kissing and touching. Then he cupped her derriere with one hand and pulled her more snuggly against him. Guessing what he wanted, she hooked her leg over his hip and shifted position so he could guide his length into her.

Valance took his time, pausing frequently to kiss her or to murmur affectionate or bawdy words in her ear. This lazy, laidback loving could not have contrasted more greatly with their earlier passionate coupling, but Honora decided she preferred this—particularly when he slipped his hand down to stroke the most sensitive part of her body. His teasing touch brought her across the brink to a long, powerful climax that left her limp in his arms.

"That was *good*," she murmured after she caught her breath. "How does this keep getting better and better?"

"It's because you happened to seduce and marry an extremely talented lover," Valance said smugly. "I assume that was the real reason you chose me at that masquerade. You must have instinctively discerned how good I am at—"

"Oh, hush," she interrupted. "You are not the only one with talent!" She set out to prove that. She pushed Valance onto his back so she could sit astride him. Then she rode him to his satisfaction. He spent himself with a deep groan, and then it was her turn to smile smugly.

"Hmm, yes, I suppose you do have some considerable ability yourself," he admitted afterwards. "I would give you top marks for that."

Honora giggled as she settled by his side. "You told me you would not grade me on my performance in bed."

"Oh, but that was only the first time. That was a practice run, as it were. But now you know what you are doing, I think it only fair for me to evaluate you, so you can improve your perfor-mance."

"Only if you want me to start evaluating *you*. And since you've set the standard so high, I will be a harsh grader." She smirked at him.

Valance wrinkled his nose. "On second thought, perhaps we should award gold stars all around and leave it at that."

"Yes, let's do that." Honora smiled at his nonsense. Then she pulled the blanket tightly around her and closed her eyes.

But Valance's words must have stuck with her, because her dreams that night were a confusing mixture of shooting stars, mathematics examinations, nursery wallpaper, and (for some reason) Mozart's 'Twelve Variations on '*Ah! vous dirai-je, maman*.'"

She awoke in the morning with the sense that she'd realized something important just before falling asleep, but she could not remember what. Maybe it would come back to her later.

Chapter Twenty-Eight

March, 1817

RATHER TO VALANCE'S surprise, his mother took seriously his suggestion that she leave the newlyweds to themselves. Shortly after his return to London, she announced that she'd had her fill of the Season. She wanted to return to Dreadnaught Hall.

"Someone ought to keep an eye on things in Surrey," she explained. "We really ought not neglect the estate."

Valance made all the appropriate responses, assuring her of her welcome whenever she chose to come back to Curzon Street. Secretly, he was relieved that he and Honora would finally have the house to themselves. Perhaps they were no longer technically in their honeymoon, but he nevertheless very much enjoyed being a newlywed.

Things kept getting better and better between them in bed. Valance could not imagine wanting to keep a mistress again. How other men could prefer to dally with the muslin company rather than devoting their attention to their wives baffled him. But perhaps, he thought tolerantly, they did not have wives like Honora. Few men could be so lucky.

Because he cared about his wife, Valance did not forget his scheme for gaining leverage over Belmont. He summoned his solicitor to discuss the possibility of investigating the death of Belmont's most recent duchess. She had died a year and a half ago, so it might be too late to uncover new information about her death, but every avenue was worth investigating.

Even so, it took nearly four weeks for the Bow Street Runner

Mr. Watson had hired to track down the duchess's former lady's maid. When he found her, the investigator reported that she would not or could not speak to him about the late duchess's final illness.

Could not, Valance mused. There were spells that could prevent a person from revealing information. Such magic was illegal, and there were few magicians powerful enough to make such a spell last for more than a few days. But though compulsion spells were illegal, there were undoubtedly some magicians willing to work them for the right price. The Duke of Belmont could afford the services of the best magicians. The possibility of magic interference could not be ruled out.

Valance decided the best course of action was to visit the lady's maid himself, to see if he could succeed where the investigator had failed. True, he had not been trained in detection, and he knew little about criminal law. On the other hand, he was a skilled magician, unlike the average Bow Street Runner.

Mademoiselle DeRose currently served a lady who lived in Bath, so interviewing her would take Valance out of town for several days. Valance did not like leaving Honora alone for so long again, but this investigation might be important.

When he proposed the plan to Honora, she raised an objection he had not anticipated.

"Can't I go with you? I like Bath, and I have not been there for years."

She lay beside him in bed, an open book still in hand. She wore her spectacles, which always incited conflicting desires in Valance. On the one hand, he thought she looked adorable wearing them; on the other hand, he wanted to take them off so he could thoroughly kiss her face.

"I would feel safer if you stayed home." He did not want to draw unnecessary attention to Honora. It would look odd for him to leave town abruptly after committing to a dinner party and a ball this week. The journey might seem even stranger if both of them left. Honora could more easily excuse his absence if he left her behind. She could simply say he'd been called away on business.

"No one is likely to hurt me." She smiled. "You are worrying about nothing."

"I do not worry about nothing, I worry about *you*," Valance explained.

He kissed her lightly on the mouth, and she put a hand on his head to keep him there so she could kiss him back, not quite so lightly. He removed her glasses and placed them carefully on the bedside table so they would not get smudged. After that, they grew further distracted and did not return to the subject of conversation until the next day.

Ultimately, Honora agreed it made more sense for her to stay behind and deliver his apologies to the few social events they had accepted. Thus, Valance set off on his own, for once leaving even his valet behind.

He arrived in Bath late on the second day of travel, but the hour prevented him from calling on Mademoiselle DeRose until the next day. Valance met with her in the private coffee room of his hotel, thinking it might be better not to attract attention at her place of employment.

Mademoiselle DeRose was a plump, middle-aged woman who, unlike Cherie, seemed to have actually lived in France at some point. And the investigator Mr. Watson had hired was right: she could not say anything about the death of her previous mistress. She happily described the duchess' character as an employer, and her taste in clothing and jewelry, but when Valance asked about her final illness, all she said was "I cannot say, sir."

"Mademoiselle," Valance said at last, "Do you know there are powerful mind control spells that can prevent a person from talking about a given subject?"

"I cannot say, sir." Her voice remained flat, but he thought he saw a flicker of reaction in her eyes.

"But there are release spells—general cancellation spells—that can undo such magic," he continued. "It might take powerful magic, but a good sorcerer or wizard could break even a strong compulsion spell. Did you know that?"

"I cannot say, sir." But she leaned forward, pleading in her eyes.

Valance reached into his waistcoat pocket and drew out a piece of notepaper he had folded into thirds and sealed with wax. From the outside, it looked like a letter. But if it were opened, one would find three of Valance's runes, including the one he'd recently developed. The cancellation rune might have been effective on its own, but combined with the two supporting marks, it became one of Valance's most powerful spells.

"This envelope contains a cancellation spell," Valance told the maid. "I poured as much of my power into it as I could—and, mademoiselle, I am generally considered a strong magician. If I hand this paper to you and activate the spell, it should break any spells or enchantments currently affecting you. All you have to do is hold the paper while I activate the spell. Do you want to try that?"

"I cannot say, sir." But she extended a trembling hand, and he took that as acquiescence.

Valance placed the folded paper on top of her open palm and tapped it, pouring a final spark of power into the spell. The effect was immediate: Mademoiselle DeRose coughed and gasped, struggling to draw breath. Then she began to weep.

Oh God, no! Not tears! He had not come prepared for a crying female. He patted his waistcoat pockets hurriedly, hunting for his handkerchief. By the time he found it, she had gotten herself under control. She used the handkerchief to wipe away the remains of the tears.

"Thank you, my lord," she said between sniffles. "I did not

understand why I could not say anything about the duchess's death. I did not realize someone had cast a spell on me. I did not know such spells were possible!" She shivered.

"So, you don't know who did it?" Valance guessed. If he could discover which magician Belmont had hired, the perpetrator might be arrested. And he or she might be willing to make a deal.

She shook her head. "I have no idea. But I know who must have ordered it. His Grace would not want me telling what I know about the poor duchess's death."

Valance drew a notebook and a pencil out of his pocket, then leaned forward. "What *do* you know about the third duchess's death? Did she die of natural causes, or not?"

"She died of natural causes, yes." But the maid frowned and nervously played with the handkerchief. "She had a lung complaint."

"Consumption?" Valance suggested. That was difficult to treat even with magical medicines. Without magic, it was fatal.

She shrugged. "As to that, I cannot say. I am no doctor. It killed her quickly, though. I always thought consumption was a slow death. This disease progressed rapidly."

"So, there was no sign of foul play?" Valance pressed. That made no sense. There had to be a reason why someone was willing to go to so much trouble to silence the maid.

"No deliberate murder, I suppose." She hesitated, frowning. "That is, I do not believe Belmont poisoned her, or cursed her, or otherwise directly caused her illness. But . . . there was neglect. Much neglect."

"Tell me about that," Valance urged.

"Her Grace coughed for weeks. *Weeks!*" Mademoiselle DeRose said indignantly. "But the duke would not send for a physician. He forbade anyone in the house to send for a physician." Her mouth tightened into a grim line.

"He did not treat her illness, then?" Valance pondered that information. Could failure to seek medical treatment constitute a legally culpable degree of neglect? He had no idea. There was probably no law that required a husband to order a physician every time his wife fell ill. After all, many people could not afford the services of a physician.

"He ordered a cough syrup from the apothecary." She grimaced and waved a dismissive hand. "The sort of cheap thing you might get for a trifling cold. A hedgewitch could have brewed better! It did not help much. But he did not call in a doctor until a week before she died. When the doctor came, he was very upset about the delay in treatment. *Very* upset." She nodded her head emphatically.

Caught up in her story, Mademoiselle DeRose needed no urging to continue. "The doctor said it would be hard to treat Her Grace, since the illness was so advanced. Her lungs were badly damaged, I suppose. Still, he prescribed a magical potion. And it seemed to help!"

"Indeed?" Valance's hand raced to jot down notes. His writing, sloppier than usual, was barely legible even to him, but he wanted to capture the interview word-for-word. He was not sure where this story was going, but it sounded important.

"But then," the maid continued, "the medicine the physician prescribed disappeared."

"Disappeared?" Valance repeated, confused. How could it disappear?

"I acted as her nurse, you understand. Because the duke, despite his wealth, would not hire a professional sickroom nurse." She snorted at that. "I gave her the medicine every four hours, as the physician ordered. But one night I got up to give the middle-of-the-night dose, and the potion was gone. We searched everywhere, but could not find it. And two days later, she died. The duke never sent for the physician again. Nor did he replace the missing medicine."

"Hmm." Valance had hoped to find more convicting evidence. A person could die of respiratory problems even with the best magical treatments, and the missing potion might not have saved her life anyway. "You think the duke deliberately took the medicine away to prevent her from recovering?"

"Yes," the maid said bluntly. "He wanted to be rid of her. He did not want to be cuckolded."

"What? What do you mean?" Valance asked sharply. "Was she unfaithful to him?" He had never heard so much as a hint about possible infidelity. The way gossip spread in the *ton*, he *ought* to have heard the rumor if there was any substance to it.

But Mademoiselle DeRose nodded. "She fell pregnant for the first time that autumn. It could not have been the duke's child, because he was in Scotland for over a month before she missed her courses. He was hosting a shooting party. He did not bring his wife to such entertainments, you understand. They would not have been suitable for a lady."

"Ah." In other words, men brought their mistresses to the shooting parties, or the host offered bawdy entertainments. Valance knew plenty of men who hosted such parties, but he had not known Belmont was one of them. Really, the more he learned about Belmont, the nastier the man seemed.

"Who was the child's father, then?" If the duchess had a lover, that complicated things. There might have been more than one man with motive to kill her.

Mademoiselle DeRose bit her lip and glanced away. "Her grace did not confide in me about her *affaires*. I have guesses, but I might be wrong. As they are only guesses, I had rather not say. The man I suspect is a good man who does not deserve to have his name dragged into a sordid story. I think, myself, that if he became Her Grace's lover, it would have been out of pity. The duke was not kind to her. Everyone knew that."

Valance bit back a bitter laugh. "Not kind" seemed like an understatement for the ages, given what he'd just heard. "So, the duke had motive to kill her," he mused aloud.

He had wondered about that. No one had ever posited a reason why Belmont would have wanted his third wife to die. Indeed, given that he had no son to inherit his title and estate, he needed a young wife to bear his children.

When people discussed whether the duke had allowed his wife to die by neglect, they shrugged their shoulders and said he was a cold, hard, cruel man. All of which was undoubtedly true—but Valance thought Mademoiselle DeRose's story explained more than it didn't.

"Oh, he had motive." Mademoiselle DeRose's voice sounded hard as granite. "He could have divorced her, of course, to keep her child from inheriting. But perhaps he thought it was easier to let her die of her lung complaint. It would certainly be cheaper than a divorce."

"Perhaps." Knowing how vindictive the duke was, Valance wondered if vengeance played a role, too. Even a duke could not necessarily get away with murder, so divorcing the duchess would have been a safer option. But a man who would punish a girl who rejected him by targeting her beloved half-sister must have a vengeful streak a mile wide.

"Is there anything else I should know?" Valance asked.

She scowled fiercely. "I hope he pays for it. I was Her Grace's maid before she married him, you know. There was a time when she was a bright, cheerful, lively young woman. He broke her, and when she betrayed him, he let her die so he could marry someone else."

"I cannot promise that he will pay," Valance warned her, "but we will do our best." He thought of something else as he closed his notebook. "Would you be willing to testify to all of this in front of the local magistrate?" He ought, perhaps, have had a magistrate interview her in the first place.

She twisted the handkerchief into knots. "If His Grace finds out I have been talking . . ."

"Yes, you might be in danger." Valance tapped his fingers on the cover of his notebook as he thought. Given Belmont's past behavior, it was not unreasonable for Mademoiselle DeRose to fear his wrath. "Maybe we should hide you somewhere."

He rubbed his face, suddenly feeling exhausted. He had

hoped to head home today, rather than lingering in Bath. He did not like being apart from Honora. But it would not be right to leave Mademoiselle DeRose in any danger. If the duke found out the compulsion spell had been broken, he might use more violent means to silence the maid.

"I do not like to leave a good position, but it would be very easy for the duke to find me if he learns I have talked." Her eyes widened with fear.

Valance sighed. "We will find a safe place for you. I promise to find new employment for you when this is over, too. Will you speak to the magistrate?"

She hesitated but ultimately nodded. "It is not right for men like Belmont to get away with such things. I will help you, for Her Grace's sake."

Valance silently hoped her testimony would be enough.

THE MAGISTRATE WHO took Mademoiselle DeRose's statement seemed to believe her, but he was not very sanguine about the outcome. "It would be difficult to prove criminal intent over a missing bottle of medication." He warned Valance.

On top of that, prosecuting a duke for a crime was an enormous undertaking. A nobleman could only be judged by his peers, meaning the House of Lords. Valance very much doubted Mademoiselle DeRose's story would be enough to convict Belmont. It might not even be enough to bring him to trial.

But if nothing else, Valance hoped to use this information to put pressure on Belmont. He was determined to make good on his promise to Honora and her family. He must protect them, and he must recover the mortgage to Grantly Manor—if he could.

Finding a safe house for the witness was more challenging than collecting her statement. Valance considered and dismissed several possibilities. In the end, he bethought himself of his mother's younger sister, who lived near Bristol. They headed there the next day.

Mrs. Barrett proved perfectly willing to house Mademoiselle DeRose. She ought to be safe enough with them. The Barretts only circulated with country gentry; they never came to London. It was extremely unlikely that anyone who knew the duke would ever learn they had added a new French maid to their household.

Since the eldest Miss Barrett was making her debut that spring, no one would think anything odd about a new lady's maid in the household. Indeed, judging from how pleased the Barretts seemed with the prospect of a genuine French lady's maid for their debutante, Valance thought it was possible that they would retain Mademoiselle DeRose even after the need for secrecy ended.

With his witness safely secured, Valance headed back to London. He had been gone for only a few days, but that seemed far too long. Some anxious part of him worried that something might yet interfere with their new-found happiness. Surely life was not meant to be so sweet? Not forever, at least.

He hoped that was nothing but superstition.

CHAPTER TWENTY-NINE

HONORA DID NOT enjoy attending balls or parties without Valance, but she had promised to make an exception for the ball that the Earl of Markham hosted at Sherborne Place. Markham, she knew, was one of Valance's particular friends. Valance had expressed the hope that Honora might get to know Lady Markham a little better while the couple was in town for the Season.

The Crosslys picked Honora up to take her to Grosvenor Square in their carriage. She was glad of their company, because Sherborne Place turned out to be the largest and most opulent London townhouse she had yet seen. It must have been three times the size of the house she and Valance leased. Everything from the marble floor to the glittering chandeliers gleamed with wealth.

Sherborne Place contained two reception rooms on the first story that could be combined into one. When the dividing wall folded away, a space the size of a ballroom opened up. Lord and Lady Markham stood at the entrance, greeting their guests. Captain Crossly, who knew Markham from the Cambion Club, introduced Honora.

Honora had known that the countess was a witch, so she was not surprised that Lady Markham's aura glittered with magic, but she was startled to see the golden gleams in Lord Markham's aura, indicating that he possessed some form of magecraft.

Valance had never mentioned that his friend was a mage, but she supposed it made sense. Most of the members of the Cambion Club possessed magical gifts.

But that was not the biggest surprise. Thanks to Jane Crossly's gossip, Honora knew Lord Markham had been a notorious rake before his marriage. Honora had naively expected to meet a dashing and perhaps sinister-looking man.

Instead, Lord Markham stood only middling high and had a snub nose. His bronze hair was the only remarkable aspect of his appearance, and even that owed more to his stylish coiffure than anything else. His smile looked friendly, but far from being an exemplar of manly good looks, he was much less attractive than Valance. Honora could not help wondering what had persuaded married women to let him into their beds. But she supposed she would never have the opportunity to ask such a question, more's the pity.

Though Honora's party arrived on time, guests already packed the room. Most of them were strangers to her. Even with the Crosslys for company, Honora felt a little lost as she surveyed the ballroom. The guests glittered with silks, satins, and jewels. Her blue and white ballgown, which she had thought very stylish, looked almost drab in contrast to some of the rich colors older women sported.

Jane introduced Honora to potential dance partners, but after only a couple of country dances, she twisted her ankle. Then she was relieved to find an empty chair near the wall. Her dance partner brought her a drink, and would have stayed with her to chat, but she could see from the way he watched the dancers that he longed to join the next set. She dismissed him with thanks, assuring him she would do very well on the sidelines.

"I am an old married lady, you know," she joked. "I will find enjoyment enough watching the dancing."

And this would have been the case, if not for the stranger who kept watching her. Honora had first noticed this mysterious gentleman while dancing. The watcher was of medium height and slender build, with brown hair. She thought she knew him from somewhere, but she did not recognize his face. Honora assumed she had met him at some previous social event and had simply forgotten his name. That happened rather frequently since coming to London. She had met so many new people, matching names and titles to faces and figures was a challenge.

But she could not understand why the stranger, whoever he was, kept watching her. It was not her imagination: the stranger really did keep staring in her direction. When Jane dropped by to chat for a moment, Honora asked if she knew the watcher, gesturing toward him with a jerk of her head so as to avoid rudely pointing.

Jane peered across the ballroom, squinting. Then she shook her head. "I don't think I've ever seen him before. But there are plenty of people here whom I don't know."

"I wonder why he keeps looking at me," Honora mused. Though, at the moment, the stranger seemed completely entranced by the punch bowl. She hoped that meant that he'd lost interest in her.

"Maybe he admires you?" Jane grinned mischievously. "You do look very well tonight. Or he might be fascinated by your jewels. It is not often you see someone with a full parure of aquamarines."

Honora remained unconvinced. Something about the pattern of colors in his aura disturbed her. He did not appear to be a magician, but Honora thought she could see a shimmer of magic about the unknown man, as if someone had cast a spell on him.

That hint of magic was not the strangest thing about the unknown gentleman. The most maddening thing was that Honora felt she knew this person, though she could not remember having seen his face. She knew this man and disliked him. It could be an irrational, random disliking, but Honora had never experienced something like that before.

Or had she? That was how she felt the first time she met the Duke of Belmont. Something about his aura had immediately repulsed her, though she had not understood why. She had, after all, never been properly instructed in reading auras. She could tell whether a person had magical abilities, and if so, what kind. But she had never learned to read people's emotions or signs of health the way some mages could. If something was wrong with this stranger's aura, she could not identify the problem.

Honora did her best to ignore the stranger. She tried dancing in the next set, but her aching ankle made dancing a misery. Not only was it painful, but she stumbled and tore the hem of her skirt. She left the ballroom, shame-faced at having been so clumsy in public. It could happen to anyone, she reminded herself as she retired to mend the damage.

Fortunately, the retiring room had everything she needed to repair the hem, and a maid stationed there to assist ladies in need. When the assistant was called away, though, Honora was left to finish her mending alone. A few minutes later, the squeak of a door hinge made her look up. To her consternation, the watchful stranger entered the room, looking very much out of place.

Honora sprang to her feet. "This is the lady's retiring room, sir. You ought not be here." Her heart pounded and the hairs on the back of her neck rose.

"I beg your pardon! I am only looking for my wife's fan," the gentleman explained. "She thinks she left it here."

Honora stared blankly at him. His explanation made no sense. If his wife left a fan here, shouldn't the wife herself be the one to retrieve it? Although she did not recognize the stranger's voice, she still felt certain she knew him. And she feared him.

"Madam?" The gentleman lifted his brows, giving her a quizzical stare. "Are you quite well?" He took a step towards Honora.

"Just a faintness," Honora babbled. "It happens sometimes. Very likely I got overheated from dancing."

She edged away from him, moving back and to the side. This close, she could better see the spell affecting the man. It looked familiar, too. She might not have seen this precise spell, but she had seen something very like it before.

Where had she seen magic like this? She frantically searched her memory. It took her entirely too long to identify the spell. By the time Honora remembered, the gentleman stood right in front of her, within arm's reach.

The spell looked familiar because it was similar to the disguise spell Valance had worked on Twelfth Night.

This stranger must be under a disguise.

A shiver of apprehension swept over her. "I had better go find my party," she said brightly.

She cast her eyes about for something to use as a weapon—just in case. Yes, there was a heavy brass candlestick on the end table next to the sofa. She slipped one hand behind her back so she could grab it quickly—though surely that would not be necessary! No one would attack her at an event like this. She was only nervous because Valance was away from home.

"Wait, if you please." Before Honora could step away, the stranger grabbed her wrist. "I wish to ask you a question, if I may."

"I am afraid I cannot stay. Please release me, sir." Honora spoke as firmly as she could, given the panic that gripped her.

But the stranger did not let go of Honora's wrist. Instead, he tightened his hold. He had a surprisingly strong grip for such a slender-looking man.

"You are hurting me!" She reached behind her and closed her free hand on the candlestick.

The stranger leaned closer. "You've led me a merry chase, my girl, but you cannot avoid me forever. We need to talk."

Belmont. Honora froze—save for her heart, which beat like a drum. This had to be Belmont in disguise. No one else would speak to her this way. No wonder she'd felt repulsed by the stranger's aura! Belmont was unquestionably the most repulsive man she knew. She must have magically recognized the duke's aura without realizing it.

She tightened her grip on the candlestick and steeled herself for action.

"I do not like to be bested by anyone," Belmont continued. "And particularly not by a girl straight out of the schoolroom."

To see Belmont's sneering expression imposed on someone else's face was disorienting, to say the least. Perhaps that was why Honora's stomach roiled.

"Let me go!" She struggled to escape his iron grip, but the pressure of Belmont's hand on her wrist did not ease up.

"I only want to talk to you," he insisted. "Surely you owe me a chance to explain myself?"

"I don't owe you anything!" Honora snapped.

Belmont stepped closer to her. This was her chance. She hefted the candlestick as high as she could and brought it crashing down on Belmont's head.

At least, she meant to do that. But she forgot that the figure her eyes perceived was an illusion. The real Belmont was taller than the illusionary "stranger" who stood before her. Consequently, she missed the top of his head and smashed him somewhere in the face. Possibly in the vicinity of his chin, though she could not be sure.

But it worked. Belmont let go of her wrist and staggered back. Honora smacked him again with the candlestick, then ran as fast as her twisted ankle allowed. She was in luck: she crashed into Lord Markham himself outside the retiring room.

"Lady Valance?" The earl sounded considerably startled.

"Someone attacked me." Honora pointed at the retiring room.

Lord Markham's jaw dropped, but he collected himself quickly. "Are you injured? Do you need a physician?"

"You have to capture Belmont!" Honora insisted. "Before he gets away."

"Belmont?" His eyes widened. "What would *he* be doing here? I don't invite the Duke of Belmont to my parties!"

Very wise of him, Honora thought, but not particularly helpful. "He's been glamoured to look like someone else—a gentleman in a blue coat. But I am sure it is Belmont. I recognized him." She stopped, not knowing how to explain the way she identified the disguised duke. It would take too long to describe her ability to read auras. "We need to capture him."

She rubbed her still-aching wrist. Even a duke could not assault a woman at a private ball and expect to get away with it. Could he?

"Of course, we will stop him," Lord Markham assured her. He stormed into the room. Then he cursed.

Honora stayed in the hallway, nursing her injured wrist. What was going on in there? She would like to have seen with her own eyes, but she could not bring herself to return to the retiring room.

Lord Markham stomped into the hallway, glowering darkly. "He got out through the window. Climbed down the lattice like a common criminal! I will send one of the footmen after him. We may catch him yet."

"Remember, Belmont is glamoured," Honora reminded him. "He will not look like himself."

Markham nodded, then went in search of a footman. Honora leaned against the wall of the corridor, feeling weak-kneed.

Jane Crossly found Honora still leaning against the wall, her eyes closed. Honora was trying to calm herself. So far, she had not been very successful.

"Honora!" Jane gasped. "Is something wrong? Are you unwell?"

"I . . . yes, I am unwell." It was not a lie. Her hands trembled and her stomach churned uneasily. She was not sure her legs could support her weight if she stood away from the wall.

Jane took Honora by the arm, lending her support. "Let us take you home. You look like you need to lie down."

"Yes, that is a good idea." Perhaps she could relax once she returned to the familiar house on Curzon Street.

But this was not the case. She had not considered how empty the house felt with Valance gone. At this hour, only a footman remained awake. Honora roused her maid and asked for a cold compress for her tender wrist. She suspected there would be a bruise tomorrow.

But the pain was nothing compared to her fear. What if the duke followed her home? He must know where she lived. He might even know that Valance was out of town. There were servants in the house who could protect her, but none of them were magicians. So far as she knew, none of the servants could box or shoot, as Valance could. She asked both the footman and Clack to spread the word of the possible threat to the household, but she would have felt far safer with her husband at home.

For the first time, she resented Valance for leaving her alone while he carried out his investigation. If she had gone with him to Bath, she would have been safe from the duke. Instead, her husband had left her behind without any protection. They did not even have a dog to keep watch!

Thinking of dogs reminded her of Bishop Barkley, and her shoulders began to shake with quiet sobs. She still missed him, and she would have given a good deal to have his company tonight. He could not have been any real protection against an attacker, but he would have been a comfort. Perhaps, she thought wistfully, they ought to get a new puppy, and train it better than poor Barkley had been trained.

Honora blew out her candle. She tucked herself into bed, put her feet on the warming pan, and tried to soothe herself to sleep by thinking about the puppy they might add to the household. But every creak startled her, and every footstep she heard outside the window made her heart pound.

Yes, she decided, she would talk to Valance about getting a new dog. Not a Yorkshire terrier, though. A pug, perhaps? A Pomeranian? She fell asleep still thinking about what kind of dog they ought to get.

THE DAY AFTER Honora's encounter with Belmont, Lord Markham called to see how she fared. He was deeply apologetic about the fact that she'd been threatened in his home. Honora assured him that she did not in the least blame her host and hostess for Belmont's behavior. She was far more concerned about what had happened after she left the party.

"Unfortunately, my footmen were not able to catch up to your attacker," Lord Markham said. "I called on His Grace this morning, but he naturally denied the whole story. He said he dined with a handful of friends last night. He even gave me their names. We can try speaking with them, but Belmont would not have named them unless he expected them to back him up."

"I *know* it was Belmont," Honora insisted. "But I have no way to prove it. No evidence to show. I can read auras, and I believe that helped me identify him. But I can't explain how I recognized him."

Lord Markham nodded. "I believe you. There were bruises on Belmont's face this morning, though his valet had tried to cover them with up with cosmetics. And you would know your magic better than anyone else." He smiled ruefully. "I know how hard it can be to describe intuitive magic. I am a weather mage, but I find it difficult to explain to anyone else how I know when it will rain or storm."

"Thank you for looking into the matter," Honora said. He really was under no obligation to help her. He might be Valance's friend, but he did not know her at all.

"I wish I could be of better service. If you *do* need anything in Val's absence, please do not hesitate to ask."

"Thank you, but I believe Valance will be home soon." Honora forced a smile, though it probably didn't fool anyone.

To her relief, Valance returned that afternoon. He must have been in a good mood, because he whistled as he entered the morning room.

"I am so glad to see you!" Honora stood up to greet him, and he swept her into a tight embrace. She rested her head against his solid shoulder, drank in his familiar scent, and knew she was safe. "I missed you."

"I missed you too." He pressed a soft kiss against her forehead. "Everything went all right while I was gone, I hope?"

Honora burrowed more deeply into his hug. She had no idea how to answer that question. She had rather not talk about Belmont, if she could help it. She would have preferred to shove the duke into the darkest closet of her mind and lock the door. But she knew she must confide in Valance if she wanted his protection.

"Nora," he prompted, "Is something wrong?"

She drew a deep breath and stepped back so she could look him in the eyes. "Yes. I believe I encountered Belmont last night, in disguise." She told him the whole story, beginning with the strange gentleman who kept watching her during the ball and ending with Lord Markham's visit that morning.

"And you are certain it was Belmont?" Valance asked sharply.

She nodded. "I recognized his aura. Besides, he said things that would only have made sense coming from Belmont."

"I see." He ran a gentle finger down her cheek. "Nora, I am so sorry. Are you all right? He did not hurt you, did he?"

"Only my wrist, where he grabbed me." She showed Valance the bruise. "That was all he did."

"I see." Valance gently turned her wrist so he could see the whole bruise. Then he kissed her on the forehead. "I warned him." He spoke calmly, almost absently, but his eyes had gone hard and distant.

Honora could only remember seeing that look on her husband's face once before. "Warned him of what?" she asked, suddenly suspicious. She no longer feared Valance's cold anger, but she could not predict what he might do when he was angry on her behalf.

"Of what would happen if he hurt you." Valance stared off into the distance for a moment, then shook his head. When he met her gaze again, the danger had left his eyes. "Listen, love, I have an errand I must do before dinner. I do not like leaving you again so soon, but it is rather urgent. I should be home in time for dinner."

Honora caught him by the sleeve before he could walk away. "Valance, I hope you are not going to do something foolish." That look in his eyes a moment ago did not bode well for Belmont.

He smiled. "No, I do not think it is at all foolish." He removed her hand from his sleeve, brought it to his lips, and kissed it. Then he left.

Honora did not feel in the least reassured.

CHAPTER THIRTY

VALANCE HAD JOINED White's as soon as he came down from Oxford, because his father and grandfather had both belonged to it. But it did not take him very long to discover that the gentlemen he was most interested in knowing preferred the Cambion Club, which employed a better set of cooks and boasted just as excellent a cellar. The only advantage White's had over the Cambion Club was that it allowed gambling. As Valance did not particularly care for gambling, this did not bother him, and he became the first Valance to join the Cambion Club.

But Valance had never dropped his membership at White's. Today he felt grateful for that, because the Duke of Belmont, not being a magician or scholar, was not a member of the Cambion Club. He patronized White's instead, and often dined there with his cronies. Valance guessed that on a sunny afternoon, the duke would most likely be found at his club.

He was right. He found Belmont chatting in the bow window with Lord Alvanley, the reigning gentleman of the club since Brummel's flight to France. Though the duke must have been a couple of decades Alvanley's senior and had never been part of the dandy set, the two seemed to be on comfortable terms. The men fell silent when Valance came to stand in front of the coveted bow window table.

"Lord Alvanley, good day," Valance said politely. He had no quarrel with the Prince Regent's friend.

He shifted his gaze to Belmont. He felt a savage surge of pleasure at the sight of the bruises on the duke's mouth and chin. Honora had caused that damage, and he was proud of her for defending herself.

"Your Grace." He did not bow or offer the duke even an inclination of the head, despite Belmont's high rank.

Belmont surveyed Valance through a silver quizzing glass. "Lord Valance, what an unexpected visitor! I did not know you patronized White's."

"I have been a member in good standing for nearly four years, though I must say I prefer the company at the Cambion Club. Your apologies, Alvanley." Valance inclined his head to the baron.

"Yes, *you* probably would." In Belmont's dry, sarcastic voice, that sounded like an insult. Valance ignored it entirely.

"I wish to have words with you, Your Grace. Will you step into another room with me?" He thought he saw a flicker of unease cross Belmont's face. But it was gone in a moment, and he might have imagined it.

"I can imagine no business you might have with me that cannot be conducted in public, Lord Valance."

"Very well." Valance drew himself to his full height and took a deep breath. "In that case, I would remind you that when you were so gracious as to call on me in January, I warned you that if you harmed anything or anyone in my household, I would shoot you where you stood. Do you remember?"

This time, Belmont clearly flinched. "I remember. What of it?"

Valance pitched his voice so that it would be heard through-out the room. "Last night, at Sherborne Place, you insulted my wife. She bears a bruise on her arm from your mistreatment. I demand satisfaction."

A silence fell over the room. Gentlemen turned to stare. A muscle in Belmont's face twitched. Valance smiled. Yes, he had rattled Belmont. Good.

"*You* are calling me out?" Belmont's gaze raked up and down Valance's substantial figure. Then he arched a single, incredulous eyebrow.

"Yes, I am." Valance spoke with feigned cheerfulness, again ignoring the implied insult. "Will you meet me?"

Belmont scanned the room, possibly trying to gauge how much support he had. He had the advantages of age, wealth, and rank. There were few men in London more wealthy or more powerful. But there were also few men in London who had fomented as many nasty rumors as Belmont. Valance had a better reputation—his only scandal was his elopement with the former Miss Grantly.

Belmont rubbed his chin thoughtfully before coming to a decision. "I will meet you, Lord Valance. I suppose you are no swordsman?" He punctuated the question with a sneer.

"On my honor, I do not know how to fence," Valance agreed.

"Pistols it is, then," Belmont granted.

As the challenged party, it was Belmont's right to choose the weapon. Choosing swords would have been to his advantage, but the rules of dueling etiquette forbade him from crossing swords with a man who did not fence. In much the same way, Valance would have been forbidden from choosing magic in a duel with a gentleman who was no magician.

The duke glanced across the room. "Lord Brandwyn? Will you serve as my second?"

"As you wish, Your Grace," Lord Brandwyn replied.

Valance did not need to glance around the room to know whom to name as his second. Though he was not on close terms with most of the men in attendance, he had spotted Lord Simon Varlow in the room when he first walked in. They had been friends in their university days.

"Lord Simon," he called. "Will you be my second?"

"At your service, Val," Lord Simon replied. "Brandwyn, shall we retire to work out the details?"

The two seconds would make the arrangements for the duel,

so Valance's business here was finished. "Good day to you, gentlemen." He nodded to Alvanley again and took his leave. A buzz of gossip rose from the room even before the door closed behind him.

Valance felt surprisingly cheerful on the walk home. He could trust Lord Simon to work out the details. All he had to do now was keep the secret from Honora. He did not want to worry her unnecessarily. He thought it very likely that if she knew what he intended, she would demand he cancel the duel. But he could not do that now that the duke had accepted the challenge. Better that she not know anything at all about it.

So, Valance said nothing about the duel that night, or the next day, or the next. The two seconds made the expected attempt to seek a reconciliation, but no reconciliation was possible as long as the duke denied having confronted Honora at Markham's ball. Belmont continued to insist he had spent the evening with friends. The seconds therefore negotiated a meeting at dawn on Friday morning at Wimbledon Common. Lord Simon arranged for a surgeon to attend in case of injuries.

The day before the duel, Valance visited his lawyer to make sure his affairs were in complete order. That night, he took Honora to bed early and kept her awake for a considerable amount of time. Fortunately, she had not the slightest objection.

So far as Valance could tell, his wife suspected nothing, and he preferred to keep it that way. He intended to leave the house while she still slept, but this plan went awry. She heard him opening the door separating her bedroom from his.

"Valance?" she called sleepily. "Where are you going?"

"Just an early morning errand." He spoke as lightly as he could. "I should be home shortly after breakfast." Or maybe even before breakfast, if all went well.

She sat up in bed and yawned. "I hope you are not doing something foolish."

"No," he said gently. "Not foolish. Something necessary. You need not worry about it. Go back to sleep, darling."

She did not seem to be fooled. She crossed her arms in front of her chest and glared at him. "You had better come back to me in one piece, because I love you."

That brought Valance back to her side, though he ought to be dressing. Lord Simon would arrive for him soon. "I will come back safe and sound," he said, though he knew perfectly well it was a promise he might not be able to keep. "Because I love you, too."

He kissed her lightly on the lips. It was the first time either of them had spoken those three words aloud. But Valance no longer had the slightest doubt. Some things in life were irrefutably true. Silver tarnished over time, gold remained uncorrupted forever, and Oliver Valance loved his wife more than anything else in the world. *Facts!*

Which was why he had to take care of the Duke of Belmont, so he would never bother Honora again. He turned to walk away, but Honora's next words stopped him in his tracks.

"Valance," she said, in a steely tone, "I know what you are going to do."

"Er, you do?" He faced her again, puzzled. How could she have known? She might be intelligent, but even she couldn't have guessed this. Could she?

"Yes. I heard it from Lord Markham. He heard the gossip at the club. He called yesterday and told me you had challenged the Duke of Belmont to a duel." Her cheeks flushed pink. "Because of me."

Valance's jaw dropped. "Markham told you?" He could not believe such a good friend would reveal his secret.

She nodded grimly. "He said I deserved to know that you were risking your life for my sake."

"Damn him," Valance grumbled. "He ought to know better than to meddle!"

Honora shrugged. "He also said you once asked him for advice about matrimony, and his advice was that a husband ought not keep secrets from his wife. I am supposed to pass that message on to you." She frowned. "He seemed to speak from personal experience, but I didn't like to ask."

Valance snorted. It was unlike Honora to show so much restraint when it came to asking personal questions. "Wise of you." If Markham and his wife had had any misunderstandings in their first year of marriage, Markham had not said a word about it.

"Very well," Valance told his wife. "It is true. I am going to duel Belmont, I am going to win, and I will come home to you. I promise."

She scowled at him. "You had better come home alive. Or I will make sure you do not sleep peacefully in your grave."

That drew a reluctant grin from him. "You aren't going to forbid me to go?"

She returned his question with one of her own. "Would you listen to me if I did? Or would you insist that you were honor-bound to meet Belmont?"

"The latter," Valance admitted. "A gentleman can't run away from a duel once the challenge has been accepted. It isn't at all the thing." The same code of honor that had forced him to marry Miss Grantly after having compromised her now forced him to face Belmont. "But I will try not to kill him. I do not want to be tried for murder."

Satisfying as it would be to put a bullet through Belmont's heart, Valance could not risk his life, his title, or his fortune in that way. A peer convicted of murder would lose everything, and so would his heir—assuming he had one.

Though it was too early to tell, Valance rather hoped there would be an heir soon. Once, that possibility had unsettled him, because he thought it would spell the end of his marriage. Now that he knew Honora would stay by his side, he looked forward to finding out what the next generation of Valances would be like. He suspected they would all ask even more difficult-to-answer questions than most children.

"I thought as much." His wife shook her head, still scowling.

"You do *not* have my approval to fight a duel, but I will not stop you from doing so."

Valance bit back the urge to laugh at the idea that Honora, who was so much smaller than him, could stop him doing anything. Then he sobered, because a woman as determined and daring as his wife might very well find a way to get what she wanted. Better not to test it!

"I appreciate that. I will return as soon as I can." He hurried from the room, knowing he had little time to get ready.

Lord Simon picked him up in his carriage, so Valance need not worry about getting himself home after the duel. If he were injured, he would need help getting to safety. The surgeon, a former military man who had attended duels in the past, already sat in the carriage. He and Lord Simon chatted lightly about famous past duels and their outcomes.

Valance ignored both of them in favor of staring somberly out the carriage window. He had presented a bold front to Honora, but in truth, he worried about what lay ahead. He trusted his ability to hit a target at twenty paces, but he had no idea how good a shot Belmont was. He did not want to die from a gunshot wound. Not now, when his life seemed so very good.

They reached the meeting point before dawn, which meant the three men had to stand around in the field making conversation. Valance paced back and forth. Lord Simon fidgeted, passing his ornamental cane from one hand to another. The surgeon, Mr. Badger, kept pulling his watch from his pocket to check the time.

But Valance did not need a watch to see that Belmont was late. The sun rose above the horizon, painting the whole world in shades of rosy light. Birds sang their dawn songs. Somewhere in the distance, a dog barked. The whole world came alive in the glorious way possible only on a clear spring morning. And still Belmont did not arrive.

"I make it half an hour past the meeting time, gentlemen," Mr. Badger said at last. "You don't suppose he has run off, do you?"

"Belmont?" Lord Simon shook his head. "He would never be able to hold his head up again if he ran away from a duel. Everyone would cut him."

"They should have cut him after his first wife died," Valance snapped.

"She fell down the stairs!" Lord Simon protested. "The coroner found it to be an accidental death. You can't give a man the cut direct because his wife took a bad fall."

Valance paused his restless pacing. "Everyone says he pushed her."

What infuriated Valance was the knowledge that Lord Simon was right. Evading a duel he had already accepted would indeed ruin Belmont's good name. But since two of his wives died under suspicious circumstances, Belmont ought not have had any reputation left to ruin.

Valance went back to his pacing. Lord Simon and the surgeon continued to make strained small talk as the minutes ticked past. The strain of waiting felt unbearable, and not surprisingly, Valance's head began to ache from tension. He pulled out his pain medication, relieved that he had thought to bring it. The coming fight was going to require all of his attention.

If this suspense continued much longer, he would start screaming at the top of his lungs. Or he would start shooting at random targets—trees and stones and treacherous looking clumps of grass. But he would look a right fool doing that, wouldn't he?

"Ah," Mr. Badger said at last, "I believe a carriage approaches." They watched as a stately town coach drew closer. By now the sun was high enough in the sky to illuminate the Brandwyn arms on the door.

"He didn't run away after all." Lord Simon sounded disappointed.

Valance's heart sank. He had begun to hope bloodshed could be avoided entirely. But when the carriage door opened, only Lord Brandwyn got out, wearing a thick greatcoat and an unhappy expression.

"Something wrong, my lord?" Valance asked. "Is His Grace indisposed?"

That would be an unexpected turn of events. Valance did not particularly want to defer today's meeting. He had rather get it over with. He was not sure he would have the stomach to come back another morning.

Lord Brandwyn looked down at the tips of his boots. "I am sorry to say His Grace seems to have fled the country."

This was so unexpected, Valance struggled to hold back a bubble of hysterical laughter. "Indeed? What makes you say that?"

"His Grace left a note at his residence explaining that he had gone to France. His servants say he left yesterday. I am very, very sorry that he behaved so dishonorably, my lords." Lord Brandwyn positively radiated shame.

"He must have been afraid to face a marksman as good as Val," Lord Simon guessed. "But my God! He will be absolutely ruined!" A mischievous grin lit up his face. "I can't wait to drop this bit of gossip at White's. It will be all over London by the end of the day."

"Yes, I am afraid it will." Lord Brandwyn was the only one who showed any sign of regret.

"I suppose my services are not needed after all," Mr. Badger said cheerfully. "But what a story I will have to tell at the hospital!" He rubbed his hands together happily.

"No," Valance said slowly, "I must ask you not to say anything. You too, Lord Simon. Not a word to anyone. We will tell everyone that we reconciled our differences and the duel was canceled."

Lord Simon gaped at him. "But why? This may finally destroy Belmont."

"Yes," Valance agreed. "And think what Belmont might do to avoid ruin."

With that threat hanging over his head, Belmont might be

willing to sell Valance the mortgage to Grantly Manor. He might finally leave Honora and Dora alone. This, combined with what Valance had learned from Mademoiselle DeRose, would provide the leverage he needed to solve the Belmont problem. Valance's lips curled up in a wicked smile.

"If you gentlemen will keep this morning's events a secret, I believe I can use that secret to very good effect." He looked each of them in the face.

"No one will hear this story from my lips, I assure you." Lord Brandwyn spoke stiffly. No doubt he was still embarrassed by the cowardice of his principal.

"Nor mine," Mr. Badger said cheerfully. "We medical men know how to keep a secret." Valance nodded, then turned towards Lord Simon, the witness who undoubtedly had the loosest lips.

"As you wish." Lord Simon's hangdog face made his reluctance obvious. "But you are robbing me of a story that would have paid for my drinks for days!"

Valance snorted. "Get a job, Simon. Then you need not sponge off your friends." Lord Simon was supposed to be reading law, but he rarely dined at the Inns of Court, nor had he taken much time to cultivate his legal connections. It seemed unlikely he would ever be called to the Bar.

"Very good advice, my lord," Mr. Badger said dryly. "If you gentlemen don't mind, I should like to get back to my surgery. I do have patients to see."

"Oh yes, of course," Lord Simon said. "Shall we head back, Val?"

Valance nodded. Now that his anxiety over the duel had passed, his stomach insisted it was time for breakfast.

Valance used the ride home to plan how he would handle the Belmont situation. Yes, he believed this would work very well. Much better, in fact, than fighting an actual duel. Belmont might have been too scared to meet him, but he would probably do much to keep his name from being further befouled. Valance could collect statements from the three witnesses and keep them safely locked up. Even if Belmont returned to England, he would not dare touch Valance's family again. Honora would be safe at last, and Valance could buy that damn mortgage and gift it to the young Sir Jacob Grantly.

"I say, Val, is that a dog sitting by your door?" Lord Simon asked.

Valance, who had been lost in pleasant thoughts, looked up in surprise. Sure enough, a scruffy gold-and-black morsel shivered on the doorstep.

He beamed. "Yes. In fact, it is the worst dog in the whole world." He thanked Lord Simon, got out of the carriage, and scooped up Bishop Barkley. "You, sir, are filthy," he told the dog. "Were you rolling in mud?"

Bishop Barkley wagged his tail and licked Valance's hand.

"I think we had better give you a bath before we let you into the morning room." Valance whistled as he walked into the house. He couldn't wait to tell Honora that their dog had returned.

CHAPTER THIRTY-ONE

March 1817

THE FIRST THING Honora did after learning of Belmont's flight to France was write to Dora, telling her sister it was now safe for her to return to London. There would be no need to maintain her disguise as "Cora Hart" now. Honora looked forward happily to launching Dora in London society. At eighteen, Dora was certainly ready to make a London debut. When Valance questioned whether London society would be ready for Dora, Honora laughed.

To her surprise, Dora promptly wrote back to say she wished to stay in Surrey until the middle of April. Peregrine wanted her help testing his meteorite trap during the annual Lyrid meteor shower. His spell, being complicated, required a sorcerer as well as a wizard to work. Dora did not want to miss seeing the spell in action.

When, Honora wondered, had Mr. Carrington become "Peregrine" to Dora? "Valance," she said at breakfast, "You don't think there could be something romantic brewing between Mr. Carrington and Dora, do you?"

Valance choked on his toast. "Um. Maybe?"

"Really?" Honora stared at him. She had not meant the question seriously. "What makes you say that?"

"Er. Just a hunch." He took a large gulp of his coffee. "When I was at the Abbey in February, Peregrine told her she would look good in Hessian boots. And he offered to take her to a boxing match. While she was disguised as a boy."

"Boxing? Ugh." Honora shuddered. She did not care for violent sports. Truth be told, she did not understand why her husband was so fond of sparring with his friends at Gentleman Jackson's. But Dora was both more adventurous and less conventional than Honora.

"That does sound like something Dora would want to do. I suppose if Mr. Carrington went with her, she would come to no harm." It would certainly be better than Dora trying to attend a boxing match on her own.

Valance stared at her for a moment, then shook his head. "Yes, if all they did was watch a boxing match, there would be no harm. But what if it didn't stop there? Can you imagine what would happen if they married? He would set fire to their furniture with his magical experiments and she would gallivant about the country garbed as a gentleman. Think of the trouble they would get into!"

Honora laughed at that picture of domestic felicity. "But it might be ideal," she pointed out. "Dora would not mind about Mr. Carrington's magic, since she is a sorceress herself. And he would not mind about the gallivanting. He does not strike me as particularly strait-laced."

Mr. Carrington had accepted his sister's romantic relationship with Miss Taylor. He would probably accept Dora no matter how she dressed. And would they really get in so much trouble if they married? Mr. Carrington was a grown man and a respected gentleman scholar. He seemed perfectly capable of looking after himself, and Dora was perfectly capable of following social rules when she chose to do so. All the couple would need was a good housekeeper and a reliable man of business to tend to their financial affairs.

"Don't say I didn't warn you," Valance grumbled.

But Honora did not share Valance's concern. On the contrary, she spent the rest of the meal trying to imagine what kind of magic Dora's children would inherit if she married into the Carrington family. The Grantlys tended to be either mages or sorcerers, but as far as she knew, all of the Carrington magicians were witches or wizards. That meant their children might inherit almost any kind of magical talent. She chuckled at the thought.

"I am glad you are so amused." Valance shook his head once more and went back to his toast.

Honora put Dora's letter aside and thought no more of meteorites. The mail contained weightier news: Mr. Watson had begun negotiations with Belmont's attorney to arrange for the purchase of the Grantly Manor mortgage. Belmont remained on the continent, and his attorney thought he might plan to take up his residence in Paris permanently. Honora certainly hoped he would stay away from England. Or at least, from London.

At first, Valance would not tell her how he intended to raise the funds to purchase the mortgage. After she reminded him of Lord Markham's advice about secrets, he reluctantly admitted he was going to sell a hunting box in Yorkshire that had been purchased in his grandfather's day.

Since Valance did not care for hunting, the sale of the estate was no great loss. Honora quit worrying so much about what his generosity might cost him. Instead, she happily looked ahead to a time when Belmont would no longer have any leverage over the Grantly family. Perhaps then, she thought wistfully, the work of reconciling with her family could begin. She would not mind if she never saw her mother again, but she did want to see Belinda, Clarinda, and Jack.

ONE MORNING, VALANCE informed her that he had an errand that afternoon. "I don't know how long it will take," he warned Honora. "But I should be home in plenty of time for the dinner party."

They were to dine with the Markhams at Sherborne Place. Honora looked forward to getting to know these friends in a quieter, less dramatic setting. At least, she hoped she would not have to fend off another attacker.

"What is your errand?" She had finished her breakfast, but she remained at the table reading a letter full of gossip from her friend Verena.

"I am going to talk to Miss Barbauld about the dog. I hope to convince her to let us keep him. I will buy him back from her if she agrees."

"I see." Honora stared at her husband, not sure how she felt about him visiting his old mistress. On the other hand, she very much wanted to keep Bishop Barkley, and she supposed it would not be right to do so without compensating his owner.

"I believe I may also owe her an apology." Valance stared down at his empty plate, as if he wanted to memorize the pattern of bread crumbs left from his breakfast. "I was not particularly kind when I dismissed her. And—there may have been things I ought to have done differently."

"I think that is a very good idea." Honora left it at that. What Valance had done prior to his marriage was not any of her business. What mattered was that she trusted him not to strike up an *affaire* with anyone now that he was married.

Even so, she spent an anxious afternoon waiting for Valance to return from his errand. What if Miss Barbauld wanted Bishop Barkley back? Honora did not know if she could stand losing her dog again.

She spent the afternoon training Barkley, just in case this was her last day with him. He still remembered "sit," but was not so good with "lie down." Honora thought it best to work on that before trying to tackle "stay."

So far, Barkley had not ruined any rugs since his return, but it was best not to think about all the furniture he had gnawed. They would have to pay hefty damages for the furniture if they ever moved out of this house.

But Honora wondered if they should simply offer to buy the little house from Lord Bloxom. She and Valance would probably spend their summers and autumns in the country, but they would need a house in London for the Parliamentary session each year. She did not particularly want to have to find a new townhouse when their lease ran out. By now, this place had begun to feel like home.

Valance had been right all those weeks ago when he told her they would make a new home together. At the time, Honora had scarcely believed it possible, given how distant and unapproachable he had been. Somehow, though, her husband had become closer and dearer to her than anyone else in the world.

All she hoped for now was that she might fall pregnant at last. Her courses had just ended, and she quietly hoped she might not see them again for a good long time. She was no longer driven merely by curiosity about pregnancy and childbirth. Now, she wondered more specifically about the family she and Valance might make together. She wanted to know what their children would be like. And, not being a particularly patient woman, she did not want to have to wait years to find out.

But, of course, it was not up to her to choose when that might happen, just as it was not up to her whether Miss Barbauld would let them keep Barkley. The fate of her little family did not lie entirely with her. All she could do was wait and hope.

CHAPTER THIRTY-TWO

WHEN VALANCE SET Cherie up as his mistress, he provided her a house in a respectable, but not fashionable, neighborhood. Most of her neighbors were merchants or middle-class professionals. The neighbors had probably been scandalized when a nobleman's light o' love settled amongst them. Perhaps that was why the curtains across the street twitched whenever Valance visited.

He felt nervous standing on the doorstep today, because he knew perfectly well that the gossips watching him would have much to say about him showing up again after not having visited Cherie for months.

Valance's nervousness about the Nosie Nellies was nothing compared to what he felt when the door was opened not by a housemaid, but by a tall, lean, golden-haired man whose perfect face was well-known by theater-goers. He had worked his way up from bit parts to leading roles in Drury Lane.

"What do you want?" Thomas Sowerby growled, clenching his fists. He stepped into the middle of the doorway, effectively blocking it.

"I would like to speak to Miss Barbauld about—"

"No," Sowerby interjected. "There is nothing you can possibly have to say to *Mrs. Sowerby.*" He put a heavy emphasis on the name. "You abandoned her months ago. *My wife* has nothing to do with you any longer. You had better leave, Your Lordship."

Valance stared, mouth hanging open in surprise. He had long suspected Cherie had a *tendre* for Sowerby, but he never expected the two to marry. He had assumed that Cherie, having grown accustomed to the life of a courtesan, would look for a new noble protector rather than a husband from her own station of life.

"Congratulations on your nuptials," he said at last, not knowing how else to respond.

"Thank you." Sowerby did not sound the least bit grateful. "You can have no business here, Lord Valance. I bid you good day, sir."

Why, Valance wondered, was Sowerby so belligerent? Did he think Valance wanted to resume his relationship with Cherie? Surely, he didn't think Valance would pursue Cherie now that she was married to someone else? Valance would never be unfaithful to Honora, but it would be particularly bad form to try to damage someone else's marriage, too.

But of course, there were men who *would* do that. Men like Belmont, who had wanted Honora even after her wedding. *He thinks I'm like Belmont*, Valance thought numbly. Valance was to Sowerby what Belmont had been to Valance: a wealthy predator from whom his wife must be protected.

Valance closed his eyes as a wave of shame swept over him. He knew he was no saint, but he had always thought himself to be an honorable man. He had believed he was a gentleman of whom his parents and his guardian could be proud. But that self-assurance crumbled in the face of Sowerby's defensive anger. Valance had once told Honora that he was not as good a husband to her as he ought to be. But perhaps the same was true of his relations with Cherie. Had he ever considered whether setting her up as his mistress was in her best interest? Or had he simply acted out of lust?

It had never before occurred to Valance to wonder what Sir John Carrington would have thought of his ward seducing a neophyte actress. But now he felt certain that his guardian would have been disappointed in him. That sent a pang through his heart. He had always valued Sir John's good opinion.

Meanwhile, Mr. Sowerby was trying to shut the door on him.

"Wait!" Valance stopped the door with his foot. "I do need to talk to Miss—to Mrs. Sowerby, about her dog. And I owe her an apology."

"An apology," Sowerby repeated. His golden brows were still lowered over his eyes, but some of the heat in his eyes was replaced by curiosity.

"Yes. May I speak to her?"

Sowerby glanced over his shoulder. "Wait here. It must be for her to decide whether she will receive you."

"Of course," Valance agreed. "I will wait."

To his great embarrassment, he spent nearly five minutes standing on the front steps, waiting to find out whether Cherie would hear him out. It must be a red-letter day for all the gossips along the street, he thought sourly. This would give them fodder for days.

When the door opened, Cherie herself stood there, wearing a simple day dress and (of all things) an apron covered in flour. Valance, stunned by this unexpected domesticity, gaped at her. He had never seen Cherie wear an apron. He had never seen her try to cook anything herself. On the contrary, she had enjoyed having servants do such work for her.

Perhaps he was not the only one who had changed over the last few months.

"You may come in, but I can give you no more than fifteen minutes, my lord." She stepped aside so he could walk in.

"That will do quite well." Valance had no desire to spend hours here. Already, he wished himself far away.

He followed Cherie to the little sitting room that had been decorated in Cherie's favorite colors before she moved in. Everything looked much the same, except for a new bookcase in one corner and watercolor portraits of family members Valance did not recognize—Sowerby's family, perhaps?—on the wall.

Cherie took a seat on the sofa, but instead of lounging, she sat up primly, with her feet on the ground and her back straight. Her face showed not a hint of a smile. Valance suspected she felt as nervous about this conversation as he did. He settled in an armchair across from her, probably sitting just as stiffly.

"My husband says you wish to talk about the dog, but I had better tell you at once, Bishop Barkley is no longer here. We were keeping him in the back garden and he ran away."

"Yes, I know. He ran back to our house on Curzon Street," Valance explained. "That is why I came to visit you."

He cleared his throat. He expected this to be a rather difficult conversation. He had, after all, given the dog as a gift to Cherie. Barkley was unquestionably hers, so far as property rights went. And Cherie did not seem to be in a particularly generous mood today. He feared she would instantly reject his request. But he had to at least try.

"As it happens," he said cautiously, "my wife was hoping she could keep the dog, as she has grown fond of him. We would, of course, recompense you—"

"You can keep him," Cherie interrupted, not even giving him a chance to offer her money. "He cannot live with us. Thomas starts coughing and sneezing whenever he is around dogs. That is why we were keeping Barkley in the garden." She crinkled her nose. "I don't think he liked being outside all the time, poor thing. That's probably why he ran away."

"I would imagine so," Valance agreed. Many dogs lived their whole lives outdoors, but a spoiled housedog would probably have a hard time adjusting. "As I said, we are happy to recompense you."

He reached into his pocket for a handful of sovereigns and placed them on the tea table with a soft clink. Barkley was not, of course, worth so much money, but Valance thought it better to err on the side of generosity.

Cherie swallowed heavily as she eyed the coins. "I would like to refuse your gold, but we might have need of it."

"It is only fair for me to recompense you for the dog," Valance reiterated. Though, in truth, the money also served as something of a guilt offering.

Cherie nodded. "I thank you, my lord. Now, is that all? For I do have chores to do." She rose out of the chair, signaling that Valance should leave.

But Valance made no move to get up. "That is not all." His heart began to pound more heavily, and his mouth felt dry. This part of the conversation would be even harder than asking to keep Bishop Barkley. "I came here in part because I believe I owe you an apology."

Cherie stared at him, then slowly sank bank into her chair. "Indeed?"

He plunged into his prepared speech. "When you spoke to Lady Valance in February, you told her that I, ah, 'led you down the primrose path' to your ruin. You are right. I did take you away from your family and from a respectable future."

He swept his eyes about the room again, thinking about her long relationship with Thomas Sowerby. "If not for me, you might have gotten married long before now. I lured you away from that possibility with promises of jewels and silk. I am sorry for that."

Cherie's eyes widened. She silently studied Valance for what seemed like half of an eternity, then shook her head. "You offered me a *carte blanche*, Oliver, but you did not force me to accept it. I chose to be your mistress. I chose to remain living under your protection, to remain faithful to you, despite—well, I think we both know there was not much love lost between us at the end." Her mouth twisted into a bitter smile.

Valance could only nod. It was true. He was not certain how Cherie had felt about him when she first became his mistress, but he knew that if she had ever been at all attached to him, that had ended long ago. They had both been unhappy for the last few months of their arrangement. Maybe longer.

What stuck out to him was the phrase "remain faithful to you." Had he been wrong about her infidelity? If so, he had treated her more badly than she had treated him. At the Twelfth Night masquerade, he'd slunk off down a hallway intending to bed a beautiful woman he had just met, without the slightest regard for his existing lover. And that lover, it seemed, had done better by him. Perhaps he had never valued Cherie as he ought.

"Even so," he told her, "I am sorry for how things played out between us, and for how abruptly I dismissed you. I am glad you seem to have landed on your feet." Those were not empty words: he *was* glad that he had not ruined her life beyond repair.

Cherie shrugged. "For now. But the lease on this house will run out, and we will not be able to afford the rent." She stared at the handful of coins Valance had deposited on the table. "Thomas wants to go into partnership with the fellow who owns that new theater, the White Rose. He thinks he can write plays that will help bring in a larger audience. All our money must go towards buying a share of the business."

"I see." Valance nodded his head as he did some quick thinking. "Well. If ever you need an investor, you should let me know." Susan's cousin was a member of the troupe at The White Rose. It was, so far as Valance could tell, a promising venture, though he was no expert on the subject.

"I will do that." Cherie unexpectedly smiled at him—not one of her artful, performative smiles, but a simple pleased grin.

She stood up again, and this time Valance took the hint and made his farewell. He walked out the door and down the steps. The twitch of a curtain across the street indicated that one of the gossips was indeed spying on him. He tipped his hat and flippantly bowed in the direction of the curtains, letting the neighborhood spies know he was on to them. Then he turned towards home.

Most likely, he would never see Cherie again, unless he saw her on the stage. Their lives would not intersect, since they moved in different social worlds. If Valance ever did invest in Mr. Sowerby's theatrical ventures, he would do so through the medium of his man of business. He doubted Sowerby would want to see him in person again.

Even so, he was glad to have mended some bridges. He knew it was not possible to undo all his past wrongs. He could only hope to do better in the future. And perhaps Honora would help him make better choices. She saw the world through a different set of lenses.

As he drew closer to home, his heart lightened, and he began to whistle. At least he had good news about Bishop Barkley!

CHAPTER THIRTY-THREE

March to April, 1817

AS PROMISED, VALANCE returned well before time to dress for the dinner party. Honora knew as soon as he walked into the morning room that his errand had been successful. He was whistling "The Parting Glass," and his step sounded light and brisk.

He greeted her with a kiss on the cheek. "You need not worry about Bishop Barkley," he said. "Cherie does not want him anymore. Her husband sneezes when he is around dogs, it seems."

"Her husband?" Honora's eyes widened. She had been under the impression that courtesans never married.

Valance nodded. "She married an actor from her troupe. A Mr. Thomas Sowerby." He smiled ruefully. "I believe she has been sweet on him for some time."

Valance sat down beside her and threaded his fingers through hers. His hand dwarfed hers, but she liked the sense of safety and security it gave her. She squeezed his hand in return.

Thinking of Cherie reminded Honora of something she had long wondered about but never been bold enough to ask. Perhaps now was the time.

"Valance, why did you let Miss Barbauld call you 'Oliver,' when you asked me to call you by your title?"

He stared blankly at her. "I thought I explained that! I wanted you to call me 'Valance' because that is what most of my friends call me." Honora opened her mouth to ask another question, but he continued speaking. "Cherie was my lover, but she was never my friend. You are both." He averted his eyes, looking surprisingly bashful. "You are the only woman who has ever been both."

Honora, momentarily overwhelmed by the sweetness of his response, could only game. Then she leaned over and kissed his cheek.

He squeezed her hand tightly. "You can call me Oliver if you want to. But the truth is, I had rather be called Valance."

"Then I will call you Valance." She grinned up at him. "Except when I call you Valentine, of course." She had not forgotten their conversation in the carriage the night they saw *Twelfth Night*. It had, after all, been a memorable evening.

He chuckled and kissed her soundly before insisting, "You most certainly will *not* call me that." But he said it affectionately.

"So," she said, returning to their original subject: "It sounds like Miss Barbauld—I mean, Mrs. Sowerby—is doing well? Is she happy with her husband, do you think?"

"I should think she was happier with him than with me. I don't think she ever cared much for me. I believe she only took up with me for the sake of the money." Valance said that matter-of-factly. Perhaps he had not been deeply attached to Illegible Scribble after all.

Honora could not argue with that. She still remembered the distaste with which Miss Barbauld had spoken of her former protector, though how anyone could call a man as honorable and tender as Valance an "oaf" was beyond her comprehension.

"Well, *de gustibus non disputandum est*," she concluded. In matters of taste, there could be no disputes.

"Quite so."

"You are to *my* taste," she assured him. "I liked you the moment I laid eyes on you."

"Do you mean to say it was my devastating good looks that led you to choose me for your ruination scheme? At last, it all makes sense." Amusement colored his voice.

"No," Honora said bluntly. She had thought him handsome

as soon as he smiled at her, but that was not what had first drawn her attention to him. "I mean that I liked your aura. I have never been taught to read auras well, but I think I could see the . . . the . . . *Valanceness* of you, and I liked that."

His aura must have hinted at some of the things that made him *Valance*: a man who was honorable, courageous, strong, and—in his own way—sweet. Just as she had been able to tell at first glance that Belmont was someone to be feared, she had sensed that Valance was someone who could be trusted.

"Tell me more about how much you like me," he suggested.

But instead of talking, she kissed him, and they became so distracted that they were actually late for the dinner party. This would not have bothered Honora much, except for the sly jokes Lord Markham kept making about newlyweds. Was it really that obvious what they had been doing before dinner?!

DORA'S NEXT LETTER begged Honora to come to Surrey for the much-anticipated meteor shower. She wanted to show off her spell work, Honora guessed. Well, it would be good to have a chance to tour Dreadnaught Hall at last. Valance had no objection, so it was settled. They took a break in the middle of the Season to witness the astronomical event.

Thus, on a cool, clear night in the middle of April, Honora found herself shivering in her pelisse in a pasture on the Carrington estate.

"Why can't we have a bonfire?" She rubbed her hands in a fruitless attempt to keep them warm. She had not brought thick enough gloves.

"The light would make it too hard for us to see shooting stars," Dora explained. "But I don't know why you're complaining. It's not too cold if you keep moving about."

"You're warm because you're dressed so snugly," Honora

retorted.

Dora wore pantaloons, Hessian boots, and a men's shirt, waistcoat, and topcoat, all cut to fit her well. Over all that, she'd put on a greatcoat that had belonged to one of the Carrington brothers. Honora thought it was a little odd that her sister continued to wear men's clothing some of the time, but she could not deny that Dora's garb looked warmer than the silk evening gown Honora wore.

"Where did you even get Hessian boots?" Honora marveled. They fit so well they must have been custom-made for Dora.

Dora grinned. "Peregrine bought them for me. He introduced me to his local bootmaker and his tailor."

"Did he now?" Honora glanced over to where Mr. Carrington stood chatting with Valance and Miss Carrington.

Honora had only arrived in Surrey yesterday and had not yet had a chance to talk to Dora alone, but she had certainly observed that her sister had grown close to Mr. Carrington. The dowager Lady Carrington seemed to be fond of Dora, too. She spoke to her almost the same way she did to her daughters. Honora found that telling.

"When is this event supposed to get started?" Valance grumbled. "It is too cold to stand about in fields all night."

Ah ha! It was not Honora's imagination. Other people felt cold, too.

"It will happen when it happens, Valance. You can't rush these things." Mr. Carrington sounded surprisingly calm for someone whose major project of the last four months was about to be put to the test. "If it doesn't happen tonight, I will be out here tomorrow night."

"Well, *I* won't," Valance grumbled. "I had much rather be in bed." He glanced in Honora's direction and winked, causing heat to rush to her face. Hopefully no one noticed her blush in the dimly-lit pasture.

"We really need to extinguish all those witchlights you lot insisted on summoning." Mr. Carrington projected his voice so it carried over half the pasture. "Or we will not be able to see the sky properly."

The various witches, wizards, and sorcerers gathered in the field grumbled, but they did as he asked, plunging the group into deeper darkness. Miss Taylor, who had been blithely ignoring everyone in favor of reading a book, complained the loudest. Abigail Carrington drifted toward Miss Taylor's chair and chatted with her until she quit grumbling.

"I do wish Cosmo was here," the dowager Lady Carrington said. "It would have been so nice to have the whole family together for once."

No one answered her, probably because this was the third time she'd said that. The first time, Miss Carrington had reminded her that Cosmo would be down in the summer for the Long Vacation. The second time, Valance had promised that he and Honora would pay a longer visit when the Season ended. That was when Honora realized that when Lady Carrington said, "whole family," she had been talking as much about Valance as about her actual children.

Valance seemed to take Lady Carrington's affection for granted. Did he know how lucky he was to have this second family in addition to his own? Honora would have given a good deal to have had such support when her mother disowned her.

Dora spotted the first shooting star. "There!" she shouted, pointing to the sky.

"It's moving in the wrong part of the sky," Mr. Carrington said. "We need one that's directly overhead for the spell to catch it." He did not sound worried, though. "Maybe the next one will be in the right position."

It took nearly an hour before a shooting star finally crossed the boundaries of the spell. The result was startling, to say the least. A flash of magical light temporarily turned the pasture brighter than day. The light was followed by an almighty thump that shook the ground and nearly knocked Honora off her feet. Valance caught her elbow and helped keep her from falling.

Honora steadied herself in time to see Dora launch herself into Mr. Carrington's arms. "Peregrine, we did it!" she shouted. He replied by kissing her heartily.

Oh. So that was how it was. Honora looked around to see other people's reactions. It was possible to see again, because someone had conjured a bright witchlight to illuminate the meteorite, which lay in the middle of a small crater.

No one else seemed the least bit surprised by the kiss. Apparently, whatever had developed between Dora and Mr. Carrington had not been kept secret from the rest of the family.

"Peregrine," Sir Roderick scolded, "it is generally considered advisable to receive permission to marry a girl before you kiss her. You ought to have waited until after you spoke to Miss Rossini's guardian to do that."

"That will be difficult," Honora pointed out, "given that we are not on good terms with the rest of the Grantly family at the moment." Uncle Robert might not be as angry with Dora and Honora as Lady Grantly was, but Honora would not bet money on the chances of him granting permission for Dora to marry.

"Perhaps I can make it a condition of forgiving the mortgage." Valance pitched his voice so that no one but Honora heard.

Just as well—Honora thought it better not to get anyone's hopes up. But she met Valance's eye and nodded.

"Oh, we can simply run off to Scotland to marry," Mr. Carrington suggested.

Judging from the sputtering sound Valance made, he felt the same dismay Honora did. Hadn't the Grantly family suffered enough scandal for one year?

"But first, we should attend this spring's meeting of the Society for Astronomical Magic. Dora, you must come with me, since you helped me with the spell."

"Peregrine," Abigail Carrington objected, "They do not allow women at those meetings. That society is only for men." Her sour expression made it clear how she felt about such exclusion.

"No? How foolish of them!" Mr. Carrington shrugged his shoulders. "Isn't it a good thing Dora already has the right clothes for the conference? They may not allow Miss Rossini into the society, but they will certainly accept *Mr.* Rossini as a member."

"Infiltrating the organization in disguise, in defiance of the rules? I like that idea." Dora grinned her most mischievous grin.

"Yes, I thought you would," Mr. Carrington replied cheerfully. "Now, if you'll excuse me, I need to take some measurements before we move the meteorite. Hannah, if you would be so good as to draw some sketches, I would appreciate it. Dora, can you summon a better light? We'll need to see well for this."

"I don't know about you," Valance murmured in Honora's ear, "But I think I had rather go to bed. Peregrine may be up for hours yet, but I don't need to witness the aftermath."

Honora opened her mouth to answer him, but a yawn forestalled her words. "I will turn in too. It was fun to watch the meteorite trap in action, but I am very tired."

She had never observed a meteor shower before, and that sight alone would have been worth standing in a chilly field, even if the spell had not worked. But it was gratifying to see Mr. Carrington's hard work pay off.

They said their good nights and began the long walk back to Carrington Hall, where a comfortable guest room waited for them. Honora tilted her head back to study the sky, just in time to catch a bright fireball streaking across the spangled heavens.

"Is it good luck to see a shooting star?" she asked Valance. "Can you make a wish on it if you see one?"

"I don't see why not." He looked down at her. "What are you wishing for, Nora?"

She smiled back up at him. "It's a secret for now. Maybe I will be able to tell you in a few weeks."

Her courses were only two days late; they might yet start any day now. But if they had not begun in a couple of weeks, she would consult a medical magician to see if she was with child. She was not patient enough to wait three months to confirm a pregnancy the non-magical way.

"Markham says married people ought not keep secrets from each other," Valance reminded her.

"Think of it as a Christmas gift," Honora suggested. "I am only concealing it to make a pleasant surprise." If she did conceive this month, the baby would be expected about Christmas time—if her calculations were correct.

Best not to get her hopes up, she reminded herself. She snuck another peek at the night sky, and when a second shooting star passed overhead, she silently repeated her wish. Perhaps it would come true. After all, good things seemed to happen to her during the Christmas holidays.

The End

About the Author

Anne Rollins is the pen name of an English professor who lives in Northern California with her family, too many cats, and an enormous collection of books. She has spent untold hours of her life rereading Georgette Heyer novels, and hopes that someday people will compulsively reread her novels, too!

Join me at the following:
annerollins.com
facebook.com/profile.php?id=100094523334798
instagram.com/annerollins23
threads.net/@annerollins23